Daisy

the Newport Ladies Book Club

Daisy

a novel

JOSI S. KILPACK

DESERET BOOK

SALT LAKE CITY, UTAH

Library of Congress Cataloging-in-Publication Data
Kilpack, Josi S., author.
   Daisy / Josi S. Kilpack.
      pages cm — (Newport Ladies Book Club series)
   ISBN 978-1-60907-008-3 (paperbound)
   1. Mothers—Fiction. 2. Pregnancy—Fiction. 3. Man-woman relationships—Fiction.
 4. Book clubs (Discussion groups)—Fiction. 5. Christian fiction. 6. Domestic fiction,
American. I. Title. II. Series: Newport Ladies Book Club series ; book 2.
   PS3561.I412D35 2012
   813'.54—dc23   2012001625

Printed in the United States of America
Lake Book Manufacturing, Inc., Melrose Park, IL

10   9   8   7   6   5   4   3   2   1

To ANNETTE, HEATHER, AND JULIE—
dear friends who were so excited and supportive
about taking this journey with me.
It's a thrill and a privilege to be loved
by such inspiring women.
I love you gals.

Acknowledgments

In the fall of 2009, Julie Wright and I went on a book tour for our newest releases. We talked almost nonstop for two full weeks. It was so much fun, and among the many things we discussed, I brought up the idea of writing a parallel book series where each book would cover the same period of time but be told from a different character's perspective. We brainstormed and in the process got really excited. We had both worked closely with two other amazing women—Annette Lyon and Heather Moore—and thought they would make the perfect partners for this project. We pitched the idea to them and they were all in. A few months later we pitched the idea to our publishers, but since I published with Deseret Book/Shadow Mountain and they published with Covenant Communications, it took some time to work out the bugs. Eventually, we made it work, and we were off and running.

This project would never have happened without the support of both of our publishers, and I am especially grateful to the team at Deseret Book—Jana Erickson, who spearheaded the process at Deseret Book, Lisa Mangum, who made the story bright and shiny, Rachael Ward for another wonderful typesetting job, and Shauna Gibby, who worked closely with Covenant to design the cover. I could not be happier with the way everything worked out, and I so appreciate everyone's flexibility and support.

Of course, this series couldn't have happened without the incredible support of Annette, Heather, and Julie. To say we had fun writing this series is a vast understatement. We had a blast, shared a few tears, took our critiques, and, I believe, are all better for having journeyed through this process. Thank you, ladies, for being such wonderful friends. The greatest blessing of my writing career has been the wonderful people I have met because of it.

I wrote *Daisy* while working on two other projects for Shadow Mountain, which upped my already hectic home life to critical levels at times. And yet my wonderful husband and children continued to cheer me on and encouraged me to keep going. Thank you guys so much for being so very good to me. I love you, love you, love you.

At the 2010 Whitney Award gala, Susan Evans McCloud was awarded the 2010 Lifetime Achievement Award. During her speech, she said, "Our Father in Heaven loves His daughters." I know that is true, and as I navigated Daisy's life, which is so different from my own, I felt that confirmation over and over again. God does love His daughters, and He is waiting for us to fall into His embrace and let Him show us what He sees when He looks upon us. Regardless of our faith, past mistakes, present trials, and heavy disenchantments, God loves His daughters. I am so grateful for my understanding of this truth, and I hope that in some way this story will help those women reading it understand how much He loves *you*.

Other books in this series:

Olivia—Julie Wright
Paige—Annette Lyon
Athena—Heather B. Moore

For ideas on hosting your own book club, suggestions for books and recipes, or information on how you can guest-write about your book club on our blog, please visit us at http://thenewportladiesbookclub.blogspot.com.

Chapter 1

"Would it kill you to take a day off, Daisy?" Paul asked over the phone.

"Yes," I said, glad he couldn't see my smile so the game would play out a little longer. "It just might."

Paul laughed, a laugh that was too high-pitched for a man of forty-four. When we first started dating six years ago, I'd found it annoying and knew I would never be able to marry a man who laughed like a teenage girl. Somewhere between that first date and a marriage proposal—complete with swans, if you can believe it—I came to love that laugh and a hundred other things that made Paul a husband-extraordinaire.

"You know I can't take time off at the end of the month—too many policy renewals," I said.

Commercial insurance policies tend to renew annually on the first day of the month, meaning that my clients bombard me with questions a week before they're supposed to re-up for another year, even though I've been reminding them for the last sixty days.

"The thirtieth is a Saturday," Paul said. "We can leave Friday afternoon after you finish your renewals and you can take Monday off. It won't set you back too far. Come on," he prodded. "You know you want to."

"You are so bad for me," I said, lowering my voice seductively. Meanwhile I flipped forward through my planner almost a month to check the dates for this romantic escapade. I had a ten o'clock meeting on Monday, November first, but I was pretty sure I could reschedule it. My hopes were rising as I flipped back a page to make sure I'd properly evaluated the weekend.

"Shoot," I said, scowling at October thirty-first. "Sunday is Halloween." It was part of the unspoken code of parenting ethics that you had to be around for any and all holidays—even pointless ones I swore were instituted by the American Dental Association and Mars Candy, Inc., as a means of job security. My next thought, however, surprised me: *Did* I have to be there? Stormy was in her final year of high school and with ten years between her and her older sister, December—who was about to make me a grandma at the age of forty-six—I'd been doing the Halloween thing for a very long time. Couldn't I take one off?

"Maybe Stormy could stay with Jared," I said, feeling my excitement build at the thought of a weekend away. Stormy didn't spend many weekends with her dad since she had things going on with her friends most of the time, but Jared *was* there. It was perhaps the only perk of having my ex-husband live just half an hour away.

"Your call, Mama," Paul said.

I scowled. He knew I hated it when he called me that. It always made me defensive of the many things I was, motherhood being only one of them. Paul, on the other hand, claimed to find my maternal aspects sexy, and I took that at face value. His fifteen-year-old daughter, Mason, lived in San Diego and found it hard to come up on the weekends now that she was in high school. She came for a couple of weeks each summer and on alternating holidays, but I knew Paul missed her.

I bit my lip and stared at the page in my planner. "I'll talk to Stormy about it," I said, hoping it would be an argument I could win. I flipped back to "Today" in my planner and wrote a note to myself.

Stormy—Halloween w/ Jared?

Then I leaned my elbow on my desk and rested my head in my hand as I continued the sweet talk with my sweetie. "So where are you taking me, Romeo?"

"It's a surprise," Romeo said.

"Not even a hint?" I pushed. It was Paul's year to plan our anniversary celebration, and I felt a thrill run through me at the possibilities. Say what you will about second marriages, but so far mine had been a wonderful ride. Maybe it was because both of us wanted to make sure this one worked, or maybe we were both grown-ups now and knew how to make better choices in a mate, or maybe we had a better idea of our future and could plan it out exactly as we wanted it to be. Whatever the reason, Paul was the sugar in my coffee, the tread on my tire, or, as he liked to say every time he brought me flowers, the Shasta to my Daisy.

"I'll give you a clue: bring your bikini."

"Nice one," I said, narrowing my eyes. Bikinis don't come in a size fourteen, but I had a very flattering one-piece with control panels in all the right places. "I don't know why I put up with you sometimes."

"Because I pay the mortgage," Paul said.

It was an offhand comment, but it pinged in my chest and I responded without thinking about it. "Careful, sailor, or you're on the next boat out of here."

That fell even flatter, and we both went quiet, having sufficiently stepped on one another's toes rather harshly. We could banter and tease all we wanted, but Paul's wife had left him without warning ten years ago, so jokes about me leaving were never funny. I wondered why I'd said it. But his comments implying that I couldn't take care of myself were equally difficult for me to take in stride. Did I say second marriages were *perfect*?

I cleared my throat. "Well, I'd better go. But the weekend sounds like fun. I'll talk to Stormy about it tonight and then give Jared a call. I'm sure it'll be a go, though; he totally owes me for Labor Day." He'd had to cancel that weekend with Stormy. He said he had a last-minute business trip, but I suspected he'd taken his newest girlfriend to New York for the opening of a Broadway play he'd told Stormy about the week before. Jared had been a theater major in college; it was probably how he'd tricked me into marrying him—he acted the part of faithful suitor. What a joke.

"Right," Paul said, also trying to recover from the awkward moment. "She's got that Shakespeare thing at school tonight, right?"

I groaned. "That's right," I said, looking at my planner again. I hadn't written it in. Instead, I had a list of errands I was hoping to do on the way home: Stop by the hair salon to pick up another bottle of my favorite shampoo—Stormy had left the other bottle at the pool on Saturday—swing by the library for a new novel, and then hit the grocery store for some more Lean Cuisines; I had brought my last one to work today for lunch. "Um, is there any way you could go solo so I can run some errands?"

"But Jared's going, right?"

"I think so," I said.

"Daisy."

The reprimand in his voice caused me to let out my breath in a huff. Paul and Jared did okay together, but Paul was always anxious about seeming as though he was overstepping his boundaries as step-dad when dad-dad was around.

"Okay, okay. Don't worry about it." I tried not to sound as annoyed as I felt. After working all day I just wanted to run my errands and go home, not sit through a high school drama performance where my daughter probably had three lines. "I'll try to leave a little early and get my stuff done before it starts."

My stuff, I thought after I hung up and looked at my list again, a familiar frustration rising in my chest. I yearned for *my* stuff, *my* time, *my* schedule. After so many years of putting *me* after *their* stuff, *their* time, *their* schedules, my patience was wearing thin. Of course, Paul was different. He was a grown man and he was wonderful about giving me my space. My girls? Not so much. I was their mother; I was supposed to put them first, but that didn't mean I didn't long to just do my own thing. I'd been so young when I first became a mother—barely seventeen—and I felt like I'd been trying to catch up with the role ever since. Now the end was in sight. If it made me a bad mom to look forward to being done with this phase of my life, well, so be it. I'd given so much for so long.

I pushed my planner to the side of my desk and opened up my e-mail folder; my break was officially over. I glanced at the clock—it was almost two. If I kept a steady pace, I should be able to leave the office by four thirty. That would give me time to get the shampoo and the microwave meals. I could go to the library tomorrow.

Eight more months, I reminded myself. That's how much longer I had before Stormy graduated from high school. She was already planning to live with Jared for the summer and then go to California State—applications were due in November. Once she was up and out, I could go away on the weekends any time I wanted to. Paul and I planned to buy a trailer and hit the open road. My office was getting closer and closer to telecommuting options all the time, so I could still work part-time. We wanted to trace the Oregon Trail, then visit the thirteen original colonies. There was so much we wanted to do, and we were so close to having the green light to do it.

For now, however, I was sentenced to high school plays, budget-busting prom dresses that were worn once, and overseeing homework.

"Eight more months," I said one last time before getting back to work.

Chapter 2

My alarm went off at 5:45 in the morning. One would think that in all the years of getting up early to help the girls get off to school, I'd be used to being up before the sun. I wasn't. Paul slept through the alarm, as usual, and I glared at him in envy as I got out of bed, as usual, grabbed my robe off the hook by the bathroom door, and headed into the hallway, as usual. It's not that I expected him to get up; I was just jealous he got to sleep in every morning and I didn't.

I turned on the hallway light, which caused me to squint, and knocked twice on Stormy's door before turning the knob and pushing it open. A pie-shaped field of light fell across Stormy's bed. I waited to hear her moving around, but after six seconds, I heard nothing.

"Don't make me turn on the lights," I warned. She knew from experience that wasn't an idle threat. I'd once resorted to a spray bottle with December—it had happened only once, though. My kids were quick learners.

"Okay," she said from the dark recesses of her cave. It sounded more like "Oooayyyy," but after all these years, I was fluent in groggy teenager.

Satisfied she was awake, I headed into the kitchen and, like a train on the track, began my daily routine. Start the coffee, switch the laundry I'd put in last night, empty the dishwasher, feed the stupid cat

Jared had given Stormy without consulting me, check the home calendar, update my planner, remind Stormy to hurry, and then—once she was eating and I was assured we were on time—take a shower.

I only washed my hair every other day and today wasn't one of them, so after I got out of the shower I put my golden-blonde locks in hot rollers that would achieve the big loose curls I loved and got dressed. Most women my age had given up any hairstyle that went past their shoulders, which might have been why I was determined to keep my hair long. It had always been thick, and I conditioned and colored it religiously to keep it in tip-top shape. So far, so good. While Stormy did her last-minute primping, I folded the laundry and cleaned the kitchen. I had this down to a science.

At 7:15 I hollered at her to double-check her backpack while I grabbed the keys out of the basket we kept by the phone.

"You know, if I had a car you wouldn't have to drive me," Stormy said, coming into the kitchen while she pulled up her backpack higher on her shoulders. She was dressed in black skintight jeans and a black-and-green striped T-shirt. Her eye makeup was too thick on her pale face for my tastes, yet she was stunning with her wide brown eyes—Jared's—and her long blonde hair—mine. The car request had become a weekly topic of conversation that never ended the way Stormy wanted it to.

"You can't al-ways get what you wa-a-ant," I sang as I headed toward the garage.

Stormy narrowed her beautiful eyes but followed me into the garage and hit the button to lift the garage door, which squeaked as it rose on its tracks. She didn't say anything until we were both in the car and I was looking over my shoulder so I wouldn't hit an unfortunate paper boy on my way out of the driveway. "I'm, like, the only seventeen-year-old in Lake Forest who doesn't have a car."

"You're, like, totally making that up," I replied with exactly the same cadence. Stormy scowled, and I bit back the real reason she didn't have a car: I was waiting for her dad to buy her one. I brought home a pretty good salary, but while Paul and I split household expenses, we kept our money separate. *My* daughter's car as well as insurance, gas, maintenance, and whatever cute seat covers she *had* to have were most certainly my expense, and I couldn't afford it unless I gave up something else. I liked my lifestyle the way it was and didn't want to adjust. It didn't help Stormy's case that I'd grown up as the second of five kids and had worn my sister's hand-me-downs until I finally had a job and could start buying my own clothes. Our family had one car, which Dad drove. The rest of us walked everywhere we went—like Jesus did, Mom told us when we complained.

I struggled to put myself through a couple years of college as a single mom after December was born, and when I married Jared, he managed the money, still hoping to be a famous actor one day. Budgets were tight. Eventually I was a single mom again, and every penny counted once more. I considered it a tribute to a good work ethic and a wise choice in my current husband that I could now live in a place like Lake Forest, a middle-class city southeast of Irvine, California. Buying a car for my daughter wasn't high on my list of priorities.

"So the one-act plays are over?" I asked, changing the subject as we wound through the neighborhoods. The school wasn't far away, less than a mile, and I knew I could make her walk, but I felt bad that she came home to an empty house every day. Driving her in the mornings helped absolve my guilt.

"Yeah, but tryouts for the school play are today. Is it okay if I stay after?"

"Sure," I said. "What are you going to try out for?"

"I don't know," Stormy said, flipping down the visor and inspecting her makeup in the mirror again. She fixed a microscopic flaw in her green eye shadow. "We're doing *Grease,* and the Thespians will get all the big parts." The Thespian Troupe was a club for kids dedicated to acting. Stormy liked the performing arts, but she wasn't a fanatic. "There are some fun musical numbers and things, so Tress and I are just going to see what we can get."

"Good," I said, glad to see her putting herself out there and having such great experiences. December had been the same way when she had been in high school, and I was proud to have raised two daughters who had avoided the pitfalls I hadn't navigated so well. "I still marvel every time I go to one of your plays—the kids are so talented. It's so different than the stuff my high school did."

"I can only imagine," Stormy said. She flipped up the visor as I turned in to the school parking lot. "But what can you expect when you have to weave the cloth for your own costumes and do everything by kerosene lamps?"

"Ha-ha," I said, giving her a playful scowl. "Isn't it a little early in the morning for old-people jokes?"

"It's never too early for old-people jokes," Stormy said, waving her hand elaborately and rolling her eyes with dramatic flair.

I slapped her arm playfully, then hit the automatic unlock on my door. "Get the heck out of here," I said, pushing her with my right hand.

"Okay, okay," she countered, just as playfully. She picked up her backpack. "I can take a hint."

"Wub-oo," she said once she was out of the car. She used to say that when she was a little girl and couldn't articulate "love you."

"Wub-oo too," I said back. She smiled, shut the door, and then turned toward the school with her bouncy step and bouncy hair. Within seconds, her bouncy friends joined her, and I headed back home where I'd take out the curlers, put on my makeup, sip my coffee while I checked my personal e-mail, and then head out for another day at the office just as Paul was waking up. He was a computer programmer for a manufacturing company out of LA and had to spend only twenty hours a week in the office. The rest of his job he did from home. Lucky jerk.

"I have a good life," I said out loud as I headed home, loving that I believed every word of it. It was even more rewarding to know that I had a good life on purpose, not by chance. I'd worked hard as a mom, an employee, and a woman to get where I was, and it had not been an easy journey.

My long-suffering Catholic mother often said "Who wants easy?" Growing up, I'd hated that phrase, and as life became more and more difficult, I came to despise it. It had been only the last few years—since marrying Paul and moving to Lake Forest, really—that I could appreciate the struggles I'd overcome. Maybe that's how everyone was— grateful only *after* the hard stuff was over—but I still wanted easy, at least sometimes.

The rest of my day unfolded pretty much like every other day. I went to work, had lunch with a coworker, then got back to work. It wasn't until I was on my way to the 405 that I remembered I was out of reading material since I hadn't made it to the library yesterday. I considered going home by way of the library in El Toro, but then I saw the sign for the Barnes and Noble in the Spectrum Mall and decided I deserved a treat. In deference to my middle-aged waistline, I'd stopped rewarding myself with bagels and cookies from Efren's Bakery and started treating myself to new books and pedicures instead. I was down eleven pounds from a year ago, so my plan seemed to be working, albeit not as quickly as I'd have liked. I took the next exit and looped around.

I spent the next thirty minutes browsing the store, looking for something that caught my eye. Joanne Fluke had a new culinary mystery—I liked those. But I'd heard a lot about *The Hunger Games;* Stormy had said she wanted to read it before she saw the movie. She'd inherited her love of theater from Jared and her love of all things fiction from me. I found the first book in the series and then practically tripped over the newest Sarah Elizabeth Phillips. After weighing all three books in my hands, I decided to splurge and buy them all. If Paul and I were going away in a few weeks, I'd need a book or two anyway. I hoped his comment about bringing a bikini meant we'd have a beach. I adored the beach, but for someone living in Southern California I spent a pathetic amount of time there.

Thinking about the weekend reminded me that I hadn't talked to Jared or Stormy about Halloween yet.

Quickening my pace toward the registers, I texted Jared about the weekend plans; I hoped I could talk to Stormy about it before Paul came home. There was an older woman talking to the one open cashier. She was dressed in a banana-yellow suit—crease-fronted pants, a long vest that reached almost to her knees, and a pink-and-yellow patterned blouse. I suspected the suit was a polyester blend since it moved nice but looked heavy. She wore matching yellow sandals and dangly yellow-and-pink beaded earrings that swung when she moved her head.

I stood a polite distance away but couldn't help overhearing.

"I'm sorry, ma'am," the college-aged cashier said. "But we have a policy against outside advertising."

"But the other bookstores were fine with putting out some of my fliers," the woman insisted, brandishing a stack of half-sheet blue fliers. "And our first meeting is on Saturday. I really think your customers might like the opportunity to join my book club."

I'd belonged to a book club several years ago, before the divorce, but it had been with a group of women from work, and I eventually couldn't fit it into my schedule anymore. I still regretted having to give it up. I admired this woman for putting one together.

The clerk explained their policy again. The woman shook her head, sending her earrings into a frenzy, and finally stepped back from the counter. "Well, I guess we know which bookstore won't be getting *my* business." She turned and saw me standing there.

I offered her a smile so she would know I wasn't annoyed with her occupying the only cashier.

"Do you like book clubs?" the woman asked.

It took a couple of seconds for me to realize she was talking to me. "Oh, me?" I said, just to make sure.

She nodded and took two steps toward me. The clerk shook his head apologetically; I smiled at him to assure him I was okay. No need for people to get uncomfortable.

"Yes," the woman said. "I'm starting one and thought the best way to find members would be to have fliers at the local bookstores, but they say it's against their policy. Don't you think that's actually a disservice to their customers?"

Oh boy. Was I supposed to agree with her? "Corporate decisions," I said, hoping to find a safe answer. "And liability issues."

"Liability?" the woman repeated, raising her penciled eyebrows. "What do you mean by *liability*?"

"Well, let's say they put out some fliers inviting people to someone's home, and then that person turns out to be a serial killer and the victim's family sues the bookstore. Their insurance premiums would go through the roof!"

"You think I'm a serial killer?" the woman said flatly.

"Oh, no," I said quickly as my face heated up, not even realizing what I'd implied. I looked past her to the clerk who was now biting back a smile while helping another woman who had passed me up when I hadn't stepped forward in line. "No, I just, well, I sell insurance so I think about that kind of thing. But I didn't mean to imply *you're* a serial killer, just that, well, liability issues are a rising problem within our litigious society as a whole, and in order to protect themselves, companies sometimes have to make policies that protect them from possible litigation. The unfortunate result is that they are sometimes unable to support community projects, like your book group, due to the necessity of protection from malignant causes." I was actually a little impressed with my quick explanation, and behind the woman's intent expression, I thought she might be too.

She looked at the stack of fliers in her hand, peeled one off, and handed it to me. "I'd love to have you in my book club," she said simply. "Do you have a pen?"

"Uh, yes," I said, carefully. She kept staring at me so I opened my purse and took out a pen. She grabbed both the pen and the flier she'd already given me and scribbled something on the back.

"Here's my address," she said. "We meet this Saturday at seven o'clock. Feel free to bring a friend or two."

"Oh, okay," I said, rather confused at what had just happened.

"I'm Ruby," she said, handing me back the pen and the flier. Finally, her expression softened and I felt myself relax. "And I'm not a serial killer, I promise."

She turned toward the door and gave the clerk a triumphant look as she marched out of the bookstore, the rest of her fliers in hand. I waited until she'd disappeared through the first set of doors before walking up to the counter to buy my books.

"Well," I said as I set my purse and my purchases on the counter, "that was interesting."

"Don't go."

I looked up from my wallet and laughed at the stoic look on the clerk's face. "You don't think I should?"

"She's totally going to poison your iced tea," he said as he began ringing up the books. "And then I'll have to testify about this whole exchange, your family will sue Barnes and Noble after all, and, like you said, our premiums will go through the roof. Just stay home." He never once cracked a smile.

I laughed again and glanced at the doors before leaning over the counter conspiratorially. "I'm a wild woman. There's no telling what I might do."

Chapter 3

Saturday—my favorite day of the week.

I slept in until almost nine, lingered over coffee, and read half a dozen chapters in *The Hunger Games.* As soon as Stormy saw it, she wanted it, but I was reading it first. In the afternoon, I helped Paul with some yard work and then took Stormy shopping for jeans; she *had* to have some colored skinny jeans, which I found disturbingly similar to the pants I wore back in high school. Jared had agreed to pay for half of the shopping spree after saying he'd love to have Stormy for Halloween. Stormy wasn't as thrilled; she was sure she'd end up babysitting Jared's girlfriend's two little kids, but she was a pretty good sport once she knew she could still go to a friend's Halloween party that Saturday night.

"Are you going to dress up?" I asked as we pulled onto the Afton Parkway on our way to the mall.

"For the party? Yeah."

"What are you going to dress up as?"

"Tress and I are going to be Playboy Bunnies."

I laughed at the obvious joke. When Stormy didn't laugh with me, I glanced at her while I slowed down for a light, and I felt my face fall. "That *is* a joke, right?"

"I'm seventeen, Mom," Stormy said, but she wriggled in her seat uncomfortably.

It was all downhill from there. By the time Stormy had found her final pair of jeans—teal skinny jeans that I thought looked ridiculous—we weren't even speaking. I'd forbidden her from wearing the costume of her choice and had even threatened to cancel my weekend with Paul if I had to in order to make sure she didn't go advertising herself as a tramp. *A Playboy Bunny?* I thought over and over again on the drive home. She couldn't be serious—could she? Didn't she realize what that would say to every other kid at the party? As a girl who, at Stormy's age, had been six months pregnant, I knew *exactly* what it said, and there was no way on this green earth that my daughter was going to send out those kind of signals. I'd always thought I'd done a good job of teaching my daughters the self-respecting nature of modesty, but apparently I'd missed something.

The car hadn't even come to a complete stop in the garage before Stormy opened her door and stomped up the stairs. I took my time gathering my purse, racking my brain for the right way to handle this. Why was I always the bad guy? So often, parenthood felt like a losing battle I could never win.

While I was stalling, I saw the book club flier on the dashboard and picked it up, giving it another look. I hadn't thought much about it since encountering Ruby at the bookstore on Wednesday, but Paul was planning to catch the Lakers game, and Stormy was going to be a *ton* of fun tonight. Maybe going to a book club with a bunch of strangers, one of whom I'd already called a serial killer, was just what I needed to salvage my weekend.

I pushed open the door and was almost knocked over by a

completely unexpected tackle-hug from the daughter who minutes earlier hadn't been speaking to me.

"Thank you, thank you, thank you," she said, squeezing the breath out of me. I had to put out an arm to brace myself against the wall so that I didn't lose my balance. "I'll dress up as anything you want me to," she said. "Oh, thank you, thank you, thank you."

I managed to push her back a little bit. "Thank me for what?" I asked.

"The car!" she squeaked, her face completely lit up.

"The car?" I repeated, beyond confused by this whole situation. Had I blacked out or something?

Stormy dug her cell phone out of her pocket. "Tress is going to freak!" She pushed a few buttons and headed toward the kitchen counter. "Tress—guess what? I'm getting a car!"

I walked to the counter and put my purse down before looking at the newspaper spread out on the island. It was open to the used car section and sitting on top was a notebook with some notes written on it in Paul's handwriting. The cars listed were things like a Kia Spectra, a Ford Fresia, and a Jetta. Girl cars.

"Paul?" I called, heading toward our bedroom where his computer was set up. I felt a little thrill run through me at the idea that he was buying Stormy a car. Part of me, I admit, was bothered that I couldn't do it, and yet I was touched that he would step in. He and Stormy got along really well, but something like this would go a long way toward making their relationship even better, and it was proof that we really were meshing into a family.

"Huh?" he said when I entered, though he didn't look up from his computer.

I came up behind him and put my arms around his shoulders, kissing his neck. "You are my hero," I said before kissing him again.

Paul laughed his teenage-girl laugh and turned his chair, allowing me to slide onto his lap. "Wow, and all I was doing was checking the NBA stats."

I smiled and nuzzled his neck again; he was a sucker for that kind of thing. "I mean about the car. She's out of her head excited, and you saved me from a really miserable day in parenthood-land."

Paul was quiet for a minute. "I'm confused," he finally said.

I pulled back. "If you wanted it to be a surprise, you shouldn't have left your notes on the counter," I said, tapping him playfully on the nose.

"Oh," Paul said, realization dawning. "You mean the car for Mason."

I froze at the mention of *his* daughter. "Mason?"

Paul nodded. "I know it's a little premature," he said, laughing nervously though his eyes danced. "But she turns sixteen in a couple of months, and I thought it would make a good birthday-slash-Christmas present. Plus, maybe she could come up more often if she had her own wheels. If I get it now, I can have it registered and outfitted in time for the holiday without having to rush anything, ya know?"

I closed my eyes and told myself not to get angry. He hadn't done anything wrong. But even if he wasn't at fault, the fact remained that what I'd thought was a *bad* motherhood day had just taken a ridiculously horrible turn.

Chapter 4

THE PLAYBOY BUNNY ARGUMENT was nothing compared to the "Paul's daughter gets a car and she's not even sixteen yet!" tirade that filled my home Saturday afternoon. Paul decided to watch the game at his brother Charlie's house in Fountain Green as soon as he realized what had happened, leaving me to deal with my daughter's temper tantrum alone. I'd never been all that good at tantrums, and reason made way for a tantrum of my own before Stormy slammed the door to her room, rattling Paul's framed D'Ottavio prints that lined the hallway.

I let out a breath and tried chanting *eight more months, eight more months, eight more months,* but it didn't ease the rock in my stomach.

Half an hour later Jared called me to discuss the situation. Thank you, Stormy. He offered to pay the insurance if I bought her a car; I told him I couldn't afford one. He told me to talk to Paul. Without getting into the details of my financial relationship with my husband, I said that wasn't an option, which invited a pointed "I see." My blood boiled.

After that *lovely* discussion, I tried to read some more, but I couldn't get into the story. I looked at the clock—it was almost six—and I made up my mind, once and for all, to go to that book club. I had just enough time to make a quick dinner of pasta and pesto sauce, prepare a plate for Stormy, eat my own plateful, and head out. Before I left, I wrote a quick note to Stormy, slid it into *The Hunger Games,* and pushed the whole book under the door of her room, though it was a tight fit. Letting her read the book before I finished wasn't much in the way of peace offerings, but I was still pretty frustrated, and it was the best I could do.

I ended up arriving at the book group fifteen minutes early, but that was okay. It gave me a chance to chat with Ruby, and laugh about how we'd met. She was eccentric, that was for sure, but she had a beautiful home, and while we waited for the others to arrive, she told me all about her late husband and the travels they'd taken. I sensed she was lonely and was surprised to realize that I could relate. Of course I had Paul and my girls and some friends at work, but I couldn't really say there were any women in my life—not even my mom or sisters—with whom I felt truly comfortable. I hadn't had many close relationships with other women as an adult since my life had always been out of the norm. While I was learning to be a mom, the girls my age were still in high school. My career was in full swing by the time most women my age were graduating from college. Ruby was almost twenty years older than I was, but I wondered if she was the kind of woman I could really become friends with. More than ever, I felt like I had room in my life to really nurture that kind of relationship.

The next member of the group, Athena, arrived five minutes before it started. I guessed she was in her thirties and tried not to envy her athletic body. I'd never had time for the kind of commitment it took to have a physique like that. Then again, maybe she was naturally thin, the same way she was naturally beautiful. She had the most striking eyes, but I worried she'd retreat if I told her so; I had the distinct impression she didn't want to be put on the spot, even in a positive way. The doorbell rang, and Ruby went to answer it, leaving Athena and me alone in Ruby's living room.

"Do you live here in Newport?" I asked when Athena didn't seem willing to start a conversation.

"Yes," she said simply.

Before I had a chance to ask anything else, Ruby was back with another woman.

"Olivia," Ruby said. "Meet Daisy and Athena."

The new woman smiled and handed a plate of cookies to Ruby.

"Call me Livvy," she insisted, blowing her overgrown bangs out of her face. Livvy nervously attempted to smooth her hair, making me wonder if she wasn't exactly comfortable with the hairstyle she'd chosen. "I know you didn't want us to bring anything, but this was a new recipe I just had to try. White chocolate chip cookies."

Ruby thanked her as the door chimed again. "Oh, I'm glad everyone is so punctual," she said, excusing herself again.

Livvy turned to us, looking flustered. She was probably close to my age—younger maybe, but close.

"It's wonderful to meet both of you. I've been looking forward to this all day," Livvy said, straightening her wrinkled top. I'd learned the hard way that you really shouldn't wear linen unless you could take care of it.

I didn't have time for a polite comment before Ruby reappeared with a young woman trailing behind her. A very young woman. How old was this girl? Nineteen?

"And this is Paige. We have one more member, but she must be running late." Ruby looked at her watch and frowned.

We all said or nodded hello to Paige, who gave a small smile and a smaller wave in greeting, and my heart went out to her. She seemed a little overwhelmed. She'd no sooner sat down when the doorbell rang yet again. Ruby smiled and bustled out of the room, returning a few seconds later with a tall woman dressed in khaki slacks and a green, collared shirt with a logo from Walgreens stitched in the corner. I could tell right away something was different with Ruby's relationship to this member; she stood closer to the girl and looked more at ease.

"This is my niece, Shannon," Ruby said with a smile. "She needs to make room for a book in her life now and again, so I'm thrilled she could come."

Shannon smiled back, but I had the distinct impression that she was here for Ruby more than for the book group. Her brown hair was pulled back into a ponytail, and I guessed she was in her late thirties. She looked tired, and I wondered what she did at Walgreens. Was she a cashier? Obviously she'd just gotten off work.

"Everyone have a seat, and we'll make the round of introductions," Ruby said, gesturing Shannon toward the white couches I'd already become familiar with. Shannon perched on the edge next to Paige, but didn't sit back all the way.

Once seated, Ruby wasted no time getting started. "As you all know, I'm Ruby Crenshaw. I just turned sixty-two last month. I've lived in this gorgeous home by myself since the passing of my husband. It's been nearly two years, but sometimes it seems as if Phil has just left for work." She paused for a breath. "I have one son who lives in Illinois with his wife. My brother and his wife—Shannon's parents—recently moved to Phoenix, though I can't imagine why they would want to live in the middle of the desert." She shook her head as evidence of her confusion, then smiled as she looked at her niece. "Shannon lives in Laguna Hills; it's wonderful to have her so close. No grandkids of my own just yet."

I'd been right about her being lonely.

"I've always read," Ruby continued, "especially when my husband traveled." She looked down at her hands and fiddled with the wedding ring she still wore, which made my heart ache a little. Paul and I had only been married for three years, but I couldn't imagine life without him. "Since I was widowed, I haven't socialized like I used to with our friends. They're always there with an open invitation, but I find it harder to enjoy myself around them since I'm always the third or fifth or seventh wheel. So I spend a lot of time cooking for myself, and reading, of course." She looked up and put on a bright smile. "That's enough about me. Let's go around the circle."

She waved toward me, indicating I was first, so I gave a quick synopsis of my family and my job, not letting my thoughts dwell on the tension waiting for me at home. "And I'm looking forward to getting to know more people now that my kids are older and I have my own life again." I laughed, but noticed that the other women just smiled politely.

Athena and Paige were too young to know what it felt like to be at this stage of life. Shannon and Livvy might understand the demands of mothering a child who thought she knew everything, but neither of them backed me up. Shannon might still be too young, and Livvy was probably a perfect little housewife, with a perfect little life, whose kids were the center of her universe. By comparison, my comment had just made me look like one of those career-driven women who counted their family low on the list of priorities. I felt self-conscious for having said something so flippant. Maybe this wasn't going to work out. I pasted a smile on my face anyway and turned to the next person.

Livvy cleared her throat before telling us about her four kids. Four! I couldn't imagine. As she continued in a hurried voice, I realized that was all she talked about—her kids. Didn't she have anything in her life outside of them? I was right about the happy homemaker judgment I'd already pronounced.

"My daughter is babysitting for me tonight, which means the kids will likely be having frozen pizza for dinner, but at least they've got homemade cookies," she said.

I could read through that, though. Livvy felt guilty for being here—guilty for doing something that, compared to the rest of her life, seemed frivolous. I could relate, but it also annoyed me.

"I haven't read a novel in a long time, so I'm hoping to get a kick start with the group," she finished.

Ruby leaned over and patted Livvy's hand.

Then it was Paige's turn. She wasn't nineteen, but she was still in her mid-twenties. "I'm sort of starting over right now," she said, shifting awkwardly in her seat. "See, I'm newly single. I have two little boys—almost seven and three. I still can't believe I'm actually divorced. It wasn't supposed to happen to *me,* you know? I mean, we were married in the temple and everything."

Temple? Was she Jewish? But she acted as though she'd said something she hadn't meant to and hurried to explain.

"See, I'm Mormon and marriage is supposed to be forever when the ceremony is in one of our temples. . . . The boys miss their dad like crazy, but he left us for another woman, and . . ." She paused again, and I could see she was embarrassed. In my mind I told her to just take a deep breath, it was okay. "I came tonight because reading is one of my few escapes—or, well, it used to be—and I miss it. I also came in hopes of making some new friends." She took a nervous bite of her cookie, and I smiled, trying to catch her eye as her cheeks flushed.

I knew she thought she'd said too much, and I wanted to hug her. I'd been there myself, and I reflected for a moment on those first few years after my own divorce. It had been like living in a haze, and I was sure I was suffering from depression on top of just plain old being overwhelmed by it all. I hoped I could have the chance to offer her some encouragement. *It gets easier,* I wanted to say, but worried I would embarrass her even more so I kept it to myself.

Ruby offered sincere regret for Paige's circumstance but said how glad she was that Paige had made this time for herself. I agreed wholeheartedly. Maybe my own adjustment period wouldn't have been so hard if I'd had other women to be close to during that time. Instead, I'd stayed pretty isolated and had put all my energy into trying to figure it out on my own.

"I'm a pharmacist," Shannon said once Paige finished. "I live in Laguna Hills, like Aunt Ruby said, and I have one son. He's twelve. I've been married for fourteen years and, honestly, I can't remember the last book I read. I think Aunt Ruby's hoping I'll develop some hobbies."

"She works too much," Ruby said with a knowing nod, but a kind smile. "I'm really glad you're here, Shannon."

Shannon shrugged, looking embarrassed, and then turned to Athena expectantly. "So, tell us about you."

Athena looked even more uncomfortable than she'd been when she first came in, but I found myself curious about her story now that we'd learned about everyone else. I hoped she wouldn't retreat from the chance to let us get to know her.

"I'm thirty-two and single," she said.

We all waited for her to continue, but she didn't seem as though she had anything else to say.

"Oh, come on," Ruby said. "There's got to be more to you than that." She smiled in a motherly way that seemed to do the trick for Athena.

"I own an online magazine called *Newport Travel.* It keeps me pretty busy . . . so much so that my boyfriend broke up with me a few days ago."

It was obvious that hadn't been what she planned to say.

"Oh, I'm sorry," Ruby said. "But you're a beautiful girl, and I'm sure you won't be single for long."

I cringed, especially since Athena looked the tiniest bit stricken by Ruby's words.

"It's not exactly what you think," she said. "I wasn't ready to move into anything deeper and . . . Karl was . . . so he ended it." I thought for sure she'd stop there but was surprised when she kept going. "He thinks I'm a workaholic." She took a deep breath, and Livvy nodded at her encouragingly. "I am. I know it. But I want to do better. So here I am."

Ruby clapped her hands together. "We'll straighten you out."

Everyone laughed.

"Well, now that we know one another, let's eat," Ruby said with a big smile while Athena recovered from what looked like shock at what she'd said. "Then we'll talk books."

The rest of the evening went smoothly. I could tell we were all a little hesitant about being too comfortable with one another, but it wasn't *uncomfortable,* and by the time we left, I was glad I'd come.

The closer I got to home, the more the reality of what was waiting for me there began to descend. I wished I had somewhere else to go, but that wasn't the case. I was the mom; I was in charge, which meant everyone's problems became my problems.

Eight more months.

Chapter 5

"Hey, Amy," I said, scanning the paper I'd just printed as I let myself into her office. "I was looking over this addendum for the Clark Construction policy, and did you ask them about—" I looked up and took in her red eyes and splotchy complexion. She wiped quickly at her eyes and ducked her head as though maybe she could hide from me. After pausing a moment, I shut the door to her office and turned the wand to close the vertical blinds on the interior window of her office, enclosing us in the privacy we needed.

"What happened?" I asked, sliding into the seat across from her desk. The policy was forgotten as I watched her face. She shook her head and looked as though she might speak before dropping her head into her hands.

"It didn't take," she said in a throaty whisper. My heart sank for her; she and her husband had been trying to get pregnant for three years. I moved around the desk and put my arms around her shoulders, giving her permission to let down her attempted façade. She leaned into me and began to sob into the sleeve of my jacket. I rubbed her back and ached with her while she let it all out.

Amy and I had worked together for almost four years, ever since she'd transferred from the Sacramento office. She was almost ten years younger than I was, but as the only two female commercial agents in the office, we tended to stick together. Paul and I had attended her wedding just two months after returning home from our own honeymoon. A year later, she'd confessed her fears to me that something was wrong. She'd expected to be pregnant by now. I'd assured her that these things took time—though they never had with me—and she began to see me as someone she could talk to.

Her mother was too sympathetic, which Amy said made her feel like a little girl. Amy's older sister already had two young children and little time to commiserate. Amy's friends were either handing their babies off to their nannies in the morning, had already decided not to reproduce, or were always offering her unwanted advice. I was none of those people. I was just Daisy, the gal at work who would cheer her on or cheer her up, depending on the circumstances. But it was getting harder to fill that role. This was Amy's fourth round of in vitro. The hormones and expectations were wearing her out. And now this one hadn't worked either. What do you say in a situation like that?

I didn't know. So I continued to hold her and, for a minute, I even let myself reflect on my own loss—the closest I could come to truly relating to how she felt right now. December had been twelve, Stormy was two, and I was pregnant, which was the only reason Jared had agreed to go to marriage counseling in a final effort to save our family. Fifteen years later, I couldn't remember if I had been excited about the pregnancy. Did I see it as the possible link that would keep us together? Did I hope it would guilt-trip him into staying? I didn't know. I *did* know that I was overwhelmed by everything that was happening to us at the time. I was desperate to hang on to my marriage, though my motives were shaky. If we could have loved that baby, could we maybe, possibly, have loved each other enough to make our marriage work?

We'd never know.

At thirteen weeks I started cramping—bad. I ended up hemor-rhaging with the miscarriage and staying at the hospital overnight after getting a D and C. I can still remember staring up at the ceiling that night, alone, exhausted, emotionally vacant, and realizing that without this baby, Jared and I had nothing else to build on. My baby was gone. My marriage was over. I had failed, again.

We stopped going to counseling. Jared stopped trying to hide the phone calls he got from a girl named Jenna, and I finally gave up. There was really nothing left to save other than the accomplishment of being married and that wasn't a good enough reason anymore. For the second time in my life, I became a single mother, only this time I had a preteen and a toddler to feel insufficient for. I had felt like a failed woman in every sense of the word, and losing that baby had been dev-astating on so many levels.

Amy wasn't in my same situation, however. She had an adoring husband and a solid career, and if her lifelong dream of motherhood was just out of reach, it still wasn't impossible. There was hope for her; she was not at a dead end, but that didn't mean it didn't feel that way for her right now.

Finally, once she wasn't clinging to me so tightly and could take a full breath, I pulled back and wiped a few strands of hair from her wet face. "What on earth are you doing in the office today?"

Amy looked at her desk; folders and paperwork covered almost every surface. "The Trodin account is past due, and Lenny needed me to train him on the new umbrella package and . . ." She wasn't con-vinced by her own excuses and let out a staggered breath. "I didn't want to be home alone." Her chin quivered but she tried to straighten in her chair. She looked up at me and asked, "Why doesn't God want me to be a mother?"

"Oh, sweetie," I said, smoothing her hair again. "This isn't about God."

"Then why doesn't my uterus want me to be a mother?"

I thought about that, and suddenly had a mental image of a cartoon uterus running down the street, pushing a stroller. I cracked a smile, and apparently Amy must have been desperate for a laugh because she smiled too. Before we knew it, we were both laughing, but pretty soon the laughter had turned to crying all over again.

"Mick knows, right?" I finally asked when we got control of ourselves for the second time. Why had he *let* her come in today?

She looked away, and it all made a little more sense.

"Amy, you need to tell him," I said sternly.

"I can't," she said, a definite whine in her voice. "He'll be so . . . sad. I've already had to tell him this three times before. *Three.* I can't even imagine forming the words." New tears rose in her eyes as she began grabbing handfuls of Mick's disappointment to add to her own.

"Do you want me to do it?" I asked. I knew it was presumptuous, but my sisters and I used to quit jobs for each other over the phone when we were in high school because we couldn't stand hearing someone else's disappointment toward us. This was kind of like that, right?

Amy's eyes went wide with hope. "Would you?" She scrambled for her purse. She pulled out her purple cell phone, toggled to a dial pad, and pressed speed dial two.

I accepted the phone and stepped out into the hall. Mick answered with a "Hello, sugar-bottom."

"It's Daisy," I said. "From Amy's office."

"Oh," he said, and though I couldn't see it, I knew his cheeks were bright red. "Is . . . everything okay?"

"Not really." I relayed to him what had happened. He was silent.

Then he cursed under his breath. "I'm sorry, Mick." Though I didn't know him well, I knew he was heavily invested in the pursuit of children. "Amy couldn't bring herself to tell you; she's having a really hard time."

"Thank you for being there," Mick said. "Can I talk to her?"

I opened the door to Amy's office and covered the mouthpiece. Amy was trying to work on the computer, but I could see that her head and her heart weren't in it. She wiped at her eyes when she turned to me.

"Mick wants to talk to you," I said.

"Okay," Amy said quietly. "Thanks for breaking the news."

"You bet," I said as I handed her the phone. I was tempted to tell her to go home, but it wasn't my place. Amy was a big girl. Instead I let myself out of her office, making a mental note to check in with her in half an hour.

As I headed back to my office, I saw Lenny walking toward me. "Are you on your way to talk to Amy, by chance?" I asked; Amy's office was the only one past mine.

"Yeah," he said with a nod. Lenny was twenty-two if he was a day, tall, thin, and ill at ease in a suit. He was the newest member of the sales staff and was trying to act and look the part, but it didn't fit just yet. I wasn't worried; none of us fit the part when we started. He'd grow into it.

"I'd give her a little time, if I were you," I said.

"Why?" he asked, looking toward her office. I could read the anxiety on his face of not being able to get the training he'd been planning on.

"Girl stuff," I said.

His head snapped back to face me, his expression fearful. "Really?" His feet started moving him back to his cubical likely before he realized what he was doing.

Before I stepped into my office, I looked over my shoulder toward Amy's office and hoped she'd be okay. I wanted to give her all kinds of comfort and assure her that one of these days, one of the procedures would work. But how did I know? I'd always felt embarrassed and guilty that I'd found myself unexpectedly in "the family way" twice whereas good, centered women like Amy had to work so hard for what came so easy to me. But then, while infertility might not have been my cross to bear, I'd had my fair share of other Goliaths.

I settled in at my desk and turned to my computer before I remembered that I'd left the Clark addendum, and the questions I had wanted to ask, in Amy's office. That, coupled with the unsettled feeling in my stomach likely triggered by my own nostalgic memories, had me feeling eager for distraction. I glanced at my door before going to Amazon.com. I hadn't managed to get to the bookstore to pick up a copy of the book for next month's book group—*The Poisonwood Bible* by Barbara Kingsolver—and there were four holds ahead of me at the library. Amazon to the rescue.

I'd never read the book, but Athena, the Greek goddess with those beautiful eyes, had recently bought it, and Ruby had read it several years ago. The landing page came up on Amazon's website and I skimmed the contents. "Five hundred and forty-six pages?" I read. "Seriously?"

I took a breath—I couldn't remember the last book I'd read that was that long. I'd even resorted to CDs from the library for the last couple Harry Potter books. "I can do this," I told myself. But I would need the book sooner than next week. I closed Amazon and looked up the Barnes and Noble where I'd met Ruby a couple of weeks ago. They had two copies in stock and agreed to hold one for me until six o'clock. I thanked them and hung up. Five hundred and forty-six pages? Beyond the ability to finish it, I hoped I would like it. I didn't have enough reading time to waste it frivolously. But then, Athena and Ruby were both poised and educated women. If they could make time for it, so could I.

Amy walked past my office a few minutes later, her purse and jacket over her arm as she looked at the floor. I was glad she was going home. After retrieving my paperwork from her now-empty office, I was back to work proofreading the latest policy when my cell phone rang. I didn't recognize the number.

"Hello, this is Daisy," I said, holding the phone against my shoulder while I corrected an error on the page.

"This is Mary Dean, one of the secretaries from Lake Forest High."

"Hello," I said, finishing up my correction as I tried to think of what this call could be about. Had I ever had a call from the high school? I marked where I'd stopped reading on the document and gave Mary Dean my full attention.

"Vice Principal Keets would like to set up a meeting with you."

"Okay," I said carefully. "In regards to what?"

"I don't really know," Mary Dean said, sounding a little sheepish. "I just schedule his appointments. He's got a ten thirty spot open tomorrow morning. Could you come in at that time?"

Right smack-dab in the middle of the workday. How convenient. "Yes," I said, scrambling for a pen so I could write down the meeting in my planner. I knew my morning was free because I always set aside Wednesday mornings to catch up on policy changes and overall file organization, but I didn't have too much of that to work on tomorrow. In that sense, the timing was good. That said, it was never good to have a meeting with your child's vice principal.

"Excellent," Mary Dean said. "I've got you down. Just come to the main office."

I finished the call and stared at the note in my planner as I tapped my pen. Stormy wasn't a troublemaker. She got decent grades. So why would the vice principal want to meet with me? The unsettled feeling in my stomach got worse. I did not have time for this! And yet, I was Mom—hooray, hooray—which meant I would have to *make* time.

I put down my pen and went back to my corrections, but my mind was rolling over possible reasons for the meeting. Truancy? Talking back to teachers? Failing classes? These were the parts of motherhood that no one had told Amy about—the moments when you felt like you'd failed somewhere but didn't know how, which meant you'd probably keep on making the same mistake. Ignorance really was bliss. I knew Amy's heart was broken, but I couldn't help wondering if she'd be quite so devastated if she knew about the not-so-bright-and-shiny moments of motherhood.

Chapter 6

Stormy acted completely ignorant about why the vice principal would want to talk to me, which meant that when I sat down on the red plastic chair in the main office of the high school the next morning I had nothing to work with. Though Stormy had assured me she didn't know what the meeting was about, she *had* looked nervous when I told her about it. Scared even, and she had spent most of the evening hidden in her room. Unfortunately, that wasn't all that strange either. Since the car brouhaha of Saturday afternoon, she'd given me the cold shoulder. It probably should have bothered me more than it did, but it was easier to be mad at her and keep my own distance when she was acting bratty.

"Mrs. Herriford?" Vice Principal Keets asked.

"Mrs. Atkins," I corrected him as I came to my feet. Herriford was Jared and Stormy's name, but not mine anymore. I'd chosen to wear my red shirt and white capris with my white sandals—a striking outfit I hoped would show the entire office that I was not a deadbeat parent, but someone who took pride in my appearance. I wasn't really sure why that should have mattered, but I always got fastidious about how I looked when I was nervous, and I was very nervous. "I've remarried."

"My apologies. I should have reviewed the file better."

I smiled my forgiveness. He was wearing a short-sleeved, button-up shirt that strained against his stomach, exposing two little triangles of a white T-shirt. I'd be willing to bet a chocolate cream pie that the students had all kinds of names for him behind his back. I could never work with thousands of teenagers. "I'm Vice Principal Keets. Thanks for coming in."

We shook hands, and he showed me into his office, where I sat in a plush-covered chair. He settled rather uncomfortably into his chair across the desk and gave me what I assumed was supposed to be a comforting smile.

"Do you know why you've been called in?"

That irritated me, but I tried to hide it by shaking my head. If they'd have told me yesterday, then I would know.

He took a breath that seemed to say "They never do" and then pulled open the drawer of his desk. He removed a manila folder and passed it across the desk to me. I regarded it for a moment, not really wanting to open it, and looked up at him with a question plainly written on my face.

"I sent a note home with your daughter last week for you to give me a call. Did you get that note?"

"No," I said flatly, and my stomach dropped a little further.

"I didn't think so." He nodded at the folder, which I took as permission for me to open it, so I did. Inside were several papers. I thumbed through them, noting the 100% written at the top of each one.

"I'm assuming I haven't been called here because of my daughter's proficiency on these assignments." I sounded calm but I was starting to panic. Why was I here?

"We instituted a policy last year stating that in order to participate in the school play, all participants needed to have a C grade or better in all of their classes."

I looked back at the papers. They were all history assignments. Stormy hated history and had always barely skated through it. This year she was taking an American government class and had whined about it constantly for the first couple weeks of school. I hadn't heard much about it since then, though.

Mr. Keets continued. "Mr. Thornston, Stormy's teacher, brought these to my attention last week. I called Stormy in, and she said you'd been helping her with her homework. I don't mean to doubt your abilities, but it's very rare that we see a student go from failing to all As in a matter of weeks. It's even more concerning when that happens shortly after the grade requirements are passed out to all those interested in trying out for the school play."

I felt my jaw tensing, but worried that Mr. Keets could tell so I forced myself to relax. That included unclenching my hands, which I had balled into fists in my lap. Mr. Keets was looking at me, and I felt obligated to say something. "I see," I said, the most neutral thing I could think of.

"Cheating is a serious situation, Mrs. Herriford."

"Atkins," I corrected without thinking. I felt my cheeks heat up. "I'm sorry. Continue."

"But seeing as how this is Stormy's first offense, we chose to go to you rather than suspend her as we did the others."

"Others?"

"We had six other students involved," Mr. Keets explained. "We're not sure how, but someone either got the answers, or found someone who knew them on their own, and shared the love, so to speak. We were able to identify six students who had the exact same answers to every question on the last few assignments, one of which was a quiz. We're still looking into it, but two of the students have had issues with this kind of thing before. They've been suspended. We'd rather this not go on Stormy's record, which is why we've called you in. It's our hope that with you involved, we can be assured this won't happen again."

I nodded, feeling about two inches high. "I'll be sure to talk to her. It won't happen again."

"I certainly hope not. If it *did,* we'd have no choice but to act more aggressively. As it is, Stormy will be asked to do some make-up assignments, and she's precluded from being a part of the school play."

Oh, she was going to be so upset. "Has she been informed of this yet?" Even through my embarrassment and anger, I was sad that she'd screwed up the one extracurricular activity she was involved in.

"Not yet. We wanted to be sure we had your support before we let her know where we stood. We'd like you to talk to her tonight, and then we'll officially meet with her tomorrow."

I would have preferred to have the sequence of events happen in the reverse order—let me mop up rather than swinging the ax. But *I* was the mother and this was *my* job. "I understand."

Ten minutes later I was in the car, the file folder on the passenger seat, gritting my teeth. I hated—*hated*—this part of motherhood—the part where everything my kids did reflected on me. I knew I wasn't a perfect parent, but I worked hard to teach my kids the difference between right and wrong, and I'd done most of it myself. Why couldn't that be reflected back once in a while?

A glimmering reminder that Stormy hadn't done anything like this before shimmered across my mind, but I still felt betrayed and stupid. Mothers should know when their kids are doing things like this. When was the last time I sat down to help her with her homework? When was the last time I asked her how American government class was going? When was the last time I talked to her about cheating and why it was wrong?

Unbidden tears rose in my eyes, and I wiped them away, angry at my emotional reaction. Angrier still that I was reacting at all. Why did this have to be about me anyway? I hadn't cheated. Stormy knew what was expected of her. She knew what was right and had chosen against it. What did that have to do with me?

Taking the morning off for the meeting meant that I had a lot to do once I reached my office—thank goodness—and I quickly lost myself in my work. Amy wasn't in today so I sent her a quick e-mail of support, but it was also a relief not to be her shoulder today. I was feeling too sorry for myself to be of much use to anyone else. I was safe, surrounded by my policies, alone in my determination to protect my clients from liabilities that could undo all their hard work. I even stayed late, not locking my office door until after six.

After a quick stop at the bookstore, it was almost seven before I got home. Paul was cooking salmon, and my stomach rolled when I stepped into the kitchen from the garage. I usually loved fish—especially when I didn't have to cook it—but apparently not when I was angry with my child.

"Is Stormy here?" I asked after sharing a quick hello kiss with my sweetheart.

"I've only been home half an hour. Haven't seen her," Paul said as he squeezed a lemon over the beautifully blackened fillet sizzling in the pan.

I put my purse down on the kitchen chair with a deep sigh.

He looked up. "Everything okay?"

"No," I said, sitting down heavily in the other chair. I proceeded to tell him about the meeting. He kept his back to me for most of the explanation, and the more I got into it, the more frustration colored my tone. He added spinach to the pan. My stomach was as excited about spinach as it was about salmon. Great—Stormy had spoiled my dinner too.

"What are you going to do?" he asked, sliding the salmon and spinach onto a platter.

"Sell her to China," I said, leaning my head against the back of the chair. "You never hear about those child laborers cheating in history class in order to be in school plays."

He chuckled. "No, really—what are you going to do?"

"Talk to her," I said with a shrug, closing my eyes as though that would help me relax. "Probably yell a little, make sure she knows what a big deal it is. Maybe I'll take away her cell phone. I don't know."

"If you approached her calmly, she might fess up to how it all came together."

I didn't really care how it came together. And *calmly* wouldn't exorcise my demons. I also hated it when people told me what to do, even Paul. "I'm not sure I can do calmly."

"You could try."

I opened my eyes, a wave of irritation washing over me. "Thanks," I said sarcastically as I got to my feet.

"What?" He turned to look at me, his face showing genuine surprise. He held a spatula in one hand.

"You say that like I'm always freaking out on her," I said, looking for some way I could share the responsibility that was sitting so heavily on my shoulders. "It's not like this is easy. She's got two parents, but I'm the only one who gets to deal with the ugly stuff and, you know what? I'm so sick and tired of the ugly stuff. I'm tired of arguing about everything. I'm tired of feeling like the bad guy all the time. I'm tired of not being appreciated, of people questioning every little thing

I do. Here I've worked hard to give her a good life, and I feel like I've created a spoiled little brat who only cares about what she can get out of people, who's constantly looking for some kind of free ride. I mean, what does she do around the house? Nothing. What does she do to earn money for the movies and new clothes and makeup? Nothing. She's lazy and rude, and now she's a cheat—how humiliating is that?" I shook my head. "I'm just tired of . . . of . . ." I didn't want to say it out loud, but the word hung there. "I'm tired of *her*. I'm tired of being *the mom*." And I was just—tired.

I looked at Paul, already feeling regret for my outburst. But he wasn't looking at me. He was looking *past* me, his expression shocked. Before I even turned around, I felt a prickling sensation of realization that I'd done something horrible. I turned to see Stormy staring at me. Not angry Stormy. Not defensive Stormy. Sad Stormy.

"Oh, hon," I said, my whole body on fire as I rewound what I had said and played it back in my head. Maybe she hadn't heard all of it, but I knew that didn't matter. Whatever she had heard was enough. She ran back to her room, where she must have been when Paul came home, and slammed the door hard enough to shake the windows. She'd already locked the door by the time I reached it.

"Stormy," I said. "Let me in."

"Go away!"

"I'm sorry. I shouldn't have said those things. I didn't mean it."

She didn't answer me, and I let my head fall forward until it hit the door. My words fell flat because, as wrong as it was to say what I'd said, I *had* meant it. And what made it worse was that Stormy knew I'd meant it. More points for Mom! I was *swimming* in maternal mistakes these days but felt absolutely sick about this one. How on earth would I make this right?

Chapter 7

JARED SHOWED UP AT MY DOOR an hour later. I shouldn't have been surprised, but I was. I'd had a few bites of salmon but couldn't stomach more than that, and although I'd tried to talk to Stormy twice through her still-closed bedroom door, she wouldn't dialogue with me. I thought I had more time to let her cool off, to think of the right way to fix things between us, but apparently I didn't because she'd called her dad for backup.

Jared didn't even say anything when I opened the door, just lifted his eyebrows as if to say, "Here I am to save the day!" He'd put on weight since we'd split up, and his hair was thinning, but he still had the looks and the confidence I'd fallen in love with eighteen years ago. I stepped aside and let him into the house.

Paul looked up from the magazine he was reading and then stood and crossed the floor to shake hands. It was always weird to see them together—my past and my present facing off. But Jared was here to face off with me, not Paul, and as soon as the niceties were finished, Jared got to the point.

"So," he said, folding his arms over his chest. He used to work out religiously, but had slacked off the last few years; it showed more than he probably wanted me to notice. "A little drama, huh?"

I wanted to slap him for being patronizing. Instead, I folded my arms too and gave him his share of the problem by relating everything that had happened at the school and how embarrassing it was and how angry I was about it.

"And so then you said you hated her and didn't want her living here anymore," Jared added when I finished.

My hands fell to my sides. "I never said that!" I looked to Paul for confirmation, but he'd stepped away from the discussion and looked as though he didn't know whether to stay or go. Betrayal surged through me. Why couldn't he, just once, stand with me instead of stepping back to let me handle the fight all by myself? He'd been there. He knew what I *hadn't* said. Unfortunately, he also knew what I *had* said and that wasn't a whole lot better.

"Well, regardless of the words you used, she *heard* that you hate her and don't want her here anymore. I came to pick her up."

"What?" I snapped. "That's why you're here—to take her with you?" I looked at Paul again, sure that this outrageousness would incense him too. He was flipping through a magazine so I turned my laser stare to Jared, who shrugged as though he had no choice in the matter—Stormy was running the show.

"Can't you see she's playing you against me?" I said, trying to sound calm even though I was anything but. "She's done something horrible, and she's trying to hide it behind *my* mistake."

He raised both eyebrows. "Sounds like you're doing the exact same thing."

I clenched my teeth together but kept from saying anything else. It wouldn't help, and I knew it. He pulled his phone from his pocket and typed in a text. I knew he was texting Stormy to tell her she could come out of her room and that he would whisk her away from all her troubles.

"She's got school," I said.

"I know that," Jared said, his calm slipping.

"She can't afford to miss school, especially now. And she's got a special meeting with the vice principal tomorrow."

"I've figured it out."

"How?" I asked, crossing my arms again, feeling the need to be defensive about anything and everything. He never took Stormy on school nights, never, not once in all these years. For him to come here acting as though he could fix everything was offensive.

"I've figured it out," he said again, this time slowly with clipped words. He spoke in a tone meant to make me feel stupid, like he had to use slow, concise words so my little brain could understand what he was saying. "I'll call you in a couple of days, when you've both had a chance to calm down."

There was that word again—calm. I took a deep breath and was about to completely tear into him and tell him what a pompous jerk he was to come pick her up without even hearing my side of things. He was wedging himself between us, and I wasn't going to stand for it.

But I didn't tear into him. For two reasons. First, I was afraid I might say too much—like I had when venting to Paul. If I'd minded my tongue then, I wouldn't have to mind it now. Second, why not let Jared try his hand at raising a teenage girl? He'd been a weekend dad most of Stormy's life and was rarely even that anymore due to her social life. He'd never gone to a parent-teacher conference. He'd never taken her to the dentist or had to explain the birds and the bees or teach her how to finish a math problem. He'd certainly never been called to the principal's office. The reason he could judge me so harshly was because he'd never walked two yards, let alone a mile, in my shoes.

I heard Stormy's door open behind me, which gave me a chance to attempt to salvage something with her there to hear it.

I raised my hands in surrender and changed my tactics. "Okay," I said, thrilled to see disappointment in Jared's eyes. He loved a good fight, and I was denying him the satisfaction of being able to rile me up even more. "I was over the top tonight, and I shouldn't have said what I said. I understand if she doesn't want to stay here right now." I wanted to turn around and make eye contact with my daughter, but I wanted her to think she was overhearing something rather than being addressed directly with these sentiments. I met Jared's eyes instead. "I'm really sorry," I said, as though having to take care of his own daughter for a couple of days was a horrible burden to put on him. He'd see what it was really like to be the custodial parent. I gave him three days—tops.

He was taken aback by my humility. Stormy moved forward, and I turned to look at her. My little demonstration fizzled. She'd been crying, and I felt horrible. "Sweetie," I said. She wouldn't look at me, and I didn't try to force her to hug me or try to touch her at all for fear she'd slap away any attempts I made. She walked past her dad and out the front door without a word, a duffel bag in hand and her backpack slung over her shoulder. Jared looked at me as though he was going to say something, but decided against it and he pulled the front door shut behind him.

Paul and I stood there for a few seconds. I stared at the door; Paul looked between me, the door, and the kitchen. "Well," he said after a few seconds, clapping his hands together. "That was fun."

I glared at him. "Thanks for your help," I said, feeling angrier than I logically thought was warranted but too emotionally fractured to curtail it. The whole day had gone from bad to worse, and I just wanted to throw it all away and start over tomorrow. Right now, I had to believe that was possible or I'd break into a thousand pieces, and I couldn't let myself do that.

"What did I do?"

"Exactly my point," I said, turning on my heel. I needed to be alone. I grabbed *Poisonwood Bible* off the counter—an excuse for solitude—and stormed into our room, shutting the door rather than slamming it, even though I was sure a slam would make me feel better.

I dropped on the bed and closed my eyes, clutching the book to my chest as I listed all the injustices that had been waged against me today. Tears rose and I choked them down. Big girls don't cry, right? After a few minutes of self-pity, and feeling rather disgusted by myself for every word I'd said since entering the house tonight, I flipped open the book and turned to the first page. I could only hope that I could lose myself completely within the words of the story. I wasn't good company, and I needed to get far away from my life. What better way than with a missionary family in the jungles of the Congo in the 1960s? Thank goodness for a distraction that could keep me from seeing myself in all my ugly glory.

What a horrible day.

Chapter 8

"I'm sorry," I said, standing just inside the doorway of the living room. I felt like a petulant child, but that wasn't undeserved. I'd gotten lost in the book for a while, but as I read about the family's interactions and saw the dysfunction there, I saw myself a little more clearly. Too clearly.

Paul looked up from his laptop set up on a TV tray and closed the lid. He leaned against the back of the couch and put his hands behind his head. I didn't want to meet his eyes, didn't want to see the censure I knew I deserved, but the silence stretched too thin and I couldn't avoid it. Paul was staring at me, waiting, but his eyes were soft, and I felt a lump form in my throat. He was a good man. That acknowledgment made me feel even worse.

"Are you okay?" he asked, and I knew he wasn't just talking about this moment. "You seem . . . out of sorts."

"I don't know what's going on with me," I said, which was true. "I don't feel like I've been sleeping well."

"That's not what I meant."

"I know," I said sheepishly. I considered telling him that I worried I was coming down with something too—hence the reason why dinner had turned me off—but I knew that wasn't what we were talking about either. He extended his arms, taking them from behind his head and holding them out as though inviting me into them. I didn't hesitate and hurried across the room to snuggle up next to him on the couch. I tucked my feet beneath me and let him put his arms around me.

"I love my daughter, but I'm tired of raising teenagers," I said, though I was distrustful of saying it out loud. After all I'd said earlier tonight, it seemed an even greater betrayal of Stormy to say it again, only using different words. "It's impossible for her to not take that personally." I sighed, heavy and laden with regret.

"Well, if I said I was tired of my wife, you might take that as a hit."

"I might."

He gave me a shoulder squeeze and kissed my hair. How was it that Paul could talk about almost anything and stay calm when I couldn't? "You're a good mom, Daisy," he whispered.

I felt the tears rise in my eyes. *Was* I a good mom? Since the moment December had been put in my arms more than twenty-seven years ago, I had *wanted* to be a good mom. But ever since then I'd felt as though I'd been trying to force myself into a mold I didn't fit. It shouldn't feel that way.

Something one of my mother's well-intentioned friends said to me when they learned I was *not* putting my baby up for adoption came back to me: "There are some choices you can't undo. You've already made one; don't follow it up with another bad decision." That comment had haunted me. Had I simply been building on that first wrong decision—getting pregnant in the first place—all these years? When that woman had shared her thoughts, I'd been seventeen years old, bloated with a baby that, honestly, freaked me out when it moved around in my belly. I took her words as a kind of challenge. I would prove I could do this. I would not give in to people's limited expectations of me.

My own friends were avoiding me by then; I had broken the illusion of invincibility that teenagers needed to justify their dumb choices. The people at church were judging me and advising me and making predictions they couldn't know were true: "You'll end up on welfare." "You'll never get an education." "You'll ruin that child's life."

I was determined, though, with the help of my eighteen-year-old Prince Charming, to prove otherwise; I wanted so badly to prove otherwise.

December was three months old, and I was still unmarried and living in Scott's parents' basement, when the bloom began to fade on the rose. Three months after that, I was living back at my parents' house and trying to ignore the "I told you so" glances from pretty much everyone. I finished my GED via night school and avoided welfare because my parents let me live at home expense-free in exchange for being able to use me as an example to my brother and sisters.

I'd tried to be the right kind of mom, but I couldn't do it on my own. And my mother's help came at a high price—mostly self-respect, independence, and good ol' pride. At the age of twenty, I moved out on my own for the first time, with more predictions of failure nipping at my heels as I went. My job as a secretary at an insurance company made it possible for me to get a studio apartment for December and me, so long as we were both content with eating ramen noodles most of the time—which we were. Mom still watched December while I was at work, but I reveled in no longer having a crib next to my bed in my childhood bedroom.

After a year with the insurance company, I received my certification to do quotes for potential clients. I added a few more certifications to diversify my potential and finally got my license to be an agent after I'd been working there about three years. As soon as I was offered an agent position—I'd been applying within the company for several months by that point—I jumped on it and moved to Los Angeles, California, where, for the first time, I had my very own office and my very own clients. December was five and didn't like going to day care after having been with Grandma every day, but what else could I do? She started kindergarten that fall and we . . . adjusted.

I had a few relationships in those first few years in LA, but nothing that took off until I met Jared through a woman I worked with. He was the sun, moon, and stars, and if I ever questioned that, he was quick to remind me of it. We were just getting serious, just beginning to talk about a future together, when—surprise—I was pregnant.

Out of wedlock.

Again.

I panicked.

I could *not* have another baby alone. Hadn't I learned this lesson already? I saw only one solution—one thing that would prove I was not some kind of bimbo idiot. I needed to get married this time. Lucky for me, Jared wasn't completely opposed to marriage.

With a weekend trip to Napa and a two-hundred-dollar ring from Kmart, we sealed the deal in a small ceremony. I sent pictures to my parents. They said they were happy for me, but why couldn't I have gotten married in a church? Jared wasn't religious, and despite my parents' refusal to acknowledge it, neither was I. The Christian ideals I'd been taught all my life had soured when those same believers had condemned me at the age of seventeen to a life of poverty and delinquency because I wouldn't part with my own flesh and blood.

Jared wanted to be an actor, which meant he waited tables and provided security at events while waiting for his big break. I continued with my career, making sure we had a reliable income, and did the best I could to juggle everything—new husband, demanding job, new baby, and a ten-year-old girl. Despite all my good intentions, however, we never quite found our groove, Jared and I, before he decided that a groove with me wasn't what he really wanted anyway.

The miscarriage right before our official separation hadn't helped my view of myself in a maternal role. Ever since, I'd harbored a secret fear that God had taken that child away from me because He knew I couldn't take care of it. I didn't necessarily disagree with Him, but it was one more reason to regard God with suspicion.

After we officially split, Jared took a job as a salesman for a computer software company in Tustin, while I stayed in our overpriced apartment in Chino before transferring to the Irvine office and tried, again, to keep up with a life I hadn't really wanted and didn't feel cut out for.

I wasn't a *bad* mother all those years, but I had a lot going on, and I couldn't honestly say that I felt like I'd ever been a good mother to my girls.

I considered saying this out loud to Paul, but it was one of those questions that came with the obligation of a specific answer. Kind of like "Do I look fat in this?" If I told Paul what I really thought about the kind of mother I'd been, he'd try to convince me I was wrong. How could he do otherwise? I was very self-aware, so manipulating people into offering empty reassurances wouldn't do me any good in the long run. I just wished I could see the job I'd done as a mom as *good enough*. Tonight of all nights, however, was not helping.

"Do you think she'll forgive me?" I asked once the lump in my throat had gone away and I'd reminded myself all over again of who I really was. Not Super Mom—just Daisy, who was trying to keep up for eight more months until she could check "Raise second daughter to adulthood" off her to-do list.

I reflected on my relationship with December. We'd had our moments when she was the teenager making me crazy, though she was never as *stormy* as Stormy was, but once she left home, we'd become pretty good friends. We talked on the phone a few times a week, and I felt like I was a part of her life in such a way that she didn't ask more than I could give, which meant I couldn't fail her. I loved that feeling.

December had her degree in secondary education and had taught junior high English in Ohio for the last three years. She hadn't renewed her teaching contract this fall, though, because she and her husband, Lance, were expecting their own child in just a few months. December was going to stay home and be a full-time mom. She was *excited* about becoming a mom. I'd never had that. Having my children had been seasons of anxiety in my life, despite the thrill it was to hold them and realize they were a part of me. I was so glad December was going to have what I didn't: a solid marriage and the ability to choose the kind of mother she would be instead of being forced into it.

"She'll forgive you," Paul said, and for a brief moment I thought he was talking about December. Then I realized he meant Stormy. "And while perhaps saying it the way it came out wasn't the most politically correct way to make the point, I don't think it hurts for her to know it's hard for other people when she screws up. She needs to be accountable."

"Yeah," I said, but I agreed only a little bit. I'd hurt her, and I hated knowing that. Her accountability didn't take away my own. Stormy's cat, Munchkin, was curled up on the chair across from us and paused in her cleaning to stare me down. I felt the censure from her too.

"Give her a few days," Paul said, standing up and grabbing my hands to pull me up with him. "And then things will be back to normal." He wrapped his arms around my waist and kissed me, long and deep. "In the meantime," he said, giving me a devilish smile. "We've got the house to ourselves. Whatever will we do with ourselves?"

Chapter 9

"What do you mean she wants to stay?" I said into the phone Saturday afternoon. I'd been reading the Kingsolver novel but wasn't even halfway through it yet. It was a long book and now lay next to me on the couch, completely forgotten in the wake of Jared's phone call.

"Look, she's embarrassed by what happened at school and with everything you said the other night. She wants to try to make a fresh start out here."

I was stunned by this turn of events. Truly and completely stunned. "Jared," I said, my voice calm only because I was still reeling from shock. "Transferring high schools is a big deal, especially in the middle of the semester of her senior year."

"I know, Daisy," he said, sounding as though he really understood that the decision was a big one. But he *couldn't* understand. If he did, he wouldn't be making this choice. "If she stays here, she can find a new place for herself, and she could still try out for the school play at Beckman. I talked to the school about it yesterday. Auditions are next week. It would be a great way for her to start meeting people right off the bat."

I closed my eyes, repeating my new mantra in my head—calmly, calmly, calmly—and raised my free hand to my eyes. I hadn't felt well all week—like my stomach knew that things weren't the way they should be—and I was feeling worse than ever right now, but I was trying really hard to ignore my physical issues and stay grounded. "I don't know that running away from this is the right solution, Jared. And I feel like Stormy and I need to fix what's between us or it'll fester." It was unusual for me to trust him with this much information; it made me feel vulnerable.

"That's the other part of this. She was really hurt by what you said, and she said that even before all of this happened that she'd felt like she's in the way over there."

That sliced through me like a razor, but it also cut my defensiveness off at the knees. "If I could take it back, I would."

I half expected him to rub it in, but he took the high road, and when he spoke his voice was sympathetic. "What's important now is that we do what's best for Stormy. I'd love to have her here. We haven't had the one-on-one time either of us would like, and maybe that's part of this whole thing too. I'm certainly willing to take my share of the responsibility." He paused, then added, "It's what she wants, D."

D. He used to call me that all the time, and I didn't like the warm reaction I felt to the nickname right now. "Okay," I heard myself say. How could I make her come back if she didn't want to? Obviously she and Jared had already planned it out. I'd been swimming against the current to even attempt putting up a fight. "But I need to talk to her. Can I come over, bring her some of her things?"

"Actually, we thought we'd come out this afternoon and pack her and Munchkin up. I'm sure you and Stormy can talk things out then. How about that?"

"Okay," I said again, broken by all of this. I wondered about Jared's girlfriend and how she might factor in to the situation, but I knew it would be inappropriate for me to ask. I had no power anymore; I'd shattered it when I'd dared say those things about my daughter out loud. Even if she hadn't been there to hear them, they were mean, and as much as I wanted to take them back, words weren't retractable.

"Good deal," Jared said.

I'd been trying hard to find something in his tone or approach to take offense to, to hold against him and use as a step to put myself higher, but not a single thing had invited my cynicism. In fact, I could turn things around and see myself reacting to the situation much worse than he was. I appreciated him handling this the way he was, even if I didn't like the result.

We finished the call, and I sat there, trying to figure out how I felt. Was I sad? Embarrassed? . . . Relieved? I clenched my eyes shut, berating myself for being so selfish. I tried to read again, but the realization that my little girl wasn't coming home made me feel raw inside. Paul was spending the day with his brother, so the house was empty. I walked to the doorway of Stormy's room and tried to be rational as I looked at the space she was leaving behind and attempted to tell myself this was okay.

I packed up some boxes and bags, and when Paul came home, I gave him the details, and he assured me that everything would be okay. Stormy and Jared came around five o'clock. Paul and Jared set about loading up the car, while Stormy and I sat on the back porch and I tried to redeem myself. I'd made some lemonade and sipped it while trying to have a very awkward conversation. Stormy was polite and respectful, but closed off. I apologized and explained how tired I was and how overwhelmed I'd felt to be called in to the school for something so out of character for her.

"You've been such a good kid, Stormy," I explained. "And I'm so proud of you for all you've done. It undid me to face something like that, but I should never have said what I said, and I'm so sorry."

Stormy looked up from her lemonade, and I was surprised to see that her mouth was tight and her eyes narrowed. An apology wasn't supposed to get that kind of reaction. "You never asked me if I did it."

I blinked and felt a sharpness in my chest. "I saw the papers, and Mr. Keets said you had claimed I'd helped you with your homework to get the grades, but I hadn't."

"I have study hall this term, and I used it to study specifically for that class. I knew I couldn't be in the school play if I didn't get my grades up; it was a big deal when they made that policy last year. It took me a while to get into the class, but then I realized that history is really like a whole bunch of stories—like a novel—and systems—like math. I did good on those assignments because I'd studied, Mom, and I said you helped me because I could tell they didn't believe I could have done it myself. They think I'm stupid."

"But he said he'd sent a note home a week before. Why didn't you give it to me when you knew they suspected you?"

"'Cause they were wrong," she said loudly. "I didn't even know those other kids outside of class, and I thought they would figure out I didn't do it."

I was horrified, and yet I hesitated to believe her. Mr. Keets had said all the answers were the same on all the students paper. "I—uh— did you tell them all of this?"

"Yeah," Stormy said, standing up from the patio chair and glaring at me. She took the last swig of her lemonade and put the glass down on the wrought-iron table between us. "They didn't believe me either."

She walked past me into the house, and I stared straight ahead. No way had that just happened. I finally pulled myself back together and hurried into the house. I didn't see Stormy right away, but Jared caught my eye as he carried a box of Stormy's clothes out to the car. He knew. I could see it in his face. He knew that I'd not only said those terrible things about my daughter, but I had, without question, believed she had cheated. I let my eyes fall closed and wanted to die.

"I think this is the last of it," Paul said, carrying an armful of clothes he'd grabbed from the closet. Jared had already disappeared outside with the box he'd been carrying. I hurried to Stormy's room, now stripped down to nothing but furniture, bedding, and a few unwanted odds and ends.

She must be in the car. I hurried outside; Stormy was in the front seat, listening to her iPod while petting Munchkin, who was curled up in her lap. I knocked on the window, and she looked up but then looked back out the windshield. I opened the door, and she pulled out one earbud, exaggerating her aggravation at having her music interrupted.

"I'm so sorry, Storm," I said. "I know that's not enough, but I am so, so sorry. I love you, so much, and the last thing I want to do is hurt you. I know I did, and I'm sorry. I feel awful."

"Love you too, Mom," she said, her voice chipper as though we hadn't just had a conversation I would never forget. There was even a glimmer of satisfaction in Stormy's eyes. "See ya." She pulled the door shut as Jared opened the driver's side door.

He smiled a good-bye. Paul came down the sidewalk and stood behind me. He didn't usually like to display affection when Jared was around, but he must have sensed the fragmentation that was taking place inside me because he put his arms around my waist and rested his chin on my shoulder as Jared started the engine. I was frozen as my baby girl drove away with her father. What had I done?

"It won't be so bad," Paul said into my ear, "having me all to yourself, will it?"

I couldn't answer; I couldn't say anything at all for fear I would admit to him what had happened and he'd lose all respect for me. I also couldn't agree with him. Yes, I wanted time with him, but not at the expense of my daughter, and I suddenly felt as though I'd traded one for the other. Was I so desperate to be free of my role as a mother that I'd unconsciously pushed Stormy away? Would she ever forgive me for this? Would I ever forgive myself?

Chapter 10

THE GUILT BECAME OVERWHELMING as I realized how easy it was to fall into a new routine that didn't involve Stormy. I slept in until seven every morning. Paul and I had coffee and toast together before I left for work. In the evenings, we watched what we wanted to on TV, or went out to eat, or drove down to the beach. My pants got looser as the knot in my stomach kept me from wanting to eat much. Who knew that not having kids around could be such an effective weight-loss plan? Paul was invited to speak at an IT convention in Philadelphia in January, and I asked for the days off of work so I could join him. Just like that.

December called from her OB appointment a few days before Halloween and let me listen to the sound of my grandson's heartbeat. I cried and made plans to visit her in Ohio the first part of February, which was when she was due, so that I could help her out. Again, it was so easy to make the arrangements since it was only my schedule I had to consider.

I told December what had happened with Stormy, but she already knew. The girls were pretty close despite being ten years apart in age. Though she commiserated with me for bumbling the incident, she was also a teacher and knew what a serious problem cheating was. She consoled me by saying she wished more parents were willing to consider the possibility that their child might be guilty rather than becoming instantly defensive.

"For every kid falsely accused, there are fifteen guilty ones screaming their innocence." She also relayed how nice it was that Stormy had the chance to build a relationship with her dad.

I tried not to take that as another personal failure, as I'd never pushed December's dad to stay in touch with her, and he hadn't. Had that created a hole in her life?

I changed the subject, and she followed. We ended up laughing over how often December found herself running for the bathroom now that she was six months pregnant, and how she and Lance were still arguing over names for their son. She was fighting for the name Tennyson—her favorite British poet—while Lance wanted something more traditional, Matthew or Samuel.

Whenever I came across Stormy's things in the house, I put them on her bed, waiting for her to start coming around and letting us repair the chasm between us. She didn't visit, though. Instead, she tried out for her new high school's play—*Phantom of the Opera*—and got a part as a ballet dancer, which she was really excited about. She'd met a couple of girls she hung out with now and then. I called her every day, but she only answered a couple of times a week, and our conversations were short and superficial. Still, overall, the change seemed to be as positive as Jared had assured me it would be.

By the time my anniversary trip weekend with Paul came around— Halloween weekend—it almost seemed superfluous to go anywhere. We had so much time together these days that it seemed silly to spend the extra money to go to Mexico like Paul had planned. But it was all reserved, so we went. Paul went parasailing while I soaked up the sun and noted that while my waistline was shrinking—I had officially fit into my size ten swimsuit—I was falling out of the top. I sure didn't remember *that* being a problem the last time I'd worn it, although Paul didn't seem to mind.

I'd always loved Mexico, but I couldn't tolerate the molé—which was my favorite. It sent me running to the bathroom to throw up as soon as we got back from the restaurant, and then kept me up half the night with heartburn. Nothing I ate sat well after that, so I settled on rice and tortillas for the rest of the trip. Paul gave me a new handbag as an anniversary gift, a beautiful red leather case that would fit my laptop and most of the contents of my purse. I gave him a battery-powered GPS unit he could use while hunting or hiking. Computer nerd Monday through Friday, outdoorsman on the weekends, was a pretty good description of the man I'd married.

I tried to get comfortable with this new life, the first time in more than two and a half decades that there wasn't a little person demanding to be taken care of, but my freedoms felt like failures somehow.

As the first Saturday in November approached—the date of my second book group—I found myself more and more excited to go. I had finished *The Poisonwood Bible* and while I didn't necessarily like the story—it was a very sad commentary about the effect one person's choices can have on everyone else's—I loved the writing and looked forward to discussing it. I barely knew the other women in the group, so it wasn't that I was excited to see *them.* Then I realized, with even more regret, that as much as I enjoyed being with Paul, I was looking forward to spending an evening with someone else. With women. He was wonderful, but I needed some texture. Book group offered something that had nothing to do with the rest of my life, and I was excited to take a break.

You really are a horrible person, Daisy, I thought.

Chapter 11

THERE WERE ALREADY TWO CARS at Ruby's when I arrived at book group. I'd been fifteen minutes early last time, and I wished I'd gotten my act together quicker this time as well. I took a minute to adjust my makeup and return Paul's text about what time I expected to be home.

Ruby must have been waiting right by the door because she opened it almost before the doorbell chime had stopped reverberating.

"Oh, Daisy, honey," Ruby said, spreading her arms and wrapping me up in a wonderful hug. Once released, she immediately turned toward the living room and I followed. "I'm so glad you're here," she said over her shoulder. She wore a plum-colored suit with a jacket long enough that it flowed behind her like a cape. I'd love the same thing in a nice eggshell. For my part, I was in jeans and a new pink top I'd bought while shopping by myself last week. The thought made me miss Stormy's fashion advice—I wasn't convinced the color was a good shade for me.

"I'm glad I could make it. Things have been a little crazy."

I took a seat and said hello to the group. Shannon and Athena weren't there, but I was greeted by Livvy and Paige and met a new member, Ilana. She was quiet, but the rest of us moved seamlessly into basic small talk. I heard a little more about Paige's job at the dental office. I hadn't known many Mormons, but I'd heard plenty about them.

Yet she looked so *normal.* I wondered why she didn't move back to Utah—where she'd said she'd grown up—now that her marriage was over, but the more she talked and laughed the more I recognized a familiar streak of independence. Mormon or not, she wanted to figure out this new life of hers by herself. I cheered her on in my mind.

Livvy was more at ease this time too. She still looked thrown together and seemed the least comfortable out of everyone there—well, maybe not Ilana, but this was her first meeting so it made sense that she'd hold back—but I was glad Livvy was making time for book group. From the things she'd said about her husband and children, I suspected she didn't do many things for herself. As we chatted, I was anxious about them asking about Stormy. In the month since I'd introduced myself, so much had changed, and I didn't want to tell anyone about what had happened, but I didn't want to lie either. Luckily, the topic never came my way. Perhaps because I kept the other ladies talking about themselves instead.

"Shannon had to work a later shift, so she'll be here next month," Ruby interjected after we'd been chatting for a few minutes. "And then Athena called me about an hour ago and said she couldn't come— something came up."

"That's too bad," Livvy said, looking genuinely concerned. "I hope it's nothing serious. Did she give any clue as to why she couldn't make it? I feel bad she's missing her own book suggestion."

"None." Ruby shook her head and took the first of the éclairs resting on a pedestal cake plate on the coffee table. "But that's why I ended up making these. Athena was supposed to bring the treats this time."

I could smell the chocolate—why could I smell the chocolate? I was hungry, but the éclairs didn't sound very good. Still, I didn't want to be rude as Ruby passed the cake plate around, so I picked up one of the small cocktail napkins and then chose an éclair, the smallest one with the least frosting.

"Could be a work deadline or something else with her magazine," I said. I'd looked up her magazine, *Newport Travel,* a few days ago. So many online magazines were being thrown together by anyone who had anything to say, and I had wondered how hers would compare. It was very crisp and included more than just information on traveling through Newport. I'd looked forward to talking to her about it. Too bad she hadn't been able to make it to group.

"I'll give her a call later to see if she's okay," Ruby said. She picked up her copy of *The Poisonwood Bible* from the coffee table and officially began with the book talk. "Since Athena picked this month's book, she was supposed to lead the discussion, but I suppose I'll have to do." She chuckled and consulted some papers she'd printed off the computer. She gave us some basic biographical information about Kingsolver and her work, then started discussing the actual book. "Okay, so my first thought was about the nature of religion and how it impacted the lives of the five female voices in the book. I believe in prayer and Jesus and all that, but I'm not much for organized religion, and books like this kind of make me glad I'm not—especially as a woman."

I couldn't help but look at Paige, who had already told us she was a practicing Mormon. I was a little surprised that Ruby would state her opinion so strongly so early in the discussion. Paige seemed to realize she'd ended up in an unexpected spotlight and she cleared her throat.

"I don't think the problem is with organized religion, per se," she said. "Throughout history, people have used religion and God as an excuse to do all kinds of terrible things. But religion was just that— their excuse. Religion has done as much to bring people together and accomplish amazing things as it has to destroy. It's powerful."

She picked up her éclair, but put it back down when no one else spoke. She looked around and must have taken our silence as a sign we expected her to say more. "You all know I'm a Mormon," she said. "Something you might not all know is that my church helps people all over the world. One of its missions is all about reaching out to those in need. In that way, I think organized religion is a really good thing, not just for its members, but for the people they can help."

Ruby leaned forward. "When you say help, don't you just mean the boys in suits who teach about your church?"

Paige shook her head and went on to describe the extensive service her church provided to all types of people. She also mentioned Mother Theresa and all the good she did as a Catholic nun. I knew all about Mother Theresa, but I kept that to myself. I wasn't just raised Catholic, I was raised *Catholic*—Sunday Mass, first communion, praying to saints, the whole thing. I never questioned it, really, just nodded and listened and tried to be a good girl so I'd never have to confess anything. It wasn't until I got older that I learned about the Crusades and politics.

Paige continued to talk about a bunch of other non-Catholic religious people—some of whom I'd never heard of. The last person she brought up was Jesus. I avoided her eyes and nibbled at the éclair, but I wasn't hungry, and sugar didn't sound good, so I returned it to my napkin.

"He was a good man," Ilana said. "I'm Jewish, so, well . . ."

She trailed off, but one look at Paige showed how hard the comment had hit her.

After another moment, Paige continued. "I guess what I'm saying is that some people get so wrapped up in one thing—and it could be a good thing, even—that they lose sight of what's most important. So that thing could be *saving* the heathen, like Nathan wanted to do in the book, even at the expense of his wife and daughters. Or it could be someone working so hard on a charity that helps people in another country but totally ignoring the needy right under their own roof. The *organization* isn't the problem. It's the slanted focus of someone who turns from devotion to obsession. And any obsession is unhealthy, especially if it's at someone else's expense."

Her voice had sped up as she reached the end of her monologue, which was too long not to sound defensive, but being a Mormon in California probably *made* her defensive.

"You make a really good point," Ruby said, nodding slightly. "I hadn't thought of it that way. Nathan used religion as a crutch to feel important and do what he wanted to do. Sort of took himself out of being responsible for anything—he could blame it all on God and his desire to serve."

Livvy squirmed in her chair. "Ooooh, that makes me hate him even more."

"I'm glad that your church is such a support to you," I said to Paige. That would have been nice when I needed people to rally around me, but that hadn't been my experience. "But not everyone gets the same kind of support through their parishes. What you said about good people in churches is true. Absolutely. And I think Paige is on to something when it comes to people using religion as a crutch—as an excuse." I paused and organized my thoughts. "From my experience, the problem comes—and all too often—when people put church before God." The final words brought up an emotion that took me by surprise, and I had to look away. Maybe they sometimes put church before their children too—maybe when their children needed them the most. "One good thing about organized religion—at least in real life, not in the book, for sure—is how it can bond families together. But if some family members are devout and others . . . *aren't* . . . religion becomes a schism and something . . . something painful." We all were quiet for a moment, and I was glad to have time to gather my thoughts. "We saw that with Rachel when she struck out on her own; she never looked back on God or her family."

"But Rachel never really looked to God at the start, either," Livvy pointed out. "She was always materialistic and vain, start to finish. She was the polar opposite of her sister Leah. Nathan's religion is his worshipful obsession, but Leah worships her father to the same crippling degree. She wants so much to please him that she very blindly accepts every crazy idea that man takes into his head."

"She does denounce her religion, though," Paige offered. Devil's advocate? "She leaves the Baptist faith behind her."

"But not God," Livvy clarified, looking a little uncomfortable. "In fact I think He becomes bigger in her mind and heart as the book progresses."

"But to say that is somehow indicative of organized religion being a bad thing isn't fair," Paige interjected. "Nathan was one man who used his religion badly, but that doesn't mean the Baptist faith in and of itself is bad. Doesn't drawing that conclusion do the very same thing Nathan did? State that one way is the right way at the expense of all other ideas?"

Wow, the conversation had quickly gone a lot deeper than I'd expected it to go, but I wasn't necessarily uncomfortable with it.

"There's a quote along these lines," Livvy said, flipping through her book. "On page one forty-one Adah says, 'I wonder that religion can live or die on the strength of a faint, stirring breeze. The scent trail shifts, causing the predator to miss the pounce. One god draws in the breath of life and rises; another god expires.' Maybe instead of God being the focal point of that quote, it's more like vision or belief or something a bit more ethereal in relation to God. Not one of us in this room believes in God the same way as another one does, but I imagine that if Nathan had respected the god worshiped in the Congo, even if he remained true to his own beliefs, the story would have been very different."

"And probably not worth writing about," Ruby said with a chuckle. "Without conflict, there's no story."

That's true, I thought, considering the need for conflict in a good story—something for the characters to overcome. Wasn't life like that too? Full of conflicts we either act against or react to? The question was whether or not I was learning from the conflicts of my life. I liked to think I was, but it was hard to see until time stretched far enough past it to give me perspective. And then one change in course, like Stormy leaving, brought everything into question all over again. Was I a better person now than who I started out as? Was I all that different from the seventeen-year-old girl who had announced to her parents that she was going to have a baby, deal with it?

Ilana leaned forward slightly and raised a hand, ready to speak. We all took the cue and listened. "I'm a bit split on the whole organized religion thing. I grew up with a pretty conservative family. We always went to temple on the Sabbath, we ate kosher, I had my bat mitzvah, the whole bit. My parents have always found strength in reading the Torah and following the laws, but as I've gotten older, I'm not so sure I believe any of it—even whether there's a God." She pointed at the book in my lap. "As far as the story in *Poisonwood* goes, I see it being just as much about the repression of women as about religion. Religion is just the vehicle the author uses to tell the story about the women and how they're kept in place and held back."

"That's a great point," Livvy said, smiling at Ilana. "And there are all kinds of political, gender, and socioeconomic themes throughout the book. Seeing only the religious connotations is missing a huge portion of the story."

Ilana nodded and leaned back in her chair, as though content to have done her part to participate.

"You don't like the éclair?" Ruby suddenly said to me, breaking the tension.

I looked around and realized everyone else had eaten theirs, even Ilana.

"I love éclairs," I quickly clarified. "Paul and I went away last weekend, and I haven't quite recovered from something I must have picked up down there. I didn't mean to waste your food, though."

Ruby sympathized immediately. "I've been getting the darndest indigestion at night myself," she said, patting her ample tummy. "Don't know what's causing it. I don't dare see a doctor in case it's an ulcer—or something worse." She said the last with a whispered tone, hinting what horrible thing "something worse" could be. "I hope your situation isn't serious."

"I don't think it's anything like that," I said. "It's probably just a bug or maybe some food poisoning. I've been a little sick to my stomach ever since, and sweets are especially unappetizing. I'm tired a lot, too—probably from not eating like I usually do. I'm sure I just need some extra sleep to kick it."

"Nausea and fatigue?" Paige asked. "Maybe you're pregnant."

My head shot up, and I stared at Paige. Did she really just say that? I forced myself to be calm, however. If I wanted to come across as the woman who had it all together, I couldn't fly off the handle when someone made a stupid comment. "That's quite impossible. I took care of that fifteen years ago." I smiled but I could feel the coldness of it. I could tell from Paige's expression that she could feel it too. It was presumptuous for her to say something so personal; I had a hard time feeling bad about my reaction.

"I'm . . . sorry . . . I didn't mean . . ."

Without warning, Livvy jumped in, patting her copy of the book and totally changing the subject. "Adah's character fascinates me." She went on to explain how Adah came to realize she limped out of habit, finding comfort in her disability.

To my relief, Livvy's attempt to change the subject worked, and the conversation continued in other directions after that. Livvy talked about her favorite parts of the book, delving into all kinds of political analogies I'd somehow missed completely. I had to admit I was surprised by Livvy's comments. I hadn't pegged her as someone with so much depth. Ilana participated more in the discussion, and we talked about the individual characters and how, even though their hardships were the same in regard to time and place and being dominated by a zealot, they all had different reactions—different kinds of growth that came from their struggles. Livvy relayed a few of her favorite quotes, and one of them was something I'd noted when I read it, but had forgotten until now.

Orleanna, the dominated wife for whom I had great sympathy—and annoyance—throughout the story, had summed up the state her life was in when the story began: "I had washed up there on the riptide of my husband's confidence and the undertow of my children's needs."

I could so relate to that, but I didn't dare say anything, especially in regard to all that had happened with my daughter these last weeks.

Paul certainly wasn't a riptide, but Jared had been. Still was. My children, much as I loved them, had felt like undertows all of my life. I looked at Livvy and wondered how she felt toward her family. Did she feel the undertow? I had a feeling she did, but that she used strong strokes to keep them all above the waterline.

"Well, it's getting late," Ruby said as the discussion started winding down. "Does anyone have a suggestion for next month's book?" She looked at Paige, who was texting. I grimaced. Older people didn't much care for the distraction of technology. "Would you like to choose it, Paige?"

She didn't look up, intent on the message she was sending.

"Paige?"

She looked up quickly and dropped the phone into her lap, clasping her hands over it. "I'm sorry, what?"

"Ruby was asking if you'd picked out the book for next month," Livvy said. "It's your turn."

"Oh, um, I'm not sure right off the top of my head. Do any of you guys have one in mind?"

We were all silent, and then Livvy cleared her throat. "Actually, *The Poisonwood Bible* reminded me of another book—very different, of course—that I read a long time ago. It's called *My Name Is Asher Lev.* Have you guys ever read it?"

"I have," I said. "Or at least I read part of it when I was dating a guy who was Jewish." I smiled sheepishly. "I stopped reading when we broke up, though, so I never finished it. It's by Potok, right?"

"Right," Ilana said.

I wondered if she'd be uncomfortable with the book, but she didn't seem to be. She'd said she was agnostic, so maybe religion just wasn't a hot topic for her either way. Certainly there was more to *My Name Is Asher Lev* than religion, just as there was more to *The Poisonwood Bible.*

"We don't have to read something Jewish your very first month," Paige said, voicing my discomfort.

"I don't mind," Ilana said, uncrossing her legs and crossing them again the other direction. "I've read *The Chosen* and really liked it."

Livvy nodded and scooted forward in her chair again. "Not that we want religion to be a theme or anything, but I loved the way that Potok delved into the interpersonal relationships, into specific practices of his orthodox life and found himself within those things but also outside of them."

I blinked. Holy moly, there was more to Livvy than met the eye.

Ruby clapped. "Sounds delightful. I've never read that one, but I visited Israel many years ago and it was wonderful." She turned to Paige. "What do you think, dear?"

"I've read something by Potok, but I don't think it was that book. I'm totally up for it."

We confirmed next month's date—December fourth—and finished things up. Livvy and Paige each had another éclair. I still felt bad about the one I had no desire to eat, so I rolled it up in my napkin in hopes no one would remember, and tucked it in my purse. Ruby walked us to the door, and we said our good-byes "until next month."

As the three of us headed down the walk, Ruby called after us. "I'll let Athena and Shannon know about the new book. See you gals next month. Oh, maybe I'll find a latke recipe so our refreshments will be Jewish! Ilana, if our meeting ends up during Chanukah, could you still make it?"

"I don't celebrate either holiday," Ilana said. "So I'll be here."

I cast a sidelong look at her, but she didn't seem annoyed with

Ruby's comment. Whatever her feelings were, she was at peace with them, which made me realize that although I had stepped away from the religion of my youth, I wasn't at peace with that division yet. The realization bothered me, but I waved good-bye while Ruby said something else to Paige, who was closest to her.

I went to bed at nine thirty, explaining to Paul how tired I was.

"You're always tired lately," he said, pouting a little. He'd wanted to go out for a late movie.

I apologized again and went to bed, but then stared at the ceiling as Paige's words came back to me. *Nausea and fatigue? Maybe you're pregnant.*

But I'd told her it was impossible, and it was. Whatever was making me feel this way was something else. I rolled over and pushed the thought out of my head. I had enough to worry about without dwelling on impossibilities.

Chapter 12

SUNDAY NIGHT I GOT A CALL on my cell phone from a number I didn't recognize.

"Hello?" I said, answering it with one hand while I continued emptying the dishwasher with the other. With only two of us at home, I was running the dishwasher only twice a week. Ironically, it made emptying the dishwasher seem like more work now that it wasn't part of my typical routine.

"Is this Daisy?"

I recognized the voice but didn't quite place it before the caller introduced herself. "It's Ruby—from book group."

"Oh, hi, Ruby," I said, smiling. "How are you doing?"

"I'm alright," she said, but I could hear the distress in her voice. "I just spoke with Athena. I called to tell her about the new book, and I found out why she wasn't there last night."

"Oh?"

"Her mother was involved in a car accident Friday night," Ruby explained. "She was killed."

I stood up straight, holding a casserole dish in my hand. "Oh, that's awful."

"I know. I'm just heartbroken about it. That poor girl. She's a tough cookie, that Athena, but there's no doubt this is a horrible thing for her to have to deal with. When I got off the phone with her, I opened my paper and found her mother's obituary. She's as pretty as Athena is; they could have been sisters. It said the funeral's on Wednesday at Saint Paul's Greek Orthodox Church in Irvine. I thought it might be nice if some of us could attend and support her."

My instant reaction was that going to Athena's mother's funeral seemed a little extreme. I'd only met Athena once several weeks ago. Didn't it seem almost . . . *pretentious* to assume I was important enough in her life that it would make some kind of difference to her if I were there? But I hesitated to say that to Ruby, who obviously thought going was a good idea. She somehow interpreted my hesitation as agreement.

"The services start at eleven, and I already called the priest to make sure that you don't have to be Greek Orthodox to attend. He assured me it was open to anyone connected to the family. He also said that it would be wonderful for us to come and that Athena and her sister are taking care of all the arrangements themselves due to their father's failing health. Can you imagine that? She's so young to lose a parent so tragically, and her father isn't well either. I just feel awful."

So did I, but I wasn't sure I could make it to the funeral. I hurried to my planner and put the casserole dish down as I flipped through the days. "Did you say the funeral was Wednesday?"

"Yes," Ruby verified. "Shannon can't make it, but if it's possible, I think Athena could use the support. Maybe we could all chip in for some flowers or something."

It was crazy to think she needed our support, but I'd caught some of Ruby's compassion and found that I did want to be there to support this new friend. Maybe it would seem weird, but maybe it was just what she needed. The other people there would likely be friends of the family, dealing with their own grief. While I was certainly sympathetic, I didn't know Athena's mother. I could be there to support Athena, if she needed it.

I stared at the page in my planner and remembered that Wednesday was my open morning. "I can go," I said, relieved to be able to say so. "And I'm still happy to go in on some flowers, or maybe a houseplant that will last a little longer."

"Oh, that's an excellent idea," Ruby said. "My sister gave me a ficus when Phil passed away. I still have it in the living room—do you remember it? It was in the corner by the piano?"

I smiled. Ruby was a very sweet woman with a big heart. "I do remember that tree; it's lovely."

"It reminds me of Phil every time I see it. I'll call a florist and see what I can find."

"Have you already spoken to Paige and Livvy?" Saying their names reminded me of Paige's comment about my being pregnant. The memory deadened some of my enthusiasm to see her again, but that made me feel bad too. She had jumped to a poor conclusion, but why should that make me uncomfortable? If anything, *she* should feel bad about what she said.

"Not yet," Ruby said. "Your name is the first one on my list after Athena; it's alphabetical by first name. I didn't tell her I was calling you gals about coming—do you think that's okay?"

"Yes," I assured her. "We'll be there to share our support any way we can."

"Right," Ruby said. "I'll give Livvy a call. Would you mind calling Paige?"

I did, a little, but it seemed petty to say so and would therefore require Ruby to make two calls instead of one. "Sure," I said. "Do you have her number?"

Ruby gave it to me, and I dialed Paige's number after I wrote the funeral details into my planner. There was a good chance it would cut into my lunch break, but my first conference call wasn't until two o'clock, so I would be okay. I'd have to look up the address of the church to find out whether it was worth going into work for an hour before the service or if it made more sense to have a lazy morning. Paige picked up on the third ring.

"Hello?" she said, sounding tired.

"Hi, Paige. It's Daisy, from book group." I could hear the sound of a TV in the background.

She paused and then said, "Oh, hi."

I hurried to explain what had happened in hopes it would cover the awkwardness.

"Poor Athena," she said when I finished. A little voice yelled for a drink, and she moved the phone away to tell him just a minute. The chaos in the background of her home made my house feel stagnant. "I'm not sure if I can make Wednesday work, though. I won't know until I get into the office tomorrow. I'd like to go if I can, and I can go in on the plant too."

"Well, why don't you give me a call when you know one way or another? This is my cell number."

"Okay," Paige said. She paused and then continued. "I've been thinking about you today," she said in a humble tone. "I'm sorry if I made you uncomfortable last night. I really didn't mean to."

"Oh, no," I said, exaggerating how *not* bugged I was in hopes it would make me seem older and wiser and confident of my position. "I wasn't bothered a bit. Don't worry about it for another second."

"Oh, good," Paige said, proving that she'd fallen for my assertions. "Sometimes I just say too much, ya know?"

"No worries," I said. "I'll look forward to hearing whether or not you can make it."

"I should know by tomorrow afternoon."

"Good deal."

The little voice again demanded a drink. I heard Paige sigh and couldn't help but try to encourage her.

"Hang in there," I said. I wasn't sure if Paige understood, but it was good for me to have a moment of empathy. She was young, alone, and raising two kids; I knew what that felt like. I also didn't want her to think I was holding a grudge.

"Thanks," she said in a soft voice. "I'll talk to you tomorrow."

Chapter 13

PAIGE CALLED ME MONDAY AFTERNOON and said she'd been able to trade her work schedule from Wednesday to Saturday. I was impressed with her determination to go to the funeral. "Will you be okay getting child care worked out on Saturday?"

"I called my mother-in-law; she lives in Orange. With Doug in Denver, she helps out with the boys when she can."

Doug must be the ex-husband. I could hear her tone change when she'd said his name. "Okay," I said. "Just keep me in mind if you need a babysitter some time. My house is a little lonely these days."

"Oh, you're sweet," Paige said in a tone that clearly communicated she wasn't really considering my offer. I couldn't really blame her. She went to church and had her own network of people there. Not only a church, but the *Mormon* church; she'd made a big deal about how focused they were on helping each other out. It was probably a good thing that she didn't take me up on it anyway. I hadn't been around little kids for a long time. I didn't really know why I'd offered. "I'll see you Wednesday."

I hung up and went back to work, but I realized that in that split second between thinking about it and offering to watch her boys, I'd really wanted to do it. I knew that had to do with Stormy being gone. I missed her. And the house was so quiet without her music blaring or her friends laughing in her room. I could use a little noise. Feeling nostalgic, I pulled out my phone and sent Stormy a text, just telling her I was thinking about her and hoped she was having a good day. I ended with *Wub-oo,* realizing we hadn't said our secret word in a long time.

She texted back about ten minutes later.

Wub-oo 2. Can I come over this weekend?

My heart leapt in my chest. I couldn't reply fast enough that it would be great to have her.

Cool. Hannah's bday prty is Friday. Can you pick me up after play practice?

Sure. Can you stay until Sunday?

Yeah. Dad's going to clean out his storage unit so I need somewhere to hide.

I should probably have been offended that her reason for coming was to get out of work, but I was so starved for positive interaction with my daughter that I let it slide right over me.

Great!!!!!

I told Paul about it when I got home, knowing I sounded pathetic about being so excited to have Stormy come. His reception of the news was a little cool. "I thought we were going to go up to Huntington Beach on Saturday."

Shoot. I'd forgotten that we'd talked about renting some beach cruisers and following the bike path along the coast before the weather got too cold, but Paul and I had had every evening and weekend to ourselves for nearly a month. Surely he could see that making a change of plans to accommodate my daughter's visit was reasonable. "Maybe we could all go."

"Stormy isn't going to want to ride a bike."

He was right. She wouldn't. "Well, maybe we could all go to Habana Cabana for dinner, and you and I can do the bikes next weekend."

Paul shrugged and went back to whatever he was doing on his computer. "Sure."

I had stopped at the library on the way home, glad to be able to borrow a copy of *My Name Is Asher Lev* instead of having to buy it, and with Paul pouting, now was the perfect time to get started on it. It wasn't as long as *The Poisonwood Bible,* but it was a pretty big book in hardback. I fixed a simple dinner of spaghetti using the leftover sauce from last week—leftovers seemed to propagate without a teenager around to eat them—and then disappeared into my room where I settled into my new evening routine of freedom and flexibility and got lost in the story of *another* religious family. I found it ironic that both *Poisonwood Bible* and *Asher Lev* were about such zealous families, but it served to deepen my principle of not letting other people determine who you should be.

I wasn't Orleanna from *Poisonwood* who danced to her husband's twisted tune in the name of devotion and fear. And I wasn't Rivkeh Lev, pulled between the love of my child and the confines of an archaic lifestyle and domineering husband. For all my mistakes and poor choices, I'd been a strong woman who thought for herself and made the best of those less-than-sparkly situations. I was proud of that. I only wished that strength felt like strength when you were in the middle of things. Right now, I was beginning to feel stagnant as my life had narrowed in focus to two things: work and Paul. Both good things, but I needed more. These books were a start, but maybe I also needed to find a hobby or take a class of some kind. I might not be Orleanna or Rivkeh, but was I becoming vague and undefined in my own right?

I kept reading, admiring Asher's passion and commiserating at the conflict it put between him and his religious community. Though not as extreme, I'd been there too. It wasn't until I'd stepped away from the church-centered life of my parents that I realized how much of my life had centered on it as well. It had been a difficult and lonely shift for me. I looked forward to seeing how things ended for Asher. I hoped they ended well. I could use a happy ending right about now.

Chapter 14

ATHENA'S MOTHER'S FUNERAL was nice, if not a little awkward, since I'd never been to the funeral of someone I didn't know. Add to that the fact that I was sitting with three women I *barely* knew in a very ornate and opulent church full of Greek people and it was hard to imagine why I *wouldn't* be a little uncomfortable. Everyone was wearing all black except Paige and me, and I leaned over to her and told her how grateful I was not to be the only one out of dress code. She laughed behind her hand, and I felt a little more bonded to her than I had before. Who knew that the Greek Orthodox wore *only* black to funerals?

Athena had looked surprised when she saw us, which was after the service when she was following the casket down the aisle of the chapel to the waiting hearse. She and a woman I assumed was her sister—same beautiful eyes—were walking on either side of a man who looked too old to be their father. He walked slowly, but kept looking around as though not sure why he was there. Athena looked tired and burdened, and I smiled slightly at her when she met my eye, hoping she felt my support. She mouthed "Thank you," and suddenly I was glad I'd come.

We followed the rest of the mourners out of the church, where several people headed for their cars. Athena, I imagined, was already in the limo that was pulling into traffic behind the hearse. The four of us had already decided not to go to the graveside service, as that seemed like something reserved for the family.

"Athena's mom sounds like a really neat woman," Livvy said. She'd worn a black skirt and shirt today—not quite the same shade of black, but it was still a good color for her. It gave her face more definition somehow, and I made sure to compliment her. She looked away, uncomfortable but pleased, and I wondered if she got many compliments. She wasn't unattractive. She had nice features and good skin; she was just . . . undone. She didn't take the time to emphasize her good qualities, and in the process, few people likely noticed them. I made a decision right then to find something about her appearance I could compliment each time we ran into one another.

The ladies talked about going to lunch, but I had to get back to work and made my good-byes. As I headed to my office in Irvine, I thought about Athena's loss. I had the impression that she was quite close to her parents. She would probably miss her mother and struggle with the void in her life her mother had left behind.

My parents were both alive and well in Chester, Virginia, living in the same house I'd grown up in. Dad still worked part-time for the manufacturing company he'd worked for since he'd been twenty-two years old. Last I heard, he'd taken up building cane chairs in his spare time. My mother kept busy with church work, and being a full-time grandma had replaced being a full-time mom rather seamlessly for her.

Mom called me once a month or so, but she'd always been a hard woman, and our conversations remained rather superficial, talking about everyone but the two of us. She was giving and always available to help, but she never hesitated to share her opinions or pull a punch. I hadn't talked to my dad for months, and the relationships with my siblings had been reduced to sending Internet jokes and prayer requests. I had only one of my sisters as a friend on Facebook, though my other siblings had profiles.

I hadn't been back to Virginia since just after Paul and I got married. I made that trip so my parents could see I could make a good choice. They'd been very nice to Paul, and the weekend visit had been just long enough to reconnect without being too much. I had left feeling good about having visited, but I also realized how far out of their world I now was.

I could be analytical and logical about the whole thing, but it didn't mean I wasn't saddened by the disconnect. I wondered if, when my parents finally passed away, I would regret not making more of an effort to have a relationship with them. But did I really *want* that to change? Did I have it in me to find a way to fix it and then maintain whatever new responsibilities came of it? The idea made my stomach—which continued to be volatile on a somewhat regular basis—even more unhappy, so I pushed past it and switched my focus to Athena, sending vibes of healing and strength her way. My parents were in their sixties, but in good health. I had more time to consider what I might want from that relationship in the future and, for now, I was content.

I realized that Athena's mother had been healthy too. She'd been killed in an accident, unexpectedly. I might not have an indefinite period of time to fix things with my mother. But then, why wasn't my mother reaching out to me? She wasn't making an effort either, which made it harder to anticipate that my own effort would be successful. The fact was, I didn't know if I could handle the rejection if I tried and failed to connect in a different way.

I pulled into the parking garage of my office and quickly pulled my mind away from my parents and back to the office, right where it belonged on a Wednesday afternoon. I knew how to get the work done, and over the years that had become a huge part of my self-confidence. Relationships were tricky, but policy renewals were something I could count on.

Chapter 15

As Friday drew closer, I was more and more excited for Stormy to come home. I cleaned her room, putting away all the things I'd been depositing on her bed for the last month, and made plans to cook her favorite dinner—beef stroganoff. I left work early and picked her up at Jared's house at five. I hadn't been to the condo he'd bought last year, and Stormy gave me a quick tour. It was about what I expected—basic furniture, not many decorations, and cluttered counters.

"Is he still dating that woman with the two little kids?" I asked Stormy as we headed downstairs. Jared had cycled through a few semi-serious relationships since the divorce but hadn't married again, which I hypocritically felt was better for Stormy. Less chaos.

"Lyssa?" Stormy asked. "No, they broke up before I moved in. She was skanky."

I didn't need more details of Jared's love life and was simply glad that he didn't have a "skanky" girlfriend around anymore. As we finished the tour, I had to admit that Stormy was comfortable here. They seemed to be making it work.

We put together an overnight bag and then took the freeway back to Lake Forest. Stormy told me all about the play and her new school. She'd made a few friends, though she didn't feel like they were totally "bonded, ya know?" I didn't bring up the cheating incident, even though I felt like I needed to apologize again, and just basked in her company.

As soon as we got home, she was on the phone to her Lake Forest friends. I was only halfway through dinner preparations when she asked if she could take the car and hang out with Tressa until Hannah's party started. I swallowed my disappointment that she didn't want to hang out with me but told her I'd save her some dinner.

"Awesome. Thanks, Mom," she said as she hurried to touch up her flawless makeup and try on a few different outfits before heading out the door. Paul had worked at the office today, so I had almost an hour after Stormy left until he came home. We had a nice dinner together, and then I worked on laundry. For more than twenty years, I had done a load of laundry almost every morning before work, but I'd managed to break the habit completely in a few weeks now that I didn't have to keep myself busy while a child got ready for school. Hence, my Friday night was full of OxiClean and Tide while Paul watched the Spurs' game on TV.

Around eight o'clock, I cocked my ear to the side—I was reading chapters of *My Name Is Asher Lev* between folding loads—and thought I heard my cell phone ringing. I was right, and hurried into the kitchen to dig my phone out of my purse, worried I wouldn't get to it before the caller hung up or it went to voice mail. I didn't recognize the number.

I pushed the TALK button and lifted the phone to my ear in one motion. "This is Daisy."

"Hi, Daisy. It's Paige."

It took me a few beats to remember who Paige was. "Oh, hi, Paige. How are you doing?"

"I'm okay," she said. "My child care plans for Saturday fell through. I was wondering if your offer is still open . . ."

"Of course it is." I said it so fast that it wasn't until the words were out that I realized I'd said yes. In the same instant, I knew I was probably her last resort and wanted to make sure she didn't know how surprised I was at my own quick response. "Bring the boys over—it will be fun." The totally weird part was that it *did* sound fun. Must be the impending grandmother status opening up new horizons. I could use the practice.

I heard her let out a breath and felt even better about saying yes. How many times had I felt ready to explode with frustration when I honestly had no one to turn to for help?

"Thank you so much," she said. "The office closes early on Saturdays, so I should be back no later than one thirty or two. You should have most of your day to yourself."

I laughed at how surprised she seemed that I was willing to help. "Don't worry about it, Paige. I've done the single mom thing. I remember what it was like."

"Thank you. I owe you one big-time."

We hung up and I consulted my planner. Shoot. Stormy and I were supposed to go shopping and then to lunch. This was the first weekend she'd come home, and I'd offered to watch my friend's kids. Impressive mothering. I considered my options. I could call Paige back with my regrets, but I already suspected I was the bottom of the barrel for her. She'd probably have to call into work if I didn't help her out. After a few more stressful minutes, I decided to ask Stormy what she thought. It was a risk because she might think I was blowing her off, but I texted her to call me ASAP.

A minute later, as I was pulling the last load out of the dryer, my phone rang. It was Stormy.

"Hi, sweetie," I said when I answered it. I could hear music and teenage laughter in the background. "How's the party?"

"Rockin'," Stormy said simply. "What's up?"

I explained the situation, ending with "It's not a big deal either way. I can cancel with her, but I just wanted to ask what you thought."

"Sure, totally do it. We can do shopping and stuff after they're gone. And it will be good training for me to be the best aunt ever!"

I laughed, loving how naturally we were getting along. And I didn't have to cancel with Paige. Nice.

"Can I stay at Tressa's until one, though?"

"Sure," I said without hesitation. Midnight was her typical curfew, but if she was willing to give up her Saturday, I could give her an extra hour.

"Awesome. Is there anything else?"

"Nope. Have a good time."

"'Kay, bye."

"Bye," I said, feeling satisfied with the way things had turned out.

I told Paul about it as we got ready for bed. He didn't say anything, but I sensed something was wrong. "Are you upset that I said I'd do it?" I asked.

"Well, it would have been nice if you'd asked me."

I remembered that I'd already ditched out on our Huntington Beach plans for Stormy; now I was letting Paige's kids take my time as well. "I'm sorry," I said for something to fill the silence. "I thought you had your day all planned out, so it wouldn't make a difference."

"It's okay," he said, but I knew he was bugged. "Maybe I'll go to the RV show in Garden Grove with Charlie. He'd mentioned it, and now that I won't be spending the day with you, I could make that work."

"I'm sorry," I said again.

He shrugged. "No biggie."

He went to bed around ten, and I stayed up, reading—this Asher book was harder to get into than the Kingsolver book had been for me—until Stormy came home. I hadn't stayed up that late in months and simply gave her a hug good night and then locked up before going to bed. Paul was snoring softly, and I didn't tell him to roll over, sure that I was tired enough that the noise wouldn't keep me up. I was right; I slept like a rock. A rock whose husband was feeling dissed, but a rock all the same.

Chapter 16

PAIGE'S BOYS, SHAWN AND NATHAN, were adorable. Shawn was seven and Nathan was three, and they walked in looking around as though this was a new and exciting adventure. Paige had brought some Legos and whispered that there was Play-Doh in the diaper bag if I allowed that kind of thing.

When she left, I had a moment of being completely intimidated by what I'd agreed to do, but Paul came to my rescue. He looked at the Legos, then at the boys and said, "Ever made a pirate ship out of those things?"

Oh, bless the saints that brought me that man.

For the next hour and a half, Paul and Shawn, mostly, worked on a pirate ship. Nathan had tried to participate, but wasn't all that interested. I turned on the TV and finally found a kid show that caught his attention. He went back and forth between the Legos and the TV, but seemed perfectly content.

Instead of being overwhelmed by having these little people around, I found myself quite comfortable. I made lunch at eleven o'clock— peanut butter and jelly sandwiches and applesauce—and thanked Paul profusely for his help when he said he had to get going. Not long after Paul left, I was cutting the crusts off Nathan's sandwich when Stormy emerged from her room. Her hair was a mess, and she hadn't taken off her makeup from the night before. She slid into a seat at the table while both boys regarded her with curiosity.

"This is my daughter Stormy," I told them.

"Your name is Stormy?" Shawn asked.

Stormy smiled at him with her black-smeared eyes. "Yep, pretty cool, huh?"

He seemed to consider that and then nodded. "I wish my name was Hercules."

Stormy laughed and told him what a cool name that would be.

I put a sandwich in front of her, and she looked up at me. "PB and J?" she said. "I haven't had that in, like, forever."

"You used to eat it every day when you were their age," I said. Remembering something, I took back the plate. I had cut the sandwich diagonally, so I took the halves and rearranged them so the corners touched together in the middle like wings. Then I got a baby carrot out of the fridge and put it in the middle of the two halves. I handed the plate back to her. "A butterfly sandwich," I pronounced, wondering if she'd remember when I made those for her.

She grinned at me. "Awesome," she said, then picked up the carrot and took a bite.

After lunch, I took the boys outside, and they entertained themselves for almost an hour playing on the apple tree in the backyard. Paul had put up a rope swing for Mason years ago, and the two boys swung and laughed and chased each other around the yard. At first I just watched them, but then I went and got my book when I realized they didn't really need me other than in a supervisory role. I was two-thirds of the way through the book, and Asher was realizing he might not be able to have both his art and his religion, when a little voice got my attention.

"Tinky."

I looked down into little Nathan's face, his blue eyes looking hesitant.

"What's that, sweetie?"

"Tinky?"

I wondered if he was talking about a game or something, and then realized he meant "stinky." Perfect.

Oh, dear. I had never changed a little boy's diaper. I led him into the house and laid him down on the kitchen floor—the tile was probably a better choice than carpet based on clean-ability. I folded a dishtowel beneath his head. I didn't mean to judge Paige, but my girls had been potty trained by two and a half. As soon as I peeled the diaper back, I was even more convinced of the wisdom of that decision. Big boys made big . . . messes.

Stormy walked in and started gagging, inducing a quick getaway, and although I wasn't so weak-willed, I found myself using just a few fingers to finish the clean up job. When I finished, Nathan scrambled back outside while I tried to recover.

"That was the nastiest thing ever," Stormy said from the doorway.

I looked up from where I was double-bagging the dirty diaper. "Just wait," I said, feigning the impression that this was no big deal. "You'll have your turn, but hopefully not too soon."

Stormy shuddered dramatically and announced she was taking a shower. I washed my hands—really, really well—and went back outside. Luckily, the boys hadn't disappeared or started bleeding during the time they were unsupervised. When Stormy got out of the shower, she sat down by the Legos, and when the boys came back in, they started helping her with the house she was building. Within minutes, both boys were jabbering away, and I realized that I was at odds again.

I'd expected this day to keep me running, yet my kitchen was clean, everyone was fed, and despite the extra energy, the day had been very pleasant. How about that. Maybe I was more prepared for grand-motherhood than I thought.

Paige showed up just after two o'clock, apologizing profusely for being late, which she wasn't.

"You weren't late," I said, laughing at how stressed out she was as I put the wipes back in the diaper bag. Stormy had helped the boys clean up the Legos and then brought them into the living room.

"This is my daughter Stormy," I said to Paige as she accepted the canister of Legos and smiled.

"Nice to meet you, Stormy," she said. "Thanks for helping with the boys."

"They're really cute," Stormy said. "It was fun. If you ever need a babysitter, give me a call."

"Oh, you babysit?" Paige asked, obviously excited to have a pro-spective sitter volunteer. Then her excitement waned. "I live up in Tustin, though. Is that too far away?"

"I live in North Irvine," Stormy said. "So it's closer than if I lived here."

I felt my face heat up with embarrassment at the admission that my daughter didn't live with me. "Stormy's just here for a visit. Jared, her dad, lives in Irvine."

"What high school do you go to?" Paige asked as she picked up a stray Lego from the floor.

"Beckman."

"Wow, that's just a few miles away from me," Paige said. "And I'm always looking for babysitters."

"Here, I'll give you my cell number," Stormy said, going into the kitchen and grabbing a pen and a Post-it note. "When I get my car, I can even drive to your place."

"What do you mean, *when* you get your car?" I asked, looking at her directly.

She handed Paige the Post-it and turned to me. "Didn't Dad tell you? He's getting me a car. I think we're picking it up on Tuesday."

"He didn't tell me anything about that," I said and winced internally at the edge in my voice. I wasn't even sure why I was so mad—Jared getting Stormy a car was what I'd wanted a few months ago—but the fact that he hadn't asked me to be a part of the decision irked me. I forced a smile but could tell that both Paige and Stormy knew it was fake. "Anyway," I said with a laugh. "We'll talk about it later." I turned to Paige and handed her the diaper bag. "Do you need help getting out to your car?"

"Nope, I'm a pro at this," she said. "Thank you so much," she said again. "I don't know what I'd have done without your help."

"You bet," I said, following her to the door. "Keep me . . . er . . . us in mind another time."

"Thanks." Paige waved to Stormy. "I will."

I waited until she was halfway down the sidewalk before following Stormy back into the kitchen. "So, your dad's buying you a car?"

"Yeah," she said brightly, pulling a soda out of the fridge. "And it's so cute. It's a Honda Civic—not the hatchback kind that looks like a bug, the other one. It's old, but it's blue, and it's not a grandma car."

"Wow, that's awesome," I said, but my tone was flat. Why hadn't Jared said anything about it to me? I didn't like being left out of the loop. I liked even less how Jared now held the hero card with both hands. First he saved her from having to live with me, and now he was giving her a car—a huge undertaking he hadn't even bothered to tell me about. My next thought was panic that he expected me to pay for half. I might be able to do that after I got my tax return, but that was a few months away. "And he's paying for it and everything?"

"I guess he got a really big sale at work, so they gave him a bonus. He said he was going to talk to you about insurance, though. Maybe you should call him."

"Yeah," I said, heading for my cell phone. "Maybe I should."

I wasn't up for an argument, so I just rode out Jared's explanation. He asked me to take care of the insurance, and I told him I would.

Stormy and I ended up meeting Paul for an early dinner at T.G.I. Fridays, and then I dropped Stormy off at a friend's house and headed home. I'd been wearing jeans all day—jeans I hadn't been able to fit into for more than a year—but they were uncomfortable after so many hours. I decided to trade them for a pair of lounge pants, but when I took them off, I caught my reflection in the mirror of our dresser. My legs had slimmed down for sure, and my backside was smaller too, but my stomach had not followed the same example. It struck me as strange, and as I looked in the mirror, it was impossible to ignore how off the proportions looked. Paige's comment about how I might be pregnant filtered through my brain, and I shook my head.

I wasn't pregnant; I was just getting old. That explained the strange shape of my body and my recent digestive issues and bouts of insomnia. That the symptoms were similar to pregnancy was just a mean trick of nature. I focused on my upper arms, which were not getting any less flabby as I aged.

I should really start doing some strength-training exercises. Maybe I could find an evening class that would work well with my schedule.

Paul had put on some weight this last year and had commented about wanting to join a gym, so maybe we could find a place that would meet both our needs. I pulled on my lounge pants and left the room, turning off the light with a snap and deciding to leave the reflection behind completely.

Chapter 17

"I'M GLAD YOU COULD MAKE IT," I said when Amy sat down the following Friday afternoon. We were at Bistro 17, a little café around the corner from the office. We'd had a few conversations since the incident in her office last month, but it wasn't as easy to connect when we were surrounded by so many male coworkers.

"Me, too," she said. She'd had her hair colored in the last few weeks, a cherry cola color that looked really nice against her skin.

"I love the hair."

She looked up as though she could see it, which she couldn't since it was pulled back in a ponytail, but she smiled. "Thanks. It's a little dramatic for me."

"Ah, what fun is it to be a girl if you're not dramatic now and again?" I was a hypocrite to say so, since I'd had the same hairstyle for the last twenty years—subtle layers in my thick blonde hair that I had pencil weaved every five weeks to hide both the gray and the natural blah brown color my roots betray as the real me. I had an appointment next week to get a touch-up, in fact. Maybe I'd go crazy and get some honey tones weaved in this time!

She smiled a little wider. "Good point."

We caught up on office small talk for a minute, making fun of Eric, another agent, who had started wearing a bow tie to work. I suspected he was desperate to stand out from every other suit in the office. Amy was certain he was a Pee-wee Herman look-alike on the weekends and was beginning a subtle intermingling of the duality of the lives he lived. After we ordered—tomato ravioli soup for me and an Asian chicken salad for Amy—I asked her how she was doing. "You look really good," I said. "Have you lost weight?"

Amy straightened her silverware on the table of the booth where we were sitting. "Yeah," she said, but there was some strange kind of apology in her tone. "I stopped all the meds and hormones, and the weight is practically melting off my hips and thighs. I'm down almost ten pounds already."

I raised my eyebrows. "You stopped taking *all* of the medications?" I didn't know details, but I knew she'd been taking quite a cocktail.

"Every one." Amy met my eyes. "And I feel great."

"I bet you do," I said. "Just taking birth control pills sent me for a loop back in the day. I don't think I'd have been able to even function if I'd been doing all the hormones and things that you've done."

"I don't think I realized how much all that was messing with me until I stopped taking them. I sleep better, I'm not hungry all the time, and Mick dares talk to me about all kinds of subjects that I used to get weepy about. It's been good." I could feel her relief, and I was so glad she had a reprieve, but I couldn't let the next question go unasked. I wouldn't be a good friend if I did.

"So, where are you at with the whole reproduction thing?"

Amy took a deep breath. "Done," was all she said.

"Done?" I repeated. Trying to have a baby had been her life for the last two and a half years. A single-word answer felt paltry in relation to the efforts that had gone into it.

"With the money we've spent, we could have traveled Europe for a full year. Instead, we vacation at SeaWorld using buy one, get one free admission tickets." She smiled at her exaggeration. "I'm thirty-five years old and don't want to spend the rest of my life chasing a dream that might not be mine to have. I'm okay with it, really."

I didn't want to question her, but her explanation felt rehearsed. "What about adoption?"

"Maybe later."

Our food came, and we both took a few bites before Amy spoke again. "Did I ever tell you Mick has a brother who was adopted?"

I shook my head; I didn't know much about Amy and Mick's life outside of the fact that they wanted to have a baby together. "He's almost ten years younger than Mick. His mom had always wanted one more child but couldn't do it on her own either. He's a nice guy, but he's pulled himself away from the family quite a bit, doesn't let himself fit in with the rest of them, and has a lot of issues with having been adopted. Mick's hesitant to adopt because of that."

"But it would be different if you didn't have biological kids, right? I mean, there wouldn't be that kind of competitive feeling."

"That's what I said," Amy said, spearing a piece of chicken. "But I can't just ignore how he feels about it. Whatever we do needs to be something we both feel good about, you know?"

"Absolutely," I said. I scooped up a ravioli and took another bite. "So, is the whole thing on the shelf for now?"

"Yep. That's even how Mick said it, 'Let's put it on the shelf for the next six months, then take it down and look at it with fresh eyes.'"

"And you're okay with that?"

Amy met my eyes, and I noticed the slightest glimmer of tears she was trying to hide. "Do I have a choice?" she said softly. She then looked away, embarrassed, and not wanting to pierce her veil of "All is well" that she'd obviously been working hard to keep up.

I went back to my soup and considered her situation. I wanted to assure her that she had choices and there was no telling what the future might bring, and yet sometimes it didn't really matter. She couldn't choose for her husband to change his mind. She couldn't choose to overcome her problems and be able to conceive. All she could really choose—the only thing she had control over—was her attitude. She was therefore choosing to accept what was, for now.

After a few more bites, I looked up and waited until she met my eye. "I'm proud of you," I said. She looked a little confused, so I clarified. "There's something very powerful about making the best of a less than ideal situation, and you're doing that." I smiled, and she looked down at her food, seemingly embarrassed by my praise.

"We do what we have to do, right?" she said, poking at her salad.

I thought about my own struggles and nodded. "What else is there?"

Chapter 18

JARED'S MOM LIVED IN SACRAMENTO, and he and Stormy went there for Thanksgiving. Paul and I went to his brother Charlie's house, and I played nice with Charlie's twenty-five-year-old girlfriend while the men watched the football games. I had to drive home because Paul was drunk by the time we left. I'd had a few sips of wine, but the whole meal just hadn't worked for me. Well, except for the mashed potatoes. I'd probably ended up eating two pounds of the stuff since nothing else agreed with me.

I wondered if something was wrong with me. I'd had digestive issues for more than a month; in fact, I couldn't remember when they'd started. They didn't seem to be getting worse, but they weren't getting better, either. In the back of my mind, a quiet voice reminded me how often I ate mashed potatoes when I was pregnant, but I drowned it out with a dozen reasons why that was just silly to consider.

Besides, thinking about my funny stomach was only slightly more prominent in my thoughts than my overall disappointment with the day. It had been many years since I'd had a holiday meal with my own family, but for some reason, this year I missed it more than I ever had before. Spending the day in a house with four adults seemed like a paltry celebration compared to what I knew must be happening back in Virginia. Mom would have made a turkey and a pineapple-glazed ham. She'd have candied and mashed yams, cherry Jell-O with pecans, collard greens—Dad was from New Orleans—and half a dozen other things she'd spent three days preparing. As a kid I had thought putting so much time into a meal was ridiculous. As I got older, I realized she actually liked doing it.

Today, all my siblings would come over with their kids, maybe even a stray aunt or uncle. The house would be bursting at the seams for hours as people filtered in and out, hugging and laughing and catching up. I wouldn't have been able to eat most of the food, and some of the people were faces I hadn't seen for years, but what I was missing was on my mind all day. I even called the house—something I hadn't done in years—and talked to as many people as I could before they needed to get off the phone in order to say grace. I hung up and stared at the phone with a lump in my throat, trying to remind myself that independence was what I'd wanted.

After we got home and Paul went to bed, I called Stormy to hear about her day. Jared's two brothers and their families had come with *their* families. There were two boy cousins Stormy's age, and they had taken her to the local skate park and showed her some tricks while Jared's mom and sisters-in-law finished cooking the meal. They'd had a traditional feast and then pie, pie, and more pie. Jared's mom had started teaching Stormy how to crochet while everyone let their bellies rest, and Stormy told me how she was going to start making flowered headbands in all different colors. They were staying until Sunday and had a slew of activities planned over those few days. Stormy had no doubt that she'd return to Irvine with mad skater skills and a bag full of headbands for all her new friends.

"That's great," I said, sounding as enthusiastic as I could. "I'm so glad you're having a good time."

"And we're going to cut down a tree for Grandma tomorrow. She got a permit and everything. Dad's going to show me how to use a chain saw."

"Wonderful," I said. I continued to encourage and applaud all she was doing, then hung up the phone and tried not to cry.

Had I ever given my daughter that kind of Thanksgiving? I loved that she was having such a good time and that Jared's family was so good to her, but I felt so . . . left out. The Thanksgiving weekend stretched ahead of me like a tired road through Death Valley. Here I'd been counting down the months until Stormy was gone, and now I wondered what I would do with myself now that she was no longer here. The shift of perspective was painful, but I couldn't block it out. I'd been working toward this for years, but it wasn't what I'd thought it would be.

I finished reading *Asher Lev*, and the ending hadn't been as happy as I had hoped—kind of like *Poisonwood Bible* had been. Asher's story was very different than mine, of course, and while I could make all kinds of little comparisons, in the end, the thing that stood out to me was the separation he felt.

He lost his family. I felt as though I'd already lost the family of my childhood and now I was losing the family I'd had since then. It hurt.

Chapter 19

I WASN'T THE FIRST PERSON to arrive at book group; Ilana was already there, as professional as ever. We chitchatted until Livvy showed up, and then we chitchatted as a group instead. Shannon, Ruby's niece, showed up a minute later. She and Ilana talked together, and Livvy and I separated. She was wearing jeans that were a size too small and a pink top that wasn't the right tone for her skin. It was a bit of a struggle to find something I could sincerely compliment, but then I noticed her toenails showing through her open-toed sandals—only in Southern California could someone get away with wearing sandals in December. The sparkly pink polish caught the light when she moved.

"I love your polish," I said.

"Oh, thanks," she said, moving her foot and looking at her toes, a little smile on her face. "I didn't realize until after I chose my color that I should have chosen something a little more Christmassy."

"Ah," I said, waving it away. "There's room for pink in every holiday."

Livvy smiled, her whole countenance brighter than it had been when she came in. Paige arrived, and then Athena showed up. Ruby made a comment about Athena being too thin, and I dared look down at my thighs spread out on the chair before looking away and sucking in my belly. I'd chosen an empire-waist shirt, but now that I was sitting, it really emphasized my stomach, which I was not comfortable with right now. My back was stiff from sitting at the computer all day, and I shifted in my seat, pressing my lower back into the cushions and making a mental note to schedule a massage. It had been too long.

Livvy said something as Paige crossed the room to Athena. "How are you?" she asked, looking concerned. Both Livvy and I stopped to listen for Athena's reply.

"Doing better," Athena said. Then she looked at all of us and thanked us for having come to the funeral. "It really meant a lot to see all of you."

Ilana made her apologies for not having been there. Shannon didn't say anything out loud but nodded. She seemed the least comfortable here, and I wondered, again, if she had come only to appease Ruby. The doorbell rang, but I didn't make the connection that it meant someone else was joining our group until a woman I hadn't met came in behind Ruby. She was black or African-American or whatever the current title was—and beautiful, with big brown eyes not much different from Athena's.

Ruby introduced her as Victoria, and she immediately shared her excitement at being part of the group and something about being afraid she'd bore us.

"She's far from boring," Ruby said. "She works in the film industry and has some amazing—and horrific—stories."

"That's true," Victoria said after she took the last open seat in the room. "But before telling you any of them, I'll need you all to sign a nondisclosure form." We all chuckled over that. It was her first week, but I felt closer to her than I did with Ilana or Shannon, both of whom had been here before.

Ruby clapped to get everyone's attention and then started out by asking everyone to share what had happened in their lives since the last time we'd met. I looked around, wondering if anyone else was uncomfortable with what Ruby had said. This was supposed to be a book club, and while we were friends, I didn't really want to share what was going on with my life.

Livvy and Paige skimmed over their updates. Victoria laughed about everything being new since this was her first week. "Trust me, you don't want all the details at once." Everyone laughed, and then Ruby turned to Shannon and Ilana who shrugged through their piddly updates as well. Athena seemed glad for the chance to talk. A lot had happened since we'd last seen her.

"Last time I was here, I made an announcement about my pitiful dating life," she said.

I was surprised. I'd expected something about her mom, not her relationships.

"The fact is, things have turned around. I'm dating a man named Grey Ronning."

"From the bookstore?" Ruby asked, again clapping her hands.

"Yes." Athena grinned broadly—I hadn't expected that either. Her mother had just died, after all. And then, just like that, she was over it and moving on? She sat back in her chair as though relieved to have gotten the information off her chest. I was confused by her behavior, even though I joined everyone else in wishing her well.

Ruby eventually turned her attention to Livvy, who cleared her throat and began the discussion about *My Name Is Asher Lev.*

"This book seems to revolve around the suffering caused from conflicting traditions. The story really deals with the decisions these three people made in their lives that ended up affecting not only their traditions, but the people they loved the most. And yet, none of them could have chosen differently, or they would have been betraying themselves."

Athena opened her copy and began flipping through several pages marked with red pencil. When Livvy noticed, she said, "I actually started underlining some of the sentences." She paused, seemingly looking for a passage. "The relationship between Asher and his father really affected me." She went on about how her mother had wanted her to date and marry a nice Greek boy.

"Is the bookstore guy Greek?" I asked.

"No," Athena said.

She flipped through the book again, still looking for something. "When Asher goes against his parents' wishes to not only become a painter, but to paint the crucifixion, I guess I was reminded of myself. Listen to what he says." She read part of the book aloud. "'I turned my back to the paintings and closed my eyes, for I could no longer endure seeing the works of my own hands and knowing the pain those works would soon inflict upon people I loved.'"

I realized that I was creasing the hem of my shirt—good thing it was cotton. I thought about how my shifts from my religious upbringing had hurt my parents. I hated thinking about that.

"I guess it really hit me hard," Athena said. "I was doing the same thing. Living a life, or more accurately, rejecting a life that those who loved me wanted me to have." She blinked back tears; I'd never seen her so emotional. She shook her head. "I don't want to turn my back anymore. Although I don't know if marriage or children are in my future, I'm willing to open my heart at least, and consider the option."

Livvy patted her hand; Athena took a breath. I wondered if she was going to talk about her mother's death. Maybe she'd needed to gear up to it, feel safe before she got into something more tender.

"I found some letters that my dad wrote to my mom," Athena continued as tears fell from her eyes, which made tears rise in my own. I was always a copycat when it came to crying; I couldn't help it. "Their marriage wasn't what I thought it was. They had their challenges but loved each other dearly." She wiped at her cheeks, explaining how she'd misunderstood their relationship.

"Isn't that true of many things in life?" Paige asked, her voice quiet, almost reverent. "We go around assuming we know or understand another person. When we find out the truth, our whole perception changes, for better—or for worse." She looked at the hands in her lap. I had no doubt she was thinking about her failed marriage. I'd spent many hours considering how perceptions could change once a relationship ended.

Livvy was the next person to speak. "This book is filled with layers of family dynamics. Each character has intense flaws, yet you can't help but relate and understand their motivations for doing what they do, even when it tears down another family member."

I rolled that around in my head. Layers. Such a great insight. The other women shared some thoughts on that, but I kept mine to myself. The layers in my family dynamics were complex, and while I knew these women struggled, it was hard to imagine any of them could understand mine. I was still embarrassed not to have Stormy living with me anymore. I missed her, but then wondered if I had done everything I could do to repair our relationship.

"Families are sticky," Victoria said. It was true, but something about the way she said it bugged me. It was almost . . . flippant.

Ilana talked about her childhood, and the expectations put on her by her family, who were practicing Jews. It was fascinating, at least in part because I, too, had been raised in a religious family, and yet with an underlying condemnation toward non-Christians. I certainly wasn't going to say that out loud, though. I just listened and learned and wondered what it was that drew Ilana away from her religion. I also found that despite her apparent confidence in her choice, I felt sympathetic toward her. Maybe *kinship* was a better word. I wondered what her relationship with her parents was like now. Did she have brothers and sisters? Did she miss them?

Victoria chimed in. "You know when Asher got into trouble with the Mashpia, which I took to mean as his school principal—I didn't take the time to look it up . . . " She looked at Ilana who nodded. Victoria continued, talking about all the creative people she spent her time with and how it would be sad if they didn't use their gifts like Asher was told to do by the Mashpia in the book.

I appreciated the thought, but felt Victoria was a little high-handed with it. This was her first group, and I felt a little like she was taking over. Ruby was impressed Victoria had already read the book, and I knew I shouldn't have been bothered since I wasn't saying much. I might have shared my thoughts if I hadn't felt like everyone else had more important things to say about it.

"Paige has the next book selection," Ruby said, turning to Paige. "Would you like to tell us a little about it?"

"Sure," she said, reaching into her purse. "I chose a classic that some of you might have read in high school or college. *Silas Marner* by George Eliot."

"Oh, I love that one," Ruby said. "It's definitely worth reading more than once."

I'd never heard of it. Paige continued speaking while the rest of us pulled out notebooks or typed the title into our phones. "I picked it because as classics go, it's pretty easy. Plus, it's short, so I figured it would be a good one to read over the Christmas holiday."

"If I'm not mistaken," Ruby said, "wasn't the author female?"

Hadn't Paige said the author's name was George?

"She was," Paige said. "Her real name was Mary Anne Evans. In her day, a lot of women had to publish anonymously or under pen names to have any chance for their work to be read and taken seriously."

The conversation veered into other topics, and as we chatted, Livvy leaned toward me. "I think those kinds of shirts are so cute, Daisy," she said out of the blue. She waved her hand. "But I can't wear them; any time I try, I totally look pregnant."

Heat instantly filled my face. This was the second book group where someone had said something about me being pregnant. I suppressed the anger and forced myself to be polite.

Ruby reached over and patted my knee. "I wonder if you are. How exciting!"

I forced a smile. "I'm *not* pregnant; trust me." I couldn't help but shoot a look at Paige, who'd been the one to bring it up last month. "I got that taken care of permanently fifteen years ago, remember? I can't get pregnant."

"I had a friend back in '87," Ruby said, not picking up on my energy. "She had a tubal ligation, and then ten years later, poof! There she was, expecting a surprise little caboose! He's a teenager now."

Everyone but Ruby seemed uncomfortable, and I tried to soften the moment and said, "That's pretty rare. I'll just make a point of not wearing this shirt again."

An uncomfortable silence settled over the room. Finally Ruby stood. "Well, let's serve up the dessert. Or, rather, the refreshments, since potato latkes aren't sweet. Ilana brought them for Livvy. Wasn't that nice of her?"

Ruby dished up the latkes, which I tried to enjoy despite being obsessed with Livvy's comment. Did I look that fat? Did I look pregnant?

"How's your father?"

I looked up to see who'd spoken. It was Paige, directing the comment at Athena.

"It's getting harder," Athena said. She looked up to see all of us listening and explained that her father had Alzheimer's. He sometimes thought she was her aunt or his younger sister, and with her mother gone, she had taken over his care, a task which sounded overwhelming. Wow. "My sister thinks we should put him in a care center now. But it's so expensive, and this is a bad time of the year to put my parents' house on the market."

"Had your mother ever talked about a care center?" Livvy asked.

Athena shook her head and pushed a piece of latke around on her plate with her fork. "Not that she told us."

"Have you checked into any of them?" I asked.

Paige smiled at me gratefully. "It might be worth looking into," she added.

"I looked up a couple of locations," Athena said. "But I feel so . . ." She looked at the ceiling as if trying to come up with a way to explain. "Guilty. I'm his daughter; he raised me and took care of me my whole life. I'm the only one who can really take care of him—my sister has three kids. It's not his fault my mother is gone; I have to take her place as best as I can. I just can't bring myself to put him away."

"You're not putting him away," Paige said quickly.

"Nursing homes are awful," Ruby said, her lips tight. She gave a quick shake of her head.

I cringed, but Paige hurried to repair it. "Not all nursing homes are the same." She told us about a care center in Utah that her church provided worship services for. "It was a beautiful place, and the residents were happy there." She turned to Athena. "Your mom was his caretaker, and she did what she thought was best. You're his caretaker now, and it's not wrong to make a choice in both of your best interests."

Athena nodded but didn't say anything else.

We ate quietly, with a few comments peppering the awkward silence. I stood as soon as I felt like I could and made my good-byes, trying to stand up straight so that my shirt would be more concealing.

Concealing of what? As soon as I stood, however, I realized I needed to use the bathroom. I already knew where it was, so I thought I'd just step in on my way out, without advertising. I'd been using the bathroom a lot more than usual, I realized, but hated thinking about that, hated the reminders of what these women had said. I wasn't pregnant. I wasn't! I couldn't be.

I washed my hands and let myself out. By the time I reached the front door, Paige was just pulling it open. She smiled at me, but then her smile faltered. I realized my eyebrows were pulled together and tried to smooth my expression.

"You okay?" she asked as I passed through the door in front of her.

"Sure," I said.

"I'm really sorry about the comments," Paige said. "I can't help but feel responsible since I brought it up last month."

I should have smiled and shrugged it off, but I didn't. Instead, I turned to Paige as she shut the door behind her. "I can't be pregnant," I said in a whisper, despite the fact that we were the only two people outside. "I can't."

Chapter 20

We stood there for a few seconds before we heard more good-byes from the other side of the door. In tandem, we started walking toward our cars.

"You're obviously worried, though," Paige said. "Why not take a test?"

"I can't," I said automatically. I was saying that a lot. It would be a waste of time and a waste of money, but . . .

"Take it at my apartment," Paige said. "There's a drugstore not half a mile away from here. Just take a test, and then you can be done with it once and for all."

"Unless it comes back positive." As soon as I said it, I clamped my mouth shut. It was *not* possible. I'd had my tubes tied fifteen years ago. I was forty-six years old. I was *not* pregnant. But the idea that had been planted a month ago hadn't ever gone away completely and to-night it had been set on fire. I could see the green shoot poking out of the ground and knew the only way to pull it out was to prove it to be unfounded. I was certain even entertaining the thought was just some sadistic way to distract myself from my other worries in life, but if that was the case, then confronting it would still be effective at moving it out of the way, right?

Paige continued. "At least this way you'll know, right? No more wondering and worrying. And I won't tell anyone the results either way."

I looked at my feet and accepted that it was time to take the test. My stomach completely rebelled at the idea, but it rebelled about pretty much everything these days anyway.

"You know you want to. Just come do it."

Livvy and Athena passed by, and Paige waved at them pleasantly as they headed toward their cars—Ilana must have been the first one out the door—then Paige turned to wave at Ruby, who was still standing at the door. I didn't even think about saying good-bye, I was totally lost in myself.

A thought occurred to me—another excuse why I couldn't do this. Not tonight. "Isn't Stormy babysitting for you tonight?"

"Yeah," Paige said. "But she'll be gone by the time you get there. Unless you wanted her to stay."

"No!" I said too loudly. That idea was horrendous. I thought about Paul—my *husband*. I should tell him I was taking the test, right? He deserved to know, didn't he? But I could barely admit it to myself, let alone share my suspicions.

"Not a problem," Paige said. "I'll be sure to have her on her way before you arrive."

"Fine," I said in surrender. "I'll see you in a few. But Stormy better not be there."

My attempt at sounding threatening only made her laugh. "It'll be perfect. I'll hurry, I promise."

Livvy's Pacifica pulled away from the curb, and Athena's slick black car followed slowly behind her. I headed to my car and could feel Paige watching me, as if she worried I would stand her up. It was tempting, but no, I was determined to get this over with. For being so young, Paige sure was pushy.

I found the drugstore and intended to take my time, but I felt like a seventeen-year-old kid again, trying to buy a pregnancy test without anyone noticing. It ticked me off that I would revert to being that stupid little girl, so I marched down the aisle, scanned the tests, and then bought three different brands. The first test I'd taken with Stormy had been negative, and I was relieved for exactly ten days. The second test had told the truth. I didn't want to think about that, however. There were few moments as difficult as telling the guy you think you might be in love with that he's tied to you for life, whether he likes it or not. I'd already done that twice—three times, if I counted the pregnancy that forced Jared and me to give things one more try until it ended in miscarriage.

Paige had texted me directions to her place. I pulled into the apartment complex in Tustin, concentrating on finding the second building on the north end. There was an empty parking space right out front, and I pulled my Prius into it, took a breath, and then pushed the button to turn off the car. I regarded the bag on my passenger seat with trepidation, hoping I had wasted sixty bucks.

I went inside and took the elevator to the fourth floor. As apartment complexes went, this one was nice. I'd seen a playground when I drove in; I bet her boys lived there when they could.

I knocked on the door with the number 425 stuck to it, and Paige opened up right away.

"You're speedy," Paige said as I stepped past her. The apartment was quiet; the boys must have been asleep. I noticed that Stormy hadn't done all the dishes. I made a mental note to talk to her about that. "Oh, and you almost ran into your daughter."

I managed to laugh, even though the thought horrified me. "Well, I'm glad I didn't."

Now that I was there I felt silly. Paige was twenty years younger than I was, and I'd raised two daughters on my own, for heaven's sake. I could take a pregnancy test by myself. But not at home where Paul might find the packaging. Oh, I so needed to get this over with. I held up the bag from the drugstore. "I bought three. Just to be sure."

Paige laughed and showed me to the bathroom. "I hope you've got enough in you to pee on all of those."

"Wish me luck," I said, jiggling the bag before I locked the door.

There was a pair of swim trunks hanging over the shower rod, and the tub faucet was dripping water on a pile of bath toys. I took my time clearing the counter to make room for the tests and laid down a doubled strip of toilet paper. I was dealing with urine after all, and if someone were taking pregnancy tests in *my* bathroom, I would want them to be considerate.

My work area prepped, I took all the tests out of the boxes and read the brief instructions on how to use them; they all worked within the same basic process. I looked at all three of them, lined up like little soldiers, and closed my eyes, offering my first prayer in I didn't know how many years.

Please don't do this to me again.

I took the tests, washed my hands, and then sat on the closed toilet with my back to the tests. I waited a full three minutes before I stood, took another breath, and turned to see my fate.

One plus sign.

Two plus signs.

Three.

Chapter 21

I HAD VERY LITTLE MEMORY of what happened at Paige's house after seeing the results of the three tests. I drove home, eventually, but I parked a few houses down the street in front of an empty house with a FOR SALE sign in the yard and a good view of the window of my master bedroom. I didn't want Paul to see my swollen eyes. It was more than an hour before Paul gave up waiting on me and turned off the bedroom light. Then I stared at the darkened window and asked myself the next question.

How on earth was I going to tell him?

Tears I thought I'd run out of crept up on me as I imagined all his possible reactions. But I didn't have enough foundation to even draw a conclusive hypothesis. Paul and I had never discussed having children together. Why would we? I had been forty-three years old when we got married, Paul had been forty, and we both had teenage daughters. He'd known early on in our relationship that I couldn't have more children.

Couldn't!

Not that I didn't *want* kids—though I didn't—but I could not physically conceive another child. I had never heard of a tubal ligation failing. I had never been told that it could "grow back." If I hadn't stared at those tests until I thought I was going to pass out, I still wouldn't have believed it. At the same time, I felt so stupid. I hadn't had a period in three months. I'd chalked it up to pre-menopause or just good luck, but I'd also been nauseated, and my breasts were swollen, and I could no longer fit into my jeans even though I wasn't eating much. I'd been through this before—not only pregnancy, but unplanned pregnancies that snuck up on me exactly like this.

How could I possibly be facing this again? How could I have not known?

I dried my tears on the sleeve of my jacket and made a decision. I was not telling Paul. Not yet. Maybe I'd come up with the right way to say it in a few days. Or maybe . . . the pregnancy wouldn't work out. The thought propelled me back to the moment when I lost Jared's baby. It had been devastating because I knew that baby was the only thing holding us together. Now, I worried about the reverse. This baby—okay, I wasn't ready to think of it as a baby—this *pregnancy* might be too much for Paul and me.

I'd be sixty-five years old when this child graduated from high school—older than Ruby—and I could honestly say at that point that I had spent my whole life raising children. I parked in the driveway so I wouldn't have to open the garage and risk Paul waking up. I got out of the car and headed toward the front door as the shock moved out of the way and anger began to rise. This was not fair! It wasn't fair to me. It wasn't fair to Paul. It wasn't fair to my daughters—I was going to be a grandmother, for heaven's sake—and it certainly wasn't fair to this . . . pregnancy.

I let myself into the house as quietly as possible, but I couldn't make myself go into the bedroom. I felt guilty and angry and completely overwhelmed. I left my shoes by the front door and went into Stormy's room. I curled up in her bed, which still smelled like her, and wished I had something else to think about. But what could possibly supersede this in my thoughts? I lay there, staring at the blank walls of the room where my daughter used to live, and thought back to the prayer I'd dared utter before I took those tests.

Please don't do this to me again.

That's why I don't pray.

Chapter 22

I'd been on autopilot before and, just as I'd adjusted to Stormy being gone, I easily fell into a routine that took me from one day to the next. I kept up at work, I kept up at home, I did what Paul wanted to do in the evenings, and I tried not to think.

Now that I knew the truth, I could finally admit that my body was changing, and it became my priority to disguise those changes. Whereas I'd lost some weight in the beginning, my shape was all wrong. I wore elastic waistband pants and pretended I was cold so I had an excuse to wear sweaters and jackets even though I was an absolute furnace. When Paul tried to be intimate, I told him I was too tired; I couldn't stand the thought of him touching my morphing body. I'd figured I was fifteen or sixteen weeks along. Would he believe that I'd only known for a week and a half?

Did *I* really believe that?

I was at work Thursday morning, verifying some client information online, and suddenly found myself on the Planned Parenthood website. I'd had a friend back in Virginia who'd had an abortion in high school. She'd insisted it wasn't a real baby, not yet, but the explanation hadn't worked for me, and I'd been horrified. For all the wild times I eventually had, I believed in the soul, and I believed that destroying a body that was meant to house a soul was a sin. But I stared at the company's logo now, thirty years later, and reviewed the arguments she'd made. What if it wasn't a baby? What if it were just cells that weren't really anything at all?

I'd let so many matters of faith fall by the wayside. Why not this one? If I believed everything I'd been taught, I was already going to hell for having gotten pregnant out of wedlock at seventeen, marrying a non-Catholic, getting a divorce, and not going to church. So what was one more black mark on my record?

Then my eyes caught the picture on my desk. We'd taken it last summer when Stormy and I had visited December in Ohio. My daughters smiled back at me.

They'd both once been a cluster of cells.

Getting rid of this would solve everything.

Could I pretend not to believe what I believed?

Was forgiveness better than permission?

I looked at the picture of my girls again and closed the website.

I got back to work, taking on a few projects that Eric was falling behind on in order to keep myself sufficiently overwhelmed at the office. I avoided Amy as though I had a communicable disease. What would she do when she found out about this?

• • •

Christmas was a few weeks away, and Paul and I talked about getting a tree, but without Stormy at home, neither of us made time for the errand. I tried to shop but ended up going around and around the hallways of the mall without buying anything other than hand soap. Why on earth did I need hand soap? I'd decided not to talk to Paul until I felt prepared for his reaction, but I couldn't imagine his reaction yet. Did that mean I didn't trust my husband? Did I think he would leave me over this? Would *I* leave if he were the one holding the key that would unravel my carefully constructed expectations of what the rest of my life would be? I walked by a life-size nativity display and stared at the baby Jesus in the manger. After a few seconds I had to look away.

Why was this happening to me?

I gave up on shopping and decided to go home, but on my way toward the exit, I saw a bookstore and remembered that I hadn't picked up next month's book yet. I stopped in the middle of the mall, and a woman bumped into me, nearly knocking me over. I didn't want to go into the bookstore and have to talk and smile at people. Autopilot could get me through only so many hours of the day. But then I remembered *Poisonwood Bible* and *My Name Is Asher Lev.* I'd been able to lose myself in both of those books. I would love to get lost again. So I went in, but I couldn't remember the name of the author, just the title—*Silas Marner.*

I asked an employee to help me find it and followed him through the stacks, ending up in the classics section. When he placed the book in my hands, I was disappointed to see how slender it was. I wouldn't get lost for long. Still, I paid for it and continued my trek to my car. I got a text from Paul saying he was going to Charlie's to work on the deck his brother was building. I was glad he'd be gone before I got home.

Paul knew something was wrong; I could tell by the way he looked at me too long. We lived in the same house, but I was avoiding him, and he knew it. Mason had come last weekend and that had been a good distraction for him. I pretended to have year-end stuff I needed to finish at the office so they could have time together.

I drove home, let myself into my empty house, and finished off the potato chips out of spite for the healthy diet I was supposed to be following. I kicked off my shoes and changed into my frumpy-comfy clothes. In the process of getting changed, I caught my reflection in the mirror again, in profile. There was a definite bump—a perfect curve where the pregnancy was taking over. I froze. For a second. Then I picked up my shoe and threw it at the mirror.

I didn't want to *be* pregnant, and I certainly didn't want to *look* pregnant. I stormed out of the bedroom and grabbed *Silas Marner* out of my purse, desperate for the escape. Paige had said it was a classic novel, so I hoped it was dark and more hopeless than my life was—like the Thomas Hardy novels we'd read in my English Literature class my sophomore year. I'd wanted happy endings for other books, but not this time. This time I wanted to read a tragedy that would make my life look a little brighter by comparison.

After settling onto the couch—I couldn't read in the bedroom because the traitorous mirror was in there—I started reading. It took me a while to adjust to the classical writing, but it was a good story, and I enjoyed the beautiful language as the book progressed. It was about a miser who treasured his money above all else until it was stolen. Then, as he's trying to find purpose again, a child enters his life. A child with bright golden hair. Stormy had had bright blonde hair when she was a baby. I kept reading, but then the story started to change. I watched the old man change with it. His longing for his money began to fade, and in its place the love for the child began to grow.

I felt my jaw clench as I tried to talk myself out of the suspicions creeping up my spine, but the parallels became stronger and stronger until I flattened the book against my chest and tried to breathe through the heated anger rising in my shoulders.

She would not do this to me, I said in my mind. *Paige wouldn't be so mean.*

But within a few more pages, I was absolutely livid. I leaned forward on the couch, bracing my elbows on my knees and holding my head in my hands. When I opened my eyes, though, I was staring at my stomach, which looked absolutely huge. I heard my phone ding with a text message, and I practically ran into the kitchen, beside myself with rage that I knew was illogical but was there nonetheless. I snorted when I saw the text was from Paige.

> I'm done with my copy of Silas Marner. Did you want to borrow
> it? How are you doing?

Oh, that girl! I stared at my purse, then looked back at the book I'd left on the living room floor.

Twenty minutes later, I pulled up to Paige's apartment complex still as mad as I'd been when I stormed out to my car. When I got to door 425, I knocked loudly and waited, my fingers clenching the book.

I heard her footsteps as she got closer and I waited. I heard the knob twisting and I waited. She pulled the door open and had the audacity to smile when she saw me standing there.

"Daisy, did you respond to my text and I missed it? I'm so sorry." She pulled the door open to have me enter, but I held up my copy of the book instead.

"I can't believe you did this."

Paige's expression fell but she simply looked confused. "Um, I'm not sure—"

"I spent my whole childhood being preached to, Paige, and the last thing I need now is for people to pretend to be my friend simply to set me up for some kind of conversion."

Paige looked over her shoulder, and then pulled the door mostly shut. "Daisy, what is your deal?"

"My *deal* is the fact that I trusted you with something that may prove to be the biggest trial I have ever faced, and you slapped me in the face with it. You are a stupid little girl who knows nothing about me or my life. The next time you want to make some kind of statement, do it on your own time." I threw my book at her; she stepped out of the way, but it still hit her in the shoulder.

Good.

I turned on my heel and headed back toward the elevators. "Wait just a second!" I heard her say from behind me. I didn't wait, and I didn't turn around until I felt her hand on my arm. Then I turned sharply enough that she fell back a step, but my aggression didn't shut her up.

"*What* are you so mad about?" Her voice wasn't nearly as submissive as I had hoped it would be.

"Like you don't know?" I lashed back, putting my hands on my hips. I was only a couple of inches taller than she was, and I suddenly wished I were six foot two.

"No, I don't know. You're making no sense."

"You totally set me up, and I don't appreciate it."

"How on earth did I set you up?" Paige asked. She held up the book. "And what does *this* have to do with anything?"

"Oh, come *on*," I said, rolling my eyes. "An old man whose greatest treasure becomes a child? Real stealthy, Paige. I don't know how I *ever* figured it out."

Paige paused for half a second, and then she laughed humorlessly.

I was ready to punch her. "You think this book was directed to you?" She shook her head. "Oh, that's a bit of a stretch, don't you think?" She put her hand on her hip. "First of all, I chose the book before you took those tests. Second, it's a classic piece of literature that has a great message for anyone who loves anyone else. It's about *people,* Daisy, not your baby. And thirdly"—she paused and her eyes narrowed—"you're being a real b . . . b . . . brat about this whole thing. You're pregnant, you don't feel ready for it, but it's a *baby,* and you treat it like it's a terminal disease. You need to grow up and—"

"You have no idea what you're talking about; no idea what—"

"Oh, whatever," Paige said. "You are out of your head, lady. If a little book unhinges you, you're trying way too hard to find a scapegoat for your misery. Frankly, I've got too many of my own problems to deal with any of yours." She threw the book at my feet, and I stared at it while the words she'd said replayed through my mind. I tried to grab onto the vapors of my rage as her words sank in, but they were fading too fast to sustain me.

Paige stared at me for another second before she turned and went back to her apartment. Her door opened, I heard snatches of canned laughter from the TV, and then her door snapped shut. I stood there for a few more seconds until the elevator dinged and I got on. I faced forward as the elevator closed with the book still in the hallway and took me back to the ground level. I went out to my car, slid into the driver's seat, and sat there.

What was wrong with me?

I felt my chin trembling, and I leaned forward until my forehead rested on the steering wheel.

I was pregnant . . . no, I was going to have a *baby.* And Paige was right. I might be forty-six years old, but I needed to grow up and face this. I had lived most of my adult life trying to prove to the people around me that I had it all together. Yet here I was, keeping a secret that was tearing me apart. I had to tell Paul, I might need to see a therapist to help me figure out how to handle this, but what I couldn't do was keep myself holed up in this shell I'd created. If I didn't trust the people I loved enough to tell them what was happening, then what did that say about my relationships? And I'd chewed out Paige, the only friend I had in this situation.

Chapter 23

THE HOUSE WAS EMPTY when I got home, and I headed for the bedroom. Could I just sleep for the next six months? Please?

I sat heavily on the side of the bed and, for the first time, brought my hands up to my stomach. I didn't think I really looked pregnant yet, just top-heavy, but I *was* pregnant. Within the next few weeks, I wouldn't be able to hide it, and I would feel this . . . *baby* move. Whether I liked it or not, my condition would soon become obvious to everyone. I needed to make a plan. The first item on that list was telling Paul.

Oh, my stomach rolled at the thought. I still, even after all this time, had no idea how he would react. But I couldn't keep waiting for some kind of inspiration, and the longer I waited, the harder it was going to be to explain *why* I had waited. I looked at the alarm clock next to our bed. It was seven o'clock. He would be back anytime.

I heard my cell phone ringing in the kitchen, so I stood up to answer it. I headed toward my purse on the counter before realizing my phone was on the table. Apparently, I hadn't put it in my purse when I went to my showdown-gone-bad with Paige. I felt so embarrassed for having reacted like that. She must think I was totally insane.

I picked up my phone. It was December's number calling, but the display said it was the sixth missed call from her number. I quickly answered it. "Hey, sweetie," I said, trying to focus on this moment.

"Mom?" December said in her trying-to-be-strong voice. "I've been trying to call you. There's something wrong. My doctor wants me admitted to the hospital."

Chapter 24

By the time Paul came home, I'd already made my flight arrangements for the next morning, and I was almost packed.

He sat on the bed while I went between my closet and my dresser, choosing clothes I knew had a looser fit. I had planned to tell him about the baby—our baby—tonight, but I couldn't do that now. Not like this; not when I was leaving.

While I finished packing, I explained that December had gone to her regular appointment yesterday but her doctor had had some concerns. They'd sent her home with instructions to follow, then told her to come back today to see how she was responding. Long story short, they told her to get to the hospital. Her blood pressure was nearing stroke level, her kidneys were shutting down, and she needed intervention quick. Lance, her husband, took her to the hospital immediately, and the doctors got her on some medication that was keeping her blood pressure stable, but it wasn't going down like they wanted.

"They're watching her closely, but will have to do a C-section if things get any worse."

"How long will she be in the hospital?" Paul asked.

"Until she has the baby," I responded.

"How far along is she?"

"Thirty-four weeks," I said, feeling my stomach drop. "She isn't due until February."

"How long are you going to stay out there?"

I turned to look at him and wished he was coming with me. Well, I kinda wished he was. I stopped my packing and came to stand in front of him, wondering if he'd noticed how fat I was getting. I touched his cheek. "I don't know," I said. "If they end up taking the baby early, I'll stay as long as I can."

Right then, I had a horrible thought. What if something happened to December's baby, and my baby was okay? I pushed that thought far away. As Paul rested his hands on my hips and looked into my eyes, I almost told him everything. For that brief moment, it seemed so plausible that he would be stunned and then excited. Maybe he'd kiss my belly and wrap his arms around my expanding waistline.

But the moment passed quickly as everything else crowded in to take its place. Now wasn't the right time; December needed to be my focus. I bent down and kissed Paul on the top of the head, then returned to my packing. My bags were by the door before I realized I hadn't talked to Stormy. I called her cell phone and explained about her sister's situation. She wanted to come with me, but since I didn't know how long I'd be in Ohio and she still had school, that wasn't an option. Luckily, she accepted my explanations.

Eventually Paul and I went to bed, but I didn't sleep much as I tried to sort through my daughter's situation along with my own circumstances. I almost prayed for December and the baby, but then I remembered my last prayer—the one I'd offered when I took those pregnancy tests. I was making progress in my own acceptance of this baby, but that didn't mean I'd let God off the hook for having done this to me. And now December? I'd been raised to believe in a loving God. But sometimes I wondered.

Chapter 25

I PICKED UP A RENTAL CAR at the Cincinnati airport and called Lance once I had finished signing the contracts. "How's she doing?"

"Fine," he said, calm as always. "She's showing some response to the medication. I hope we didn't call you out here for nothing."

"No, I'm glad you called," I said. Was I ever. "The rental car has a GPS so I should be there soon."

I found the hospital easily enough, and within an hour of my plane landing, I was marching down the hall of labor and delivery. When I stopped a nurse and asked where my daughter was, she showed me to December's room. I could see right away how swollen she was. Her hands and her face were round almost to the point of looking painful. She teared up when she saw me, and I hurried over to hug her as tightly as I could.

"Oh, sweetheart," I said when I pulled back. We were both crying. "Are you okay?"

I stayed for the rest of the afternoon, talking or being silent as the situation warranted. Mostly, December was just scared, but the doctors were optimistic that they could hold off labor a little longer. Lance came that evening; he'd gone into work to make notes on his different projects in case someone needed to step in for him next week. I stayed for another hour before finally admitting I was dead on my feet. I'd left

California at six o'clock that morning, and the flight was catching up with me fast. I hugged December, made Lance promise to call me if anything happened, and followed the GPS directions to their house in an older suburb with big trees and cracked sidewalks.

I was dragging when I finally shut the front door behind me but still went about making up a bed on the couch. It had only been a few months since I'd last been here, but I could see the changes in December's little home. There was a car seat still in the box in the corner of the kitchen. On top was a pile of clothes and tiny little baby things. I touched a baby-sized baseball cap and felt a lump form in my throat. December had told me all about the baby shower her friends had thrown for her last weekend. She'd been absolutely glowing in the photos she'd posted to Facebook, but in hindsight, I remembered noticing that her face looked a little rounder than usual. I'd chalked it up to pregnancy weight gain, but more had been going on, and no one knew it. I'd sent her a gift certificate for Babies "R" Us.

Would a better mother have done something more personal?

The extra bedroom where Stormy and I had stayed when we visited last summer had been painted a light green—very calming. I sat down in the rocking chair, a hand-me-down from Lance's mother, and began rocking back and forth. The crib wasn't set up yet, but the pieces were stacked against the wall. Lance still hadn't finished moving out the desk that had been in here when it was an office. I thought about trying to set up the crib, or at least move the desk out into the living room, but I didn't feel up to it. I didn't feel up to much of anything.

I closed my eyes and let the rocking motion soothe me—or I tried to. It was hard to let go of the tension, both what I'd left behind and what I'd come to. Facing December's impending motherhood while hiding my own was very surreal. But how could I tell anyone about it now? December needed my help and attention. It would take away from her if I suddenly made an announcement. Was I grateful for the excuse? If I was being totally honest, I would have to say that I was, but that didn't mean I felt good about it. Paige's words were fresh in my mind. I still needed to grow up, but when would I find the time for that?

Chapter 26

I FELL ASLEEP IN THE ROCKING CHAIR and woke up around two o'clock in the morning when Lance came through the front door.

"I thought you were going to stay at the hospital," I said as we met in the living room.

"All they had was a chair," he said, stretching out his back. "And my back is killing me. December has her phone, though, and I made her promise to call."

I'd forgotten that Lance had injured his back a few years ago in a waterskiing accident. He looked like he was in a lot of pain. Come to think of it, my back wasn't feeling all that swell either.

"I meant to borrow an air mattress for you to use like we did over the summer," Lance said as he retrieved a prescription bottle from a kitchen cupboard.

"The couch is fine," I assured him, not wanting him to worry about something so trivial. "She was okay when you left?"

"Yeah," Lance said with a heavy sigh. "I'm hoping she'll sleep better if she's not worrying about me."

He offered me their bed, but I refused. He needed it more than I did. We both turned in, and while the couch wasn't all that comfortable, it was better than the rocking chair. I slept until almost eight and then made coffee and instant oatmeal for breakfast. Lance was still asleep, so after getting dressed, I left him a note and headed for the hospital.

On the way, I stopped at Kmart and, for the first time in years, headed to the baby department. I couldn't believe how much stuff there was. Surely there hadn't been so many things when my girls were little. I looked for several minutes before I found some preemie-sized pajamas, the dress kind with a drawstring at the bottom that I'd always preferred when my girls were little. They were so small, though. I shook my head, hoping that everything would be fine from here on out and December's baby would wait until it was due. I knew better, though. The doctors were taking it one day at a time, but no one expected December to take my grandson to term.

I grabbed some socks and little knit caps, then one of those bouncy chairs for good measure. I did not think about buying two of everything to stock myself up; instead I thought only of December and what she would find helpful. When I passed the women's sleepwear department, I chose a set of blue silk pajamas for December, size large, so that she'd have plenty of room to recover in them.

She looked about the same when I got to the hospital except that the medication made it hard for her to focus her eyes, so she looked drugged. She said she'd slept, but then fell asleep as soon as I stopped talking. Lance came at almost noon, horrified he'd slept so late. I grabbed lunch in the cafeteria, called Paul and Stormy with an update, and walked around the hospital, feeling stir-crazy and wishing I had taken up knitting so I would have something to do. I'd never tended a bedside. It was very boring now that I was no longer terrified.

I returned to the room in time to hear the tail end of the nurse's conversation with Lance. "I've notified the doctor, and he'll come in and talk to you both, but I just wanted you to be aware."

I picked up my pace and stepped into December's view. Her eyes were wide and glassy. The nurse left as I hurried to December's bedside. "What happened?"

Lance repeated what the nurse had said: December's blood pressure wasn't responding as well as it had been yesterday and had been slowly increasing all day. They'd given her something different, but unless she showed marked improvement in the next hour, they were going to have to induce labor.

Lance and I both assured December she would be fine. I pointed out a few situations I knew of where babies had come early and everything had turned out great. December, who had kept things together so well, broke into tears.

The doctor came, reviewed the chart, and explained everything very calmly. A nurse changed the IV bag to something new. An hour passed, and they took December's vital signs. The new medication wasn't working. The baby was showing signs of distress. I was going to become a grandma . . . today.

Chapter 27

"YOU DID GREAT," I SAID, brushing December's hair from her face.

She'd insisted on attempting natural labor, but at six AM Sunday morning, when she hadn't progressed as they'd hoped, they ordered a C-section. The epidural made her even sicker, and she cried through the whole procedure even though she couldn't feel anything. As soon as the doctors delivered the baby, he was taken to the Newborn Intensive Care Unit. He was six weeks early, and his cry sounded like a mewing kitten. Lance kissed December's forehead before following the NICU team down the hall at her insistence.

Her body was shaking; one of the nurses had assured me it was a reaction to the epidural, but it was frightening to watch.

"You did great," I said again, trying not to cry anymore, wanting to be strong for her. I'd never seen December so undone. She'd always been very even-keeled, solid. It made me reflect on the fact that childbirth and motherhood pushed all of us to our limits sometimes. She'd gotten off to an intense start, but she was a mother now. My little girl was a mom.

She opened her eyes that were still dilated from the medication. "He's okay?" she asked in a shaky voice.

"He's strong and healthy," I said, repeating what the nurse had said before they hurried him to the unit, just in case. "And he's beautiful."

But judging from the expression on the nurse's face at the computer on the other side of December's bed, though, everything wasn't fine just yet.

"You need to get some rest," I told her. "We've got everything covered."

"I want to see him," December said.

"You'll see him later," the nurse answered, though the question hadn't necessarily been directed toward her. "Your mom's right. You need to rest. I promise your little man isn't going anywhere."

I nodded my agreement, still smoothing December's hair, touching her arm, doing everything I could to assure her that everything was okay.

"I'm cold," December said.

"I'll get you another heated blanket," the nurse said. "But it's the medication that's making you cold, and it'll wear off."

The nurse left, and I stayed, hating that I couldn't do more. I started humming, needing something to calm my nerves if not December's. After a few bars, I realized I was humming "Ave Maria." I almost stopped. How long had it been since I'd sung a hymn? But December's eyes were closed, and the music seemed to be comforting her. I kept humming as I moved around to the head of the gurney to continue stroking her hair.

The nurse came back and put the warm blanket over December, who pulled it all the way up to her chin. She was still trembling, but it seemed to be lessening. After a few minutes, the nurse wheeled December's gurney down the hall to a private room. It was another fifteen minutes before she was settled, and she fell asleep almost immediately. When the nurse came in to update her chart, I followed her out of the room. She was about my age, but taller.

"So, what happens now?" I asked.

The nurse turned to me in the hall. She explained that they were watching December carefully but didn't expect anything else to happen. Her blood pressure was already coming down, though it might be a few weeks before it was back to normal. They were keeping an eye on her kidneys as well. She was young and strong, and therefore was probably going to be just fine.

"Thank you," I said, realizing as I faced this woman that I had an opportunity to get some answers of my own. "Um, could I ask you something else?"

"Sure."

"Um, have you ever heard of tubal ligations not working?"

"Oh, sure," the nurse said, as though it happened all the time. "Especially the ones they were doing ten or twenty years ago. They'd often knot the tubes, or clamp them instead of cutting and cauterizing. With the older procedures, the younger the patient, the more likely that the tubes could grow back together, or grow around the clamps—that kind of thing." She paused. "Your daughter's awful young to make that kind of decision, though, and preeclampsia isn't something she needs to fear should she decide to have another baby. It's most common in first pregnancies."

I shook my head. "This isn't about my daughter; it's . . . something else." I shifted my weight to my other foot. "If that happens—the tubes growing back—and a woman gets pregnant, is there an added risk to the baby?"

"Not really," the nurse said. "Unless, of course, it's an ectopic pregnancy. That can be pretty common in those kinds of situations, but assuming the baby implants correctly, it's just like a normal pregnancy."

I was glad to hear that; I knew I was past the ectopic pregnancy stage. My reaction surprised me, though. Was I *glad*? "Good, I was just, you know, curious." Though why anyone would just be curious about something like that was beyond me.

"It would be important, though, for the woman to get good pre-natal care, especially if she were older and not expecting to get preg-nant—which is usually the case in pregnancies following failed tubals. Older moms have increased risks to both her health and that of the baby."

I didn't like the way she was looking at me and I smiled really wide and nodded quickly. "Thanks," I said, and turned away.

Older moms. Grandma-moms. I was going to be one of them.

Chapter 28

DECEMBER WANTED TO NURSE, but her colostrum hadn't even come in yet, and Tennyson—Lance gave up arguing about names when he saw December in labor—was so small that he struggled to even take a bottle. The doctors had to put him on a feeding tube. December cried about that, too. She'd worked so hard to come up with a birth plan that reflected all her goals and expectations, but it had unraveled completely. She couldn't see her baby until she was well enough, and she was still sick from the medication they'd pumped through her veins. Lance and I took turns rubbing her feet and bringing her glasses of water.

It was almost seven o'clock Sunday night when I presented myself at the NICU and washed up as though I were going to perform a surgery or something. I put on the gown then followed the nurse to the tiny Plexiglas box where my grandson lay, hooked up to tubes and wires. I was shocked to see him like that, and I stared for several seconds until a nurse approached me.

"Would you like to hold him?" she asked.

I looked up at her. "Can I?"

She indicated for me to pull up one of the many rocking chairs placed around the room. It took a few minutes for her to adjust Tennyson's wires and tubes correctly, but then she handed me his tiny little body and helped me settle him on my chest. She put a blanket over both of us, and I adjusted our position until I could look into the swollen, scrunched up face.

"I'll be back in a few minutes," the nurse said before pulling a curtain around us to give us some privacy.

I could feel the faintest heartbeat against my chest, and emotion filled me up from top to bottom. Tears rose in my eyes. "Hello there, Tennyson. I'm your grandma. Can you believe that?"

He puckered his lips, and I laughed, deciding to take that as an answer that it was hard for him to believe it too. "You sure know how to make an entrance," I whispered, overcome by the spirit of this infant child. I went on to tell him about his mom and dad, as though I were his tour guide for this new adventure he'd undertaken. I talked about Stormy, about California, and all the fun things we would do when he came to visit. I told him about Paul and then . . . then I told him about my baby—his aunt or uncle—and struggled to wipe my eyes with my shoulder as I imagined holding my own child this same way in not too many months.

I could barely breathe with the understanding that filled me in that instant. I'd been taking a journey to accept this, tiptoeing closer, but suddenly, it was so *real*. I wasn't simply carrying a baby—I was carrying *my* baby. And I would hold it soon, and love it, and nurse it, and raise it up into a whole person, like December and Stormy.

How terrifying. How exquisite.

In that instant, I felt like I was in the eye of a storm. I knew my journey wasn't over, but for the first time, I felt a glimmer of excitement and positive anticipation. The fact that I was having a baby was as unbelievable as ever, but a different kind of unbelievable. This disbelieving moment was sweet and tender and somehow invigorating.

"We'd better put him back."

I blinked up at the nurse, who was standing a few feet away. I hadn't heard her approach but nodded my agreement. Again, returning Tennyson to his crib was a process that took a few minutes, but eventually I was looking through that Plexiglas box again, watching the little person who would now be a part of the rest of my life.

As I stared, the eye of the storm passed by, and my fears returned. I didn't want this. I wasn't ready. I couldn't do it. But the moment of understanding I'd had helped ease some of my fears. Just knowing I *had* felt that assurance was something. Surely I would get there again, to stay. I could only hope.

Chapter 29

SUNDAY BECAME MONDAY, and after heading to the hospital in the morning, I spent three full hours in the cafeteria on the phone with my office, helping them find their way through the work I'd left on my desk. Year-end was not a good time to be a no-show, and I was reminded, twice, of the mandatory training meeting Thursday afternoon about upcoming procedure changes, effective January first. I could not miss it.

By two o'clock I was finally able to put aside the urgent work and tune back in to December. She was looking better, feeling better, and though she'd been able to go see Tennyson with Lance that morning, she was ready for another trip. I couldn't believe she could walk already, but I stayed at her side and steadied her as we made the slow trek to the NICU.

"The nursery isn't ready," December said. "At the house. It's not done."

"I'll work on it when I go back tonight," I assured her. "It'll be ready by the time you come home, I promise."

"When do you have to go back home?"

My stomach sank. I wanted to stay so much, but I knew I couldn't. "I need to be back by Thursday."

December didn't say anything, but a few moments later she

sniffled, and I saw her wipe at her eyes with the sleeve of the new pajamas I'd bought her.

"Oh, sweetie," I said, feeling tears come to my eyes too. "I'm so
sorry. I wish I could stay longer." I had tried to come up with any way I
could make it work, but there were no options. There were things that
needed to be done that only I could do. "I can probably come back out
for Christmas." I cringed at the expense, but was willing to swallow
it. If I worked late and got ahead of my policies, instead of behind, I
could probably take a few extra days for the holiday.

"I need to sit down," December said as we passed a bench in the
hallway. I helped her gingerly sit, and once I let go of her arm, she
wiped at her eyes more completely. Her chin still trembled and for a
moment she looked so much like the little girl she had once been.

"I can't do this," she said under her breath, bringing her hands to
her face. "How can I do this? I'm not ready."

"You're doing wonderfully," I told her, rubbing her back and stroking her hair. "You're already up and walking, and you're not as swollen
as you were yesterday."

She shook her head, and her shoulder-length brown hair fell forward. "He's not coming home with me," she squeaked. "They're keeping him here. Lance has to work—he has to—and I can't drive myself
to the hospital until I'm off my medication." She began to sob, then
put a hand to her belly as though it hurt her.

I pulled her into my arms and held on as tight as I dared while
trying to think of her options. I automatically thought back to the
resources I'd grown up expecting to be there and make up the
difference—church and family. But December didn't have either of
those things. I hadn't raised her with a church, and she had no family
here in Ohio.

"Do you have friends who could take turns bringing you to the hospital?" I asked.

She shrugged and was trying to stop crying as though embarrassed by the breakdown, but I felt horrible. I was supposed to be the person helping her right now, and I could stay only two more days. I had the crazy idea I should just quit my job and fix this. But there was Paul and Stormy to consider, bills to pay, and health insurance to keep. After another minute, December apologized, and I helped her walk the rest of the way to the NICU. The nurse led us to Tennyson's isolette and asked if December wanted to hold him.

She unbuttoned the top buttons of her pajamas so he'd have more contact with her skin. The nurse said she'd come back in a minute to see if she could help December nurse. December seemed to lose all her tension and worry once Tennyson snuggled into her chest. She wrapped the sides of her pajama top around him, and then the nurse settled another blanket over the top of them, wrapping them together like a cocoon. December rocked slowly back and forth, closing her eyes as though soaking him up like the rays of the sun. After a few minutes, she opened her eyes and looked at me. "Could Grandma come?"

"Grandma?" I repeated. Was she talking about me or . . . my mother? Here I'd been trying to find solutions and the obvious one hadn't even been a consideration. I was equally quick to discount it. "She's a long way away," I said, but then felt bad. It *was* an option, and while my mother and I weren't all that close, December had had a bond with her from the first few years of December's life.

"I know, but when I talked to her last week, she said to let her know if I needed anything." December's eyes became a bit more pleading. "I could really use her help after you leave."

"I'll call her," I said, realizing that I hadn't even called to tell her about her great-grandson being born.

"Thanks, Mom," December said, closing her eyes and looking more relaxed. Which is why I would call my mother and ask her to fill the role I couldn't fill in my daughter's life. Again.

Chapter 30

LANCE CAME TO THE HOSPITAL after he finished work. The poor boy looked exhausted, but I sensed they wanted to be alone so I kissed December and drove back to the house where I set to work cleaning the house, doing the laundry, and organizing the baby things December hadn't expected to need for several weeks. Even the newborn clothes looked huge. Maybe I could find some more preemie outfits tomorrow. I couldn't move the desk out of the nursery by myself, so I did everything else I could think of besides that.

My cell phone rang around eight o'clock. I took a deep breath when I saw it was my mother calling me back. When I'd talked to her earlier, she'd been abrupt with me, saying she'd see what she could do. I'd hung up the phone more tense than ever, realizing that one of my biggest stumbling blocks about being a mother was the relationship I had with my own. It had never been a good one, and even after raising two children, I feared my children would feel toward me the way I felt toward her. Except they didn't. Not really.

"Hi," I said when I answered the phone.

"Daisy, hi," she said in her abrupt way. My mother *was* a nurturer, but if you didn't know that, you wouldn't guess it right off. She'd always been blunt and sharp at the same time, and I had to consciously keep myself from taking offense. "I've worked it out with your father and your sisters for me to come out tomorrow."

"So soon?" I'd planned to fly home on Wednesday and hoped that maybe she and I would miss each other.

"Yes, yes, it all came together. I'll be able to stay a week."

"Wow, a whole week." I knew I shouldn't be jealous that she could stay longer than I could, but I was. "December will be so grateful."

"The poor thing," Mom said, though she still had that clipped tone that seemed at odds with her words. "Hard to start out motherhood this way."

I clenched my jaw. How about it being hard to start out motherhood as a seventeen-year-old single mom? I'd never had sympathy from my mother for *my* start. But I was instantly embarrassed by my thoughts. What was wrong with me?

"She's struggling," I finally said. "It's good of you to come."

"Of course," Mom said. "I wouldn't let anything stand in my way."

Like I was, I thought, thinking of how I had to go back to work. "Do you know when you'll be here?"

"I hope to get an early start, which should put me there in the afternoon."

"You're driving?"

"Certainly. I can't afford to jump on a plane; plus, I'll need transportation while I'm there. When does December come home from the hospital?"

"Wednesday morning," I said. "My flight leaves that afternoon."

"Well, I guess I'll see all of you tomorrow, then."

"Yeah, drive safe."

"I will."

I hung up and wanted to scream. I didn't want her to come to

December's rescue. She hadn't wanted me to even *keep* December. Did she ever think about that? Had she ever admitted she'd been wrong about me and my potential?

While straightening up the living room, I found a book about pregnancy and childbirth and sat down on the couch to read it, taking note of how little I had done to prepare. What if I wasn't healthy enough for this? I had been sick and not eating well. What if that hurt the baby? I read until I was sufficiently overwhelmed, then put the book back where I'd found it. I still couldn't believe this was happening.

Chapter 31

MOM ARRIVED AROUND SIX o'clock Tuesday night. She came right to the hospital and organized December's side table, forced Lance to have a meal that included vegetables, and asked a hundred questions of the NICU nurse that hadn't even crossed my mind.

Basically, she made me look and feel like an idiot as she effortlessly took over. I retreated to the sidelines and let her run the show. She was efficient and smooth, and, based on December's reaction, calming. December had been emotional all day, hating that tomorrow she would go home empty-handed. Now that Mom was here, though, she was taking it in stride. My insignificance seemed to know no bounds. We finally left the hospital around eight thirty, and I was glad to be alone in my rental car. It gave me time to prepare for being alone with Mom at the house.

"Well," Mom said when we shut the front door of December's house behind us. "Are you hungry?"

"Not really," I said. "I had a sandwich at the hospital while you went to the NICU."

"I was thinking of making some popcorn," Mom said, heading into the kitchen. "Do you think December has some popcorn—preferably not microwavable? It's good to end the day with fiber."

"I have no idea if she has fiber or not," I said, sitting down heavily and letting the couch cushions envelop me. I might never stand up again.

"You mean popcorn."

"What?"

"You said you didn't know if she had fiber or not. You meant popcorn, I think."

I waved a hand through the air. "Popcorn. That's what I meant."

"I know. That's what I said you meant."

I stopped talking and just breathed deeply, leaning my head against the couch and trying not to think about my mom watching me, judging me, and juggling a hundred questions in her mind that she didn't dare ask. I'd hoped Lance would have come home with us to diffuse the tension, but the doctors had Tennyson on a two-hour feeding schedule, and Lance wanted to be at the ten o'clock feeding with December.

I closed my eyes and must have drifted off to sleep, because the next thing I knew, a hand on my knee startled me awake. I blinked to see my mother's face above me. She handed me a large pink mixing bowl.

"She had popcorn," Mom said, taking a handful from the bowl. "And a Whirly Popper." She smiled, causing a firework of wrinkles to appear beside both eyes. She'd stopped coloring her hair since I'd seen her last, and her gray curls were soft around her face. "I put extra butter on, just how you like it."

She must have caught me off guard because I laughed, taking us both by surprise. "You're the one who likes extra butter," I said. "You only blame it on me."

She smiled even wider and shrugged. "You like extra butter too, so we can share the blame." She sat down next to me on the couch, and we munched in silence for a few minutes.

"How's Stormy?" Mom asked. I felt myself bracing.

"Good." I hadn't told her that Stormy was living with Jared, and I hoped I wouldn't have to. "She's in the school play, *Phantom of the Opera*. It'll run through the end of January."

"Wonderful," Mom said. "She's a talented girl."

"She is."

"And how's Paul?"

Guilt descended. I took another handful of popcorn. "Good," I said. "Working hard."

"Good," Mom said.

We'd run out of things to talk about already. It was my turn to command the small talk. "How's Dad?"

"Hanging in there," Mom said. "His doctor thinks he needs a new hip. Maybe this summer—I don't know."

We worked through updates on my siblings, Mom's sisters, and Dad's mom, Grams, who was still alive and kicking at the age of ninety-one. Well, maybe not kicking.

"We should get a five-generation photo," Mom said. "Hopefully Grams will hang on that long."

"That would be fun," I said. "Maybe we can all come to Virginia this summer, before Dad's surgery." As soon as I said it, though, I realized I might have a baby of my own by then. I felt the blood drain from my face.

"Wouldn't that be nice?" Mom said, nodding.

Another silence descended. I couldn't think of anything to say.

"And how are you, Daisy-Day? Is everything all right with you?"

For some reason, her question initiated a wave of emotion I was desperate not to show. Nothing was all right with me, but my mother was not someone I would share that with. She never had been.

For as long as I could remember I hadn't trusted her with my emotions. I shrugged and stared into the popcorn bowl. "Fine," I said. "Everything's fine."

"I've been worried about you."

I hated being worried about. It implied that I might need help from someone, that I might be incapable of handling whatever I needed to handle on my own. "I'm fine."

Mom seemed to accept that. "He's sure a beautiful baby, isn't he?"

"Yes, he is," I said.

"Though the name is quite strange."

"Alfred Lord Tennyson is December's favorite British poet," I said, feeling a little defensive and yet pleased to know this detail about my daughter. "It holds special significance for her."

"Well, regardless, it's wonderful to see her taking this step in her life, isn't it? Babies are magical."

"Magical?" I repeated, unable to block how unmagical it had been when I had brought my baby home. "Hmmm."

Mom interpreted my response as a desire for explanation. "Well, they're just amazing little souls fresh from God. They bring healing and happiness, joy and celebration with them. It's remarkable, the spell they can cast on people. You can see it in December's eyes when she looks at him; she's instantly in love. It's a beautiful thing seeing a mother and child together like that, especially this close to Christmas."

I blinked at my mother and felt my anger boiling. I had a distinct memory of coming home from the hospital to a house decorated for Christmas. "You never said anything like that to me when I had a baby around Christmastime."

"Well, your situation was never quite like December's, was it? You never had this kind of stability."

"So maybe only some babies are magical, then? If you're not ready to be a mom, then the child is less valuable?"

I could feel her looking at me with her stoic stare; I looked straight ahead as she answered.

"That's not what I said. This isn't about you."

I laughed without humor. "Of course it isn't," I said, standing and wishing I had taped my mouth shut.

"Why are you so angry all of a sudden?" she asked as I passed in front of her as though I had somewhere I could go to get away from her.

"Never mind," I said, rubbing at my eyes and reconsidering the sleeping arrangements. Maybe I should go to a hotel. Obviously I couldn't control myself very well right now. "I'm tired."

"So am I," Mom said. She rose and headed into the kitchen to rinse the cereal bowls Lance and I had left in the sink that morning.

I took off my shoes and eyed the couch that would be my bed. Mom had already set up the inflatable bed she'd brought with her in the nursery. She never missed a detail. The hotel was sounding better and better.

From the kitchen, Mom said, "I'd caution you to be careful comparing your situation to December's. It's not the same."

"Oh, that's right," I said in an almost offhand manner. "I'm the sinner. I forgot."

Mom shook her head and turned to face me. "I did not come here to fight with you, Daisy."

"I know. You came to help December because she's done it the *right* way."

Mom turned back to the sink, but she was out of dishes, so she wiped down the counter as a way to keep from having to look at me.

"She *has* done it the right way. Don't let your jealousy get in the way of her success."

"It was thirty years ago." I wasn't sure who I was saying that for. Me or her? Shouldn't I be over this thirty years later?

"You're the one who brought it up, dear."

She turned to face me but didn't say anything else. I took that as a challenge. "I'm so tired of feeling judged."

Mom shook her head and actually rolled her eyes before turning back to the sink where she wrung out the washcloth and laid it perfectly flat over the divider in the sink. "You *want* to feel judged."

My eyebrows shot up. "I want to feel judged?"

"It makes you feel superior."

I sputtered and could feel the heat in my face. "That makes no sense at all, Mom," I said. "I have no need to feel superior, but I don't deserve the censure, either."

Mom's shoulders lifted as she took a deep breath. "When have I censured you?" she asked. "When have I put you down or called you out on anything? You act as though I'm continually harping on you or being critical of your choices. When have I done it? Give me an example."

My mind was reeling. "Only one?" I spat out, but I was stalling. Suddenly I couldn't latch on to anything, so I went with the easiest one. "When I got pregnant with December, you wanted me to give her up for adoption. You had a prayer meeting for me, for heaven's sake."

"If Stormy were pregnant, wouldn't you ask her to at least consider adoption?"

The calmness of her question only antagonized me more. "I wouldn't tell her to do it."

"Did I tell you to do it?"

"Yes!"

"When?"

I hunted my gray matter. I dug and searched for it, but now that I'd been called on the carpet, I didn't know how to answer. *Had* she told me to give December up for adoption, or had it been only a suggestion, something to consider? I remembered going to Catholic Charities, where the nuns had talked to me about the blessing of a child being raised by parents who had covenanted with God and each other, but I didn't remember why I'd gone there.

I was starting to feel confused by the fact that I knew—I *knew*—my mother was overbearing and blunt to the point of being rude, but she didn't lie. She didn't. But if she hadn't made me feel forced somehow, why was I so angry?

Mom sighed and folded her arms. "Let me tell you a little bit about seventeen-year-old Daisy," she said, her face absolutely serious. "She was beautiful and smart and talented—everyone loved her. She might not have been the most popular girl in the school, but I would be surprised if there was anyone who didn't like her. She wanted to become a nurse. Do you remember that?"

I did, but it seemed so long ago that it didn't feel real anymore.

"So, there she was, this smart, unpretentious, good-hearted girl. She started dating a boy her father and I didn't approve of. We wanted you to be with people who would support the values we felt were so important. He wouldn't do that. We knew it, yet you lit up when he entered the room. You had always been independent, but suddenly you weren't coming home on time, you were lying about where you'd been, you didn't want to go to Mass or youth group."

"More judgments," I cut in. "The fact that I didn't believe what you believe put me on the outside as soon as I dared say it. It was unfair to judge me for having different beliefs than you did."

"And you're not judging me for believing different than you?" she asked, cocking her head to the side. "Church can help us find God, and then it helps us stay close to Him. It's a vehicle, Daisy, not a destination in and of itself. But you were suddenly not interested. In our experience, not wanting to worship means there is unrequited sin in need of confession, but you wouldn't go. We were really starting to worry about where this boy might take you, when you came home one day to say you were pregnant. You weren't tearful. You weren't repentant. You saw it as a shortcut to a grown-up life."

I felt a shudder rip through me as for a moment I was that seventeen-year-old girl again, telling my parents about the wonderful thing that had happened. It hadn't been what I believed, exactly—I was terrified—but I had presented it to them completely different because I thought it would make me seem more mature, more capable. Strong.

Mom continued, but her words hit me differently now. "Your father and I spent hours on our knees seeking the Lord's help with this. We did not see December as the end of you or your life, but we saw that your journey would be very different and that you had no idea what you were up against. You moved in with Scott. You promised us you would get married, and then, when you didn't and instead moved back home, you didn't even thank us for the help. You never did, really. I cared for December while you finished school. I took her to get her immunizations, I took her to the park to play, and I even stayed up with her when she was sick so that you could get your rest."

I hadn't thought about those things, but she was right. I felt sick.

"As soon as you had a good job, you were ready to leave, and you acted as if we'd somehow been holding you back, making things so hard for you. You were determined to prove that you could do this on your own. Even as we admired your spunk, we worried about you very much. You were a nineteen-year-old girl with a GED under your belt, barely a year of college, and a toddler in the backseat. I still watched December after you moved out, and though you were gracious enough, you still treated it like it was my job.

"Then you moved to California and disappeared completely from our lives. I was heartbroken. I realized that at least part of my being there to help you and December was due to the hope that it would get us to a point where you and I could be closer. If I helped you, surely you would soften toward us." She shrugged. "But then you didn't call. You didn't visit. You just went on with your life, and through it all, you've treated the past as though *we* somehow damaged you, hurt you, treated you badly. When the fact is, Daisy-Day, we didn't."

Her voice had softened in direct proportion to my tension increasing.

"We loved you, and we worked hard to support you in a bad situation, but what you wanted was a celebration. You wanted to somehow be applauded for being a pregnant teenager. You wanted baby showers and accolades, and there was no way we could give you approval for something we didn't see as a good thing for you. We love December, and we can't imagine a life without her in it, but that doesn't mean we weren't justified in our disappointment. You were not ready to be a mother, and we were worried about your future. That you've done well is wonderful, and we are proud of you, but please don't judge us so harshly. If you are truly honest with yourself and look at the situation from the perspective of a grown woman rather than a teenage girl, I think you'll see a very different picture than the one you've chosen to paint in your head."

She pushed away from the sink and passed by me, heading into the nursery. The door clicked shut behind her, and I stared into the place where she'd been standing. I didn't know what to think about what she'd said. I wanted so badly to believe it wasn't true. And yet, my mother didn't lie, and there was something about the version of events she'd relayed to me that felt . . . real.

I got ready for bed in a daze and said hello to Lance when he came home around eleven. Mom didn't come out of her room. Lance went to bed, and I settled onto the couch, staring at the streetlight shining through the miniblinds and thinking over what my mom had said.

I remembered thanking her when I would pick up December from her house after I'd moved out, but did I ever thank them for letting us stay? Did I ever try to make up for the extra burden I'd brought into their home and lives? The more I thought about that time of my life, the more embarrassed I became. I'd treated their help as my right. I'd expected my mother to take care of December just as she took care of my younger siblings. I expected it, took it for granted.

I'd been lying on the couch for half an hour when I heard a door open. I closed my eyes, pretending to be asleep, until I heard the bathroom door close. Then I peeked over the back of the couch. The nursery room door was open; Mom was the one in the bathroom. I feared I'd never get any sleep if I didn't at least try to chip away at the ball of guilt and shame growing in my stomach. I stood outside the bathroom, waiting for her. The toilet flushed. The sink turned on, then off again. She opened the door, saw me, and then shut off the bathroom light, but not before I saw her red, swollen eyes. She'd been crying. Over me.

"Thank you," I said. It came out in a gruff whisper. I cleared my throat and tried again. "Thank you for taking care of me and December back then, for letting me come back home and for . . . coming out here now. I . . ." I had to take a breath to keep from crying. "I'm sorry I never properly thanked you before now. I hadn't realized that I'd been so . . . entitled and unfair."

"Well, thank you for that," Mom said, but she wasn't giving in completely. The walls were back up. "You're welcome."

"And I'm sorry," I said. "For judging you guys so harshly. You deserved better than that."

She was quiet, and then her soft hand touched my arm. For my mother, any kind of physical touch was a powerful statement. "I love you, Daisy-Day, and I've never wanted anything other than your happiness. I'm very sorry you felt that I was in the way of that."

I shook my head, words failing me. We both stood there in the dark hallway, facing one another and yet not looking each other in the eyes.

"I love you too, Mom," I said, and wondered if I had ever said that to her before. We weren't an affectionate family, and we didn't say things like that often.

She gave my arm a squeeze before dropping her hand. "We'd best get some sleep," she said. "I'm determined to get that desk into the hall before December gets home tomorrow."

We said good night before retiring to our beds. I lay facing the window for what felt like a long time. *I love you, Daisy-Day,* kept repeating itself over and over in my mind, and for the first time in a long time, I allowed myself to believe that was true. I was forty-six years old and felt like I still had so much growing up to do.

Chapter 32

PAUL PICKED ME UP AT THE AIRPORT, and the anxiety I'd been feeling all the way from Ohio dissipated long enough for me to fully enjoy the reunion hug and take solace and comfort in the look in his eyes as he smiled at me.

"I missed you," he said, leaning in to kiss me on the mouth. I could feel how much he'd missed me with the intensity of his kiss and responded in kind. I so wanted to believe everything was going to be okay between us.

I could have stood there forever, just looking into the face of the man I loved. "I missed you too," I said. What if I told him right now about the baby we'd created?

A car behind him at the curb honked. Paul had parked too close, and the guy couldn't get out.

Paul gave my hand a squeeze and then opened my door before hurrying to put my bags in the trunk. We pulled into traffic outside LAX and made our way home. I had considered going into work for a few hours since I'd missed four whole days, but I was exhausted and intent on what lay ahead of me.

At home, Paul took my bags in, and I called Stormy—who had just gotten out of school—and updated her on her new nephew. I'd talked to her every day I'd been gone and appreciated how the situation had brought us together. She mentioned she was babysitting for Paige on Saturday night. I experienced a little shudder of memory at the mention of Paige's name. I didn't know what to do about that situation but took it as a good sign that she'd still called Stormy to watch her kids. I asked Stormy if she could stop by the house after she finished up.

"Maybe you could stay over that night," I offered.

"It'll be late, like eleven," Stormy said. I took that as proof that Paige was going on a hot date, and it made me sad to think that our budding friendship had come to such a place that she likely would never tell me that type of thing again.

"It's okay if you come in late. I'll wait up for you. I need to talk to you about something." My stomach tightened at saying that out loud. I had crossed the threshold between hoarding my secret and letting it spill out.

"What?" Stormy asked.

"I'd rather discuss it in person. So, can you come over on Friday after you're done at Paige's?"

"Yeah, I guess."

We finished the phone call, and I let out a breath, hoping that I could make it through the rest of the week. I put my phone on the counter and headed toward the bedroom, where my suitcase and husband had disappeared to. I thought back to the time I'd spent with my mom in Ohio. It had been different from any other interaction I could remember having with her, and I felt a soft spot inside me grow a little at the new perspective. The words she'd said when I vented about Church and God still rang in my head.

Church can help us find God, and then help us stay close to Him. It's a vehicle, Daisy, not a destination in and of itself.

I reflected on the things Athena had said about her mother and what she'd learned since the funeral. Maybe there was time for me to do better, to be a little more lovable.

The sound of running water broke into my thoughts. Paul came out of the master bathroom, a satisfied smile on his face. "I'm running you a bath," he said, crossing the room to me. "And while you unwind, I'll throw together some dinner. Sound good?"

I put my arms around his neck and nearly asked him to join me in the bath before I realized that would be pushing the inevitable conversation way up, and I wasn't ready for that. I needed this evening—this reminder of all the good things we had together—to help prepare the foundation I would need to build on later tonight.

"You are adorable," I said.

He smiled, kissed me again, and closed the bedroom door behind him as he headed for the kitchen.

The bath was wonderful. I gathered my hair on top of my head and clipped it in place before undressing. The smell of the lavender bubble bath Paul had thought to add wrapped around me as I slid into the water. It was hot. Too hot? Just in case, I adjusted the temperature of the water still streaming from the faucet—one of so many accommodations I was going to have to make in the coming months. I took a deep breath and looked down to see my belly poking up just above the water. I stared at the curve for a long time, trying to hold on to the realizations I'd had at the hospital, trying to remember the excitement I'd felt amid the fear.

When the water began to cool and my nerves began to tighten, I got out, dried off, and looked at myself full on in the mirror. I wasn't going to be able to hide this much longer; it was time to stop trying. I pulled my silk robe off the hook and put it on. It was impossible to tie the thin fabric in a way that disguised my belly, so I didn't even try, simply tying the sash above the mound which, again, made the truth inescapable. I fixed my hair so that it looked casually undone, but still flattering, and began adjusting my makeup before realizing I was stalling.

When I entered the kitchen, the smell of salmon was heavy in the air, and I remembered the last time Paul had cooked it—and I hadn't been able to eat it. Now I knew why. Soon he would too. I was glad the nausea had passed so I could enjoy the food this time.

He turned from the stove, and I caught the look that went from my face to my body, then back to my face. He wouldn't know what to think of it—he didn't have enough information to draw the right conclusion—but it had caught his attention.

I drew a shaky breath, but I couldn't say the words yet. I slid into a kitchen chair. A moment later, he set down a plate with a large piece of blackened salmon and some steamed squash.

I smiled up at him. "This is wonderful," I said as he sat down across from me.

"You haven't even tried it yet," he said, picking up his fork, but his manner was reserved. Were the pieces coming together for him?

I cut myself a bite and tried to calm my nerves. It tasted as good as I knew it would, and we ate in silence for a few minutes. I focused intently on the flavors and textures, truly putting myself into every detail of this moment as I prepared for the moments that would follow.

The fact that he didn't ask me about the trip, or start any kind of conversation made me even more anxious. Finally, I put down my fork. "There's something I need to talk to you about."

He raised his eyebrows and placed a bite of fish in his mouth.

"Um, it's . . . not a conversation we ever expected to have."

Flashes of memory spun through my mind. Me sitting on the

hood of Scott's truck, almost thirty years ago, crying about how my parents were going to kill me, begging him to marry me and make this all better.

Ten years later, knocking on the door of Jared's apartment while December waited in the car. As soon as he opened it, I blurted the whole thing out. I didn't cry that time, just stared at him with a "What are you going to do about it?" expression.

Calling Jared on the phone at work to tell him that, surprise, the very thing that had brought us together was happening again and we *had* to give our marriage another chance. Two weeks later I put a note on his car that said never mind, I wasn't pregnant anymore. Go ahead and move forward with your attorney.

"Sounds serious," Paul said, bringing me back to *this* moment I felt I had lived too many times already. But Paul wasn't Scott or Jared. He was Paul, and I loved him. We were good together.

"It's serious," I said. "But in a good way, I hope."

He put down his fork and braced his elbows on the table, resting his chin on his knuckles and looking at me with those intent blue eyes of his.

"Remember when we were first together and talking about our children?"

He nodded.

"And I asked you if you wanted any more, and you said not really?"

He nodded again, but his eyebrows pulled together. Apparently my belly hadn't given me away, and the idea that I could be pregnant was so far off his radar it wasn't even a possible direction of this conversation. I took a breath and pushed forward, needing to get through this.

"And I said that was good, because I had taken steps to ensure I wouldn't have any more."

He nodded a third time, still trying to anticipate.

"Something went wrong."

Silence hung as heavy as the smell of salmon in the air.

"What do you mean, something went wrong?"

"I've always thought getting my tubes tied was a for-sure, no-way, never-gonna-happen procedure that guaranteed I would never get pregnant again."

He said nothing, did nothing. He just stared at me.

"Something went wrong," I said again. I took a deep breath and felt the emotion rise in my chest. The rest of the words tumbled out in an ungainly heap. "I'm pregnant, Paul. I didn't mean for it to happen, I didn't think it *could* happen, but it did, and I tried to ignore the signs for a long time, but I finally took a test—well, three tests—and they were all positive. I think I'm sixteen or seventeen weeks into this and . . . yeah."

He blinked at me, then sat up straight in his chair. "You're pregnant," he repeated. His tone was completely even and dangerously calm.

I nodded and picked up my napkin to wipe at my eyes. I willed him to take my hand, or come around the table and lay his head on my belly. I needed him to tell me that everything was okay, that *we* were okay, that we were in this together, and that, above all, he loved me. He just sat there. I looked into my lap and continued wiping at my eyes, waiting, silently pleading that he would save me from this awful feeling of the unknown. I heard the legs of his chair scrape against the tile, and I looked up to see him standing. He didn't meet my eye as he left the table. He didn't come to my side.

"Paul?"

He didn't answer me. Instead he disappeared into the master

bedroom. I was on my feet and heading in his direction when he came back out, keys in hand. The panic set in.

"You're leaving?"

He didn't say anything, just looked at my belly, then walked past me toward the garage.

I followed him, and the first sob broke. "You're leaving me!"

"I'm going out," he said.

"Now?" I cried, tears coursing down my cheeks. "We need to talk about this. We need to—"

He pulled open the door, stepped into the garage, gave me a cold look, and slammed it in my face.

Chapter 33

HE DIDN'T COME HOME.

I didn't sleep well. In the morning, I clicked back into that autopilot mode I'd become so good at. The house was eerily silent as I got dressed—it was getting harder to find clothes that fit—fixed my hair, tried to disguise the puffiness around my eyes, and made myself some scrambled eggs. December's pregnancy book had talked about how important protein was for the baby. I took some small comfort in doing this one thing right.

At work, I was grateful for the backlog of files that kept me sufficiently overwhelmed so I wouldn't think about the phone call I hadn't received from my husband. I had been sure he would want to talk once the idea settled. My phone was silent except for a text message from Amy, who had been looking at me strangely across the conference table at our morning meeting.

Are you okay?

My reply was brief.

It's been a long week.

I hadn't run out of work to do, but my back started to hurt around seven o'clock. I couldn't remember the last time I was the last person at the office. I shut down my computer, organized the piles of work I needed to take care of tomorrow, and headed home. The windows were dark when I pulled up. The house was empty.

I turned on the kitchen light, then sat on the living room couch. Should I call him? Should I keep waiting? I was tempted to be angry— I was sure the anger was in there somewhere—but then I thought about the process I had to go through to come to terms with this myself. He was doing the same thing, right? I was desperate not to judge him too harshly.

He didn't come home again.

The next morning, Friday, I was beginning to feel some anxiety about running out of work when Amy entered my office. She shut the door behind her and sat down in the chair on the other side of my desk. She'd lost even more weight and looked beautiful in a pair of black slacks and a cranberry-colored blouse. She leaned forward and looked me squarely in the face.

Panic swirled around me like a hurricane.

"What's wrong?" she asked, her wide eyes staring me down while the sincere concern in her voice demanded an honest answer.

I couldn't tell *her*. But I couldn't *not* tell her either. She'd find out eventually—everyone would. I sat there for several seconds, trying to find a way to be honest and still preserve her feelings.

"What's wrong?" she asked again.

I felt the tears rise and shook my head. "I don't want to tell you."

She said nothing, and when I looked up at her, she had leaned back in the chair, looking as though she were trying to interpret what I meant. "You don't want to tell *me?*"

I'd already run off my husband. I'd run off Paige, too; my tantrum still embarrassed me. I didn't want to lose Amy, but I was tired of playing games with people. I could not save her from this. I was powerless against the truth that would soon be very apparent. So I told her.

"I'm pregnant."

It landed like a brick on the desk between us. Amy's eyes went wide, a flash of envy sparked behind them, and then, in the next moment, her expression went blank. "You are?" There was no recrimination in her tone. Instead, she reached across the desk and took my hand. "Really? I thought you were . . . done."

"So did I," I said, waiting for her expression to harden as her true feelings came to the surface. But her face stayed soft, her expression confused, perhaps, but open.

She started asking questions, and I answered them, still waiting for her to cry or get angry or something. Instead, she was supportive and excited, even when she realized that this wasn't necessarily a good surprise for me. She asked how Paul felt about it, and I completely fell apart and told her I hadn't heard from my husband in thirty-six hours. When I recovered, she asked if I'd been to a doctor yet.

"No," I said, embarrassed. "I've only known for a few weeks, and then I was in Ohio with December, and then I told Paul and . . ."

"Do you have a good OB?"

"I've just gone to a clinic for my yearly stuff," I said. "I couldn't even tell you the name of the last doctor I saw."

"Hold on," she said. She left the office, and I focused on taking deep breaths and trying to digest the fact that the one person who seemed to have the most reason to *not* be happy for me, was. She came back a minute later and handed me a piece of paper. "Dr. Christiansen is the doctor Mick and I have been working with. He specializes in pregnancies that aren't necessarily standard—like in vitro, or high risk, or, I'm sure, failed sterilization. He's really wonderful."

I stared at the paper and then looked up at Amy. "Thank you," I said, and I meant every word. She came around the desk, and I stood up so we could hug. I held on tight, needing her strength, needing her support. She stepped back after several seconds and smiled.

"You're going to be okay," she said. "This is a good thing."

I couldn't help but feel a sting in my heart. Even though her tone and her expression were sincere, those words couldn't have been easy to say. But she'd said them anyway. That was remarkable.

After she left, I sat back down and stared at the name and phone number on the paper she'd given me. I was already into my second trimester, and he was a specialist, which meant that getting an appointment was probably impossible, but I sure didn't want to ask anyone else for a recommendation. I called the number, explaining to the receptionist that I was a new patient. When I told her my age and how far along I was, she put me on hold. Thirty seconds later, she was back on the phone. "How about Monday morning?"

"This coming Monday?" I said, looking at the calendar. "You can see me that soon?"

"We keep a few slots open for situations like this, and Amy Shawton called a few minutes ago to refer you—we always try to work with referrals from other patients. It's important that you're under a doctor's care as soon as possible."

"Okay," I said, seeing this as a good sign. "I'll take it."

I wrote the appointment into my planner and allowed myself to feel a little better. I was eating right, I had a friend to support me, and I had an appointment with the doctor. Those things didn't completely tip the scales against everything else, but they were a start.

I was on the couch at home around eight o'clock, flipping between channels and crying my eyes out when I heard the garage door open. *He's home,* I thought as my heart leapt in my chest. I jumped up from the couch—well, kinda jumped since my body didn't respond as quickly as my adrenaline did.

It had been two full days since I'd seen or heard from Paul, and although I'd gone to call him half a dozen times, I'd chickened out. I kept telling myself I was giving him the chance to process this, that's all. I wiped at my eyes and smoothed my shirt, but my hand stopped on my extended belly. I swore it had doubled in size in the last two days. I wished I could hide it for this meeting.

The sound of the garage door closing spurred me into the kitchen, so I was waiting for Paul when he came in. He opened the door and saw me standing there. We both just looked at each other. Then he looked away and came all the way inside.

"I picked up Chinese," he said as the door shut behind him. "Do you want some?"

Chinese? That was his lead-in? "Um, no thanks."

He nodded his acceptance and put the white plastic bag on the counter before opening the cabinet and pulling out a plate. "Do you mind if I watch the Clippers game?"

"No," I said, watching him dish up his spicy chicken and ham fried rice, wondering when he would recognize that the elephant in the room was still there.

He finished loading his plate, grabbed a beer out of the fridge, and went into the living room, where he sat down and turned the channel on the TV. I hovered in the doorway for almost two minutes, waiting for him to initiate the inevitable conversation. When he continued ignoring me, I felt I had no choice but to start things off myself.

"Are we going to talk about this?" I asked over the shot clock buzzer.

"Not yet," he said with finality, his eyes glued to the TV.

"When?"

"I don't know."

The anger I knew was within me flared briefly, but I didn't want it to best me. I'd already agreed to let him take the time he needed, just as I had done. I nodded my acceptance of his terms, but he didn't look at me, so he didn't see it. I stood there for another minute and then went into our bedroom.

Paul was home, but I was still very much alone.

I fell asleep before he came to bed.

The next day was Saturday, but I went into the office anyway, since I'd be missing part of Monday for my appointment. When I came home, there was a note from Paul saying he was at Charlie's putting the finishing touches on the deck. He was going to stay there overnight, and then they were going fishing in the morning. I told myself that I thought it was a good idea for him to spend time with his brother and take things slow, and then pushed it out of my mind while I made my-self a sandwich for dinner and then baked cookies.

Stormy had confirmed she was coming over after she babysat for Paige and would stay until Sunday. I needed some extra fuel to get me through yet another announcement—hence, the cookies. After telling Stormy, I would tell December, and my parents—ironically, they were the ones I was least worried about, and not just because of the tête-à-tête Mom and I had had in Ohio. I wasn't seventeen years old anymore. They'd be happy about this baby because they knew I could handle it. And I could, but I wasn't looking forward to explaining it to people and having to navigate their reactions.

It wasn't quite eleven o'clock when Stormy came in through the front door. She had her overnight bag over one shoulder, and I was glad we'd have enough time together for her to ask whatever questions she needed. I hoped we could use this as another way to pull us closer together. I gave her a hug and invited her to sit down at the table, where I had a plate full of freshly baked Rolo cookies waiting. After pouring her a glass of milk, I sat in the same seat Paul had been sitting in when I'd told him the news two nights ago.

"Sheesh, Mom, you're kinda freaking me out here."

She had no idea.

I had rehearsed all kinds of ways to tell her, but I was tired, so I just said it. Her eyes went wide, and while she digested the bombshell, I filled in the details. When I finished, she was breaking a cookie into little pieces on the plate.

"So," I said, feeling myself tense up when she didn't say anything or even look at me. "How do you feel about this?"

She shrugged and dug the caramel out of one of her cookie pieces with her fingernail. "Okay, I guess."

"It's certainly a surprise, isn't it?" I tried to keep my tone light.

"Yeah."

"It's kind of cool that you've been babysitting Paige's kids so much lately, huh? So you know a little more what it's like to have a little kid around."

She looked at me, her eyes narrowed slightly. "I'm not going to babysit for you all the time."

I felt my cheeks heat up. "I didn't mean that," I said. "I just meant that now that you'll have a little brother or sister, it's nice that you've had some experience with children."

"I guess." She went back to her cookie massacre.

"You don't seem very happy," I finally dared say out loud.

"Are you happy?" she asked, looking up again.

"I'm getting there," I admitted. "It's been a . . . journey. But holding Tennyson reminded me of you and your sister and how much I love you. It's hard not to feel excited about doing that again."

"You don't even want to take care of me," she said, an edge creeping into her tone.

"That's not true," I said quickly, feeling slapped even though I had prepared myself for her to say something like this, based on our recent history. I had convinced myself that if she brought up what I had said, I would take the opportunity to clear the air between us once and for all. Mom had said babies were magical; I was counting on it. "I would do anything to take back what I said that night, Stormy, and I'm horrified by the way I handled that whole situation. I do love you, so much, and—"

She pushed away from the table. "I'm going back to Dad's."

Tears, again, blurred my vision as she stood. "Please don't," I said. The catch in my voice caught her attention, and she looked at me, anger and sadness wrapped up in her features. "I'm sorry, Storm, for what I said, for the kind of mother I've been to you. I'm sorry for making you feel less important than you really are to me. It hasn't been fair to you, and I'm sorry for all of that." I was about to add a "but" and explain why none of that should have anything to do with this new baby, but that wasn't fair. It had everything to do with this baby.

She stared at me, her eyes starting to get shiny with tears of her own.

I held my breath, willing her to stay.

She turned around and headed for the front door. I felt like a balloon that had been popped when the door slammed behind her, and I deflated back into my chair where I covered my face with my hands and sobbed over the mess I had made of everything in my life. The hope I had so cautiously cultivated for this meeting broke into a thousand pieces. Every good thing I'd ever had I'd somehow squandered. And now, I was going to start all over again with a new baby who deserved so much better than this.

Chapter 34

"THANK YOU FOR COMING with me," I said to Amy after we'd been sitting in the waiting area of Dr. Christiansen's office for ten minutes. She'd called me on Sunday to see how I was doing. When she found out that Paul wasn't planning to go to the appointment, she asked if I wanted her to come.

"You're welcome," Amy said, looking up from her magazine. I was reading *Parenting* for the first time in a dozen years. She was flipping through *National Geographic*. I wished I dared ask her how she felt about this, if it was painful for her, but I wasn't ready to support her possible answers.

I felt so battered by Paul, who'd come home early Sunday morning but continued to be distant, and by Stormy, who hadn't called me all weekend, that I was too desperate for support to risk having to hear of how this must burden Amy.

I'd talked to December every day. Tennyson was off the oxygen and was taking a bottle; December had a breast pump she used religiously now that her milk had come in. Each time we called one another, I'd told myself to tell her about the pregnancy. Each time, I chickened out. Her trials of being a new mom traveling to the hospital three times a day were not over yet, and I couldn't bring myself to burden her even more. Although Stormy wasn't talking to me, I'd texted her to ask that she not tell December until I was able to. She'd texted back with a simple *okay*.

The nurse called me back, and Amy stood to the side while the nurse took my vital signs and drew some blood. I avoided looking at the scale once I stepped onto it. I was well aware of the fact that I weighed more now than I had when I'd been nine months pregnant with December; I didn't need to see it. The nurse showed me into a room, and I undressed from the waist down per her instructions, then sat on the examination table. Amy knocked a minute later, and I told her she could come in. It was a little weird to have her there; we hadn't been what I would call close friends before now, but I was still starved for the support and glad not to be alone.

The doctor came in a few minutes later—he was actually younger than I was, which was strange, but he seemed very nice and personable. He and Amy exchanged a few pleasantries before he turned to me and we got to work creating my chart—the paper synopsis of my whole reproductive life.

"How many pregnancies have you had prior to this one?"

"Three."

"How many live births?"

"Two."

"How many abortions?"

I startled. "None," I said strongly. Just remembering the dark moment when I'd briefly considered that option coated me with shame.

"Miscarriages?"

"One."

"How far along were you when it happened?"

"About thirteen weeks."

"Were there any complications?"

"Yes, I hemorrhaged and ended up getting a full D and C that required me to stay overnight at the hospital."

"How many living children?"

"Two," I said. Should I tell him I'd become a grandma last week?

"Marital status?"

"Married." Sorta.

"But this was an unplanned pregnancy, correct?"

His question surprised me. Had I told him that? But everything was such a blur I probably had. "Yes."

"Okay," he said, nodding as he scanned his notes. He looked up at me and smiled. "I understand you made the decision a long time ago not to have more children, so it would be understandable if this change of circumstances didn't fit into your future plans."

His comment took me off guard. "If you're talking about an abortion, there is—"

"No," he said strong and firm. "That's not what I'm talking about at all."

I blinked at him, confused for a moment. "Adoption?" I hadn't even thought about it. My family, everyone at church, and even my friends had pushed me that way with December. When I discovered I was pregnant with Stormy, I was a different woman in a completely different situation—few people brought up the fact that I had a baby six months after the wedding. I was now forty-six years old; I'd raised two children and knew what I was getting into. I wasn't a desperate teenage girl unable to meet the needs of a child.

Why would he bring up adoption to me?

Dr. Christiansen continued before I could put the thoughts running through my head into words. "I know your situation isn't exactly typical in regards to women who usually choose adoption for their baby, but it is something you should at least consider. I can assure you that there will be no judgment from me should that be the right choice for you. Many wonderful couples could provide this baby with a loving home and a bright future. An open adoption would even allow you to maintain limited contact."

The room was silent when he finished. I was stunned. Then I noticed the briefest look pass between Dr. Christiansen and Amy. He smiled at her, and I turned to see her smile back at him. She saw me looking and quickly glanced into her lap.

Amy had a loving home and could provide a bright future for a child. Was *that* why she was here?

"Just think about it," he said casually as he turned to the counter and pulled some gloves out of the box. "Just because you've conceived this child doesn't mean you're obligated to raise it, if that isn't what you want to do. Adoption is a heroic thing, not a selfish decision, and no one will judge you harshly for asserting the decision you made years ago when you chose not to have more children. Biology cheated you, so don't feel as though you don't have any other choices because of that."

He put on his gloves and instructed me to lie back on the table so he could continue the exam, but I didn't move.

"Just lie back," he repeated. "This will only take a few minutes."

"No," I said, shaking my head and wrapping my arms around my waist.

Amy spoke up. "Daisy, just—"

I silenced her with a look. I didn't have to say anything else. She looked away, then at Dr. Christiansen for help.

"I don't think this is going to work for me," I said as calmly as I could. "I'm sorry for taking your appointment. I'd like to leave."

I could see in his eyes that he knew what I was thinking.

"No one is going to push you in a direction you don't want to take," Dr. Christiansen said. "So let's not jump to conclusions about—"

"What conclusions?" I cut in, staring him down and trying to hold back the emotional avalanche taking place inside of me. We all went silent, no one willing to say out loud what we all knew. My head was tingling. Amy wanted my baby? Was this a bad movie? Was this really happening?

"I need to get dressed," I said.

He and Amy left, and I hurried to put my clothes back on. I felt violated but forced myself not to give in to the despair creeping over me. Maybe I was wrong. Maybe the pregnancy hormones were making me paranoid.

Amy was in the waiting room when I came out, and as soon as I saw her, I knew my suspicion wasn't paranoia. She looked guilty and couldn't meet my eyes. I didn't look at her as I headed to the door. We'd driven to the appointment together, and I wasn't going to leave her here, so I didn't stop her from coming with me, but I was furious and deeply, deeply hurt.

We got in my car, and I turned on the radio. Loud. Tom Petty and the Heartbreakers sang about an American girl, and I used every bit of willpower to hold back the tears.

You can cry later, I told myself. *When you're alone.*

Amy didn't say anything until we arrived at the elevators in our office building. The silent car ride had been excruciating, and the idea of being in that little box with her right then was repulsive.

"I'm taking the stairs," I said, turning toward the door next to the elevator. The door shut behind me, and my shield began to waver.

I took the stairs slowly, trying to put myself back together before I reached my office, wondering if I could afford to take yet another day off. With each stair, I felt like I was imploding as everything began to wriggle to the surface of my consciousness. Paul. Stormy. Amy, too. The door to the stairwell opened below me.

"You don't even want it." Amy's voice wasn't loud, but it echoed through the concrete stairwell.

I stopped where I was and closed my eyes for a moment before I turned and looked down the flight of stairs. She was crying, and she stared at me with such a pitiful expression that for the briefest moment I saw this from her perspective. I was old, tired, and struggling with my teenage daughter. When she looked at me, she saw a woman who did not deserve—or want—what she wanted the very most in the whole world.

"And it's not fair to the baby to be where it isn't wanted. I just thought . . ." She paused for a breath. "I just thought maybe this was God's way of answering both of our prayers."

Heat rushed through me. "You don't know anything about my prayers," I said, my voice shaky. "I'm sorry for your situation, Amy, and I don't deny how hard this is for you, but while this is something I didn't expect, and while it's made me reconsider everything I ever planned for, this baby belongs to *me*."

"But you don't want it," Amy repeated, tears rolling down her cheeks. "You're just going through with this because you have to."

"I don't *have* to," I said. "I *want* to." My words surprised me.

I wanted to? Really? When I couldn't even call it a baby three weeks ago?

"I would be a better mother," Amy said, her voice low. "I can give it a better life."

I felt tears come to my eyes, not only from the pain her words inflicted, but because I couldn't say she was wrong. "I'm sorry," I said, my voice quivering. "I don't understand why this has happened the way it has for either of us, but I love this baby, Amy, and I'm going to do the best job I can to give it the life it deserves."

Amy stared at me, then crumbled onto the bottom step and dropped her face into her hands as she began to cry even harder. Her sobs reverberated through me, and she looked up, her red face suddenly full of rage.

"Go away!" she screamed at the top of her lungs, her hands clenched into tight fists. I shook at the power behind her words. "Get out of here!"

She folded over herself and put her arms over her head as though trying to protect herself from an avalanche. She began rocking back and forth, wracked with the torment she must have been holding back since I first told her I was pregnant.

I turned and continued up the stairs, knowing there was nothing I could do to help her and trying to swallow the lump in my throat. Once on my floor, I kept my head down as I navigated the hallways toward my office. I locked the door behind me before closing the vertical blinds to shut me off from the rest of the office. I dropped my face in my hands.

What monster could be coming for me next?

My husband was avoiding me. My daughter was ignoring me. The only friend I felt I had in this world had betrayed me, and I was scared to death to tell anyone what was going on for fear that they, like everyone else, would be equally horrible. I felt fractured and wobbly on my foundation. Did I have a foundation anymore? I was completely and utterly alone.

I had no one, not one person, to buoy me up, to tell me it would be okay. The future I had so perfectly crafted for myself was dark and empty, and while I was trying hard to take comfort in the optimistic moments I had had over the last two weeks, and while I wanted to believe what I'd just said to Amy, they were only tiny pricks of light amid a heavy canvas of utter darkness. Could the glimmers of excitement and the moments of capability compare to losing everything else? I was not up to the task of meeting any of the responsibilities in my life, let alone taking on a new one. My throat tightened, and I curled around myself like the burning edges of paper. I'd just told Amy I loved this baby and that I could give it the life it deserved. I'd lied.

I can't do this, I screamed in my mind to anyone who might listen to me. *I am going to fail at this, too.*

And then the face of Paige Anderson came to mind. At any other time, I think my pride would have prevented me from reaching out to her. She had good reasons to never speak to me again. But I was drowning, and she was the only person I could think of who might give me the motivation to keep swimming toward a shore I could only hope was still there. I knew that she had confidence in that shore. That she had confidence in my ability to do this.

Or, at least, she did once.

Sniffling, I pulled my phone from my purse and toggled through my contact list until I found her number. I hit the call button and put the phone to my ear, barely holding it together.

She didn't answer.

I really was as alone as I thought I was. I lowered my head onto my arms crossed over my desk and gave in to the sorrow, the loneliness, and the despair that I felt foolish for trying to overcome in the first place. I couldn't even handle the pregnancy. How was I supposed to raise this child once it was here? Why had God done this to not just me, but to this child as well? What kind of sick joke was this?

I startled when my phone rang. I nearly ignored it, but lifted my head to check the caller ID. It was Paige. I scrambled for the phone and answered before I'd figured out what to say.

"Daisy," she said carefully, reminding me of all the ugliness between us—ugliness I was responsible for. I didn't know how to make it right. I didn't know how to explain. I didn't even know what I needed right now. I was still crying, and I took a shaky breath and tried to say something, but it came out in a stuttering sob. I was such a mess.

"Daisy?" Paige said again, this time not quite so careful. "What's wrong?"

Chapter 35

IT WASN'T PAIGE WHO CAME to my office forty-five minutes later; it was Livvy. Paige couldn't get off work, and when she'd called back to tell me that Livvy was on her way, I didn't even care that I didn't know Livvy very well and that she was going to see me at my absolute worst. I didn't care that Livvy in some ways embodied every fear I had about becoming lost in those riptides and undertows. I felt as though I'd existed in a state of animated suspension since crying to Paige on the phone and being assured that everything would be all right. I hung on to her promise as tightly as possible, and told myself that Livvy, therefore, must be part of that commitment.

By the time Livvy found her way to my office, she'd already told my boss I was leaving; I didn't know how she'd figured out who my boss was, and I didn't care. She packed my purse for me then led me to the parking garage, smiling and nodding at everyone we passed. I could see them all looking at me, evaluating me, trying to figure out what was going on. Amy was nowhere to be seen, and I was glad we didn't have to pass her office. Just getting out of there was a huge weight off my shoulders. I forced myself not to think about coming back tomorrow and trying to explain myself.

What was there to explain? I was pregnant, my husband had emotionally left me to fend for myself, and one child wasn't speaking to me while the other one simply didn't know what was going on with me yet. Was there a better reason to fall apart?

Livvy followed me home in her car, and by the time we got there, all I wanted to do was curl up in a ball and cry myself to sleep. Livvy wouldn't have it.

"You haven't eaten lunch, have you?" she asked.

I looked at the clock. It was 12:30. I shook my head and noticed how Livvy brightened, as though glad to have something to do.

"Why don't you lie down—I'll have something ready in a jiffy."

I didn't have to be told twice. My head was pounding, my eyes felt like sandpaper, and my feet were so heavy. I lay down in the bed Paul and I used to share and stared at the door as tears came, again, and I searched for understanding, *again,* and found nothing.

A few minutes later, Livvy stood in the doorway and invited me into the kitchen. I didn't want to go. I wasn't hungry, but she'd worked so hard at it, so I slid into a chair at the table, glad she'd made a sandwich for herself as well so I wouldn't be eating alone.

"Tuna with spinach leaves," Livvy said as I lifted the top piece of bread from one of the sandwiches to inspect its contents. "I have anemia issues, especially when I'm pregnant, and this is what my OB called a lunch of champions. I ate it every day. It's packed with protein and iron."

I smiled at her as my stomach growled. "Thanks." She must have found the spinach Paul used for his wilted spinach salad.

"So," Livvy said after we'd each made our way through the first half of the sandwich. I was sure it was delicious, but I wasn't really tasting anything. "Do you know what you're having?"

"No," I said. "I haven't been to a doctor." I paused. "Well, actually I went to a doctor this morning, but it didn't work out."

Her pale eyebrows pulled together. "What didn't work out?"

"The doctor," I said. "If it hadn't happened to me, I would be sure it was a poorly written soap opera episode."

"Really?" Livvy didn't ask me to tell her about it, but I did. She had her hand over her mouth by the time I finished, her forehead wrinkled with shock.

Once she knew I had finished, she lowered her eyebrows and blinked her wide eyes at me. "That's so awful," she said. "You poor thing."

I didn't like the pity, even if I deserved it, so I took another bite of my sandwich.

"I bet you could turn him in to the medical board for that," Livvy said. "That's a horrible thing for him to have done."

"I suppose I could," I said, though I hadn't even thought of it. "But I'm not sure I have the energy."

"And you still need to go to a doctor," Livvy summed up. "Paige said you were about fifteen weeks?"

"Closer to seventeen, I think, but I'm so big." I framed my growing belly with my hands. "Maybe I'm further along than that." I stared at my belly, the housing for this baby who had no idea the turmoil it brought with it. I looked up to see Livvy looking at me with an expression of longing on her face that made me feel horrible. Did she want more children too? And here I was the unappreciative brat.

"You make a cute pregnant woman," Livvy said, startling me.

How could I be cute? I was a forty-six-year-old grandma.

"I don't know about that," I said, embarrassed and yet loving that someone had said something positive. I pulled at my purple top, the color represented empowerment and strength—for all the good it had done me. "Paul's never liked me in purple," I said, imagining how a few weeks ago he would have teased me about it. Now, he likely wouldn't even see me wearing it. "He once called it a color for old ladies and little girls." I laughed. It had been a joke, but saying it now made him sound sort of horrible. "It's always been one of my favorite colors, though, so he's learned to deal with it."

It wasn't until I stopped talking that I realized I might not have to deal with his complaints much longer. I hoped I was wrong and that he'd tease me about wearing purple again. Silence stretched between us, and I endeavored to change the subject. "How many children do you have, Livvy?" I knew she'd mentioned it during our first book group where we all introduced ourselves, but I couldn't remember what she'd said. So much had happened since then.

"Four," she said. "Of my own, at least. Nick has two kids from his first marriage, but they're grown. His oldest has two kids of her own."

"Oh, wow, you're a grandma," I said. She was younger than I was by at least five years. "You're not old enough. Do you love it?"

"I think I *would* love it," she said as her smile faded. "I don't get to see them much. Nick has been a little . . . hard on his kids." She shifted in her seat, and I sensed she'd said more than she wanted to. I liked talking about her life, though. It kept me from thinking about my own.

"Oh," I said, wondering if Nick was hard on Livvy as well as on his kids. Maybe that was why she seemed so . . . mousy sometimes. I felt bad for the negative thought. The woman had dropped everything to rescue me and make me lunch.

"I'd have loved to have had more," Livvy offered up, tearing off the crust from the remaining half of her sandwich. "Wasn't in the cards for me, though."

More guilt. I looked down at my plate and took another bite.

"It's funny how that works, isn't it?" she said.

I looked up at her and hurried to swallow. "What?"

"Pregnancy and babies. I can't think of a single woman I know who has exactly what she wants in regards to that. It seems everyone wants more or fewer than what they have."

I hadn't ever thought of it that way, but it made me feel bad to be one of the women who wanted fewer than she had. Or *almost* had. "You enjoy being a mom, don't you, Livvy?"

She smiled at me. "I do. Well, most of the time. The whole teenager thing is taking its toll on me, but I really do enjoy being their mom, even when they hate me."

"I can't imagine your kids hating you," I said, thinking about Stormy and how difficult our relationship was right then. But I knew that was my fault. I didn't imagine Livvy ever said things like I had said about Stormy.

"Oh," she said with a laugh. "Trust me, they do. Just like I hated my mother, and my mother hated hers—at least for a while. Part of growing up, I suppose. Don't you have a teenage daughter?"

"Yes, and an older one," I said and gave her a brief recap of December and Stormy. She loved hearing about Tennyson, and then she told me about her kids, really lighting up when she spoke of them.

"So you're a grandma, too," she said. "We're definitely too young to be running around with people calling us Grandma. I could have sworn I had to be collecting Social Security before getting that title."

I laughed. She had such a way with words.

"You love your kids a whole lot," I said.

"I do," she said, nodding. "They're my world."

"I wish I were more like that," I heard myself say. "I'm not sure I ever really enjoyed my kids the way I could have."

"Then it must be exciting to have another chance," Livvy said with a smile. "I sometimes think about what a better mother I would be now, as opposed to when I was in my twenties with so much growing up left to do."

"That's a good point," I said, and it was. I hadn't thought about how much more efficient I was in running a home these days. I felt a flicker of hope that surprised me. What if I was a better mother to this baby than I had been to my girls? How good a mother could I have been to December at seventeen? After talking to Mom last week, I'd realized how much I'd relied on her to take care of my baby. Stormy was different, and I could see that I was better in my role of mom with her, but I'd had a new marriage and financial issues, too. This baby would be different, and maybe not all those differences were bad.

"So, is your husband getting used to the idea?" Livvy asked.

Time to look at my plate again. I shook my head. "I'm not sure he's going to stick it out." After I said those words, I was shocked I'd been able to get them out of my mouth.

She was silent, and when I looked up at her, she was quickly blinking away tears. She tried to smile but Livvy wasn't someone who hid her thoughts. "I'm sorry," she said quietly. "No wonder this is so hard for you."

I simply nodded. No wonder.

Livvy stayed until three o'clock, catching up on my laundry and mopping my kitchen floor while I took a nap. Before she left, she tapped on the door, and I got up long enough to give her a hug. She wasn't as soft and powdered as Ruby, but she was a sincere hugger, even if I sensed she was a little uncomfortable. We barely knew one another, and yet suddenly she was exactly what I needed. She'd brought peace with her and let me talk about stuff that had smoothed me out somehow. I thanked her for coming and taking care of my home for me.

"It's what I do," she said, shrugging one shoulder. "I love it; it makes me feel connected to the people I care about."

"My mom's like that," I said. "Always doing stuff for people." Was that how she felt connected? Showed her love? Had I misinterpreted her all these years?

"Sounds like my kind of woman," Livvy said, and a mask of sadness descended. I remembered what she'd said about losing her mother, and for an instant, I wondered if I would be so missed by my daughters. But I took it a step further. Was there time to repair our relationships? Was there time to make myself miss-able?

"Thank you," I said, hoping that my sincerity was apparent. "I know it couldn't have been easy for you to give up your entire afternoon, but I feel so much better. I was in a very dark place."

"I know all about dark places," Livvy said. "And it's often someone else who needs to help you get out of it. I'm glad I could be that hand for you to grab on to. You call if you need anything at all, okay?"

"I will."

"Promise?" she said, cocking her head to the side as though questioning my commitment.

I laughed, but tears filled my eyes at the same time. She cared about me. Genuinely cared. I had misjudged her as someone who'd lost herself in the people she loved, as though that were a bad thing. Reality was very different. I could learn a thing or two from this woman. "I promise."

Chapter 36

PAIGE HAD GIVEN ME the name of the doctor she'd had for Nathan, Dr. Cortez, who had a practice in Mission Viejo. I made an appointment for the week between Christmas and New Year's and told myself he wouldn't be like Dr. Christiansen and that there was nothing to be afraid of. I'd put off telling December about the baby for too long, so I finally picked up the phone on Wednesday evening, three days before Christmas.

She was very quiet, and I felt myself slowly turning to stone as I waited for her response.

"Wow," she finally said. The fatigue was thick in her voice, and I regretted, again, having to tell her this right now. "Um, congratulations."

"Yeah," I replied, playing with the zipper on my jacket. "Quite a shock."

"Yeah," she said back. "It'll take some time to get used to the idea of having a sibling younger than my son."

"I know," I said. "It took me a while to wrap my head around it."

"So, why didn't you tell me when you were out here?" I hated that she sounded hurt. I hadn't wanted to hurt her, but I felt as though one way or another I was hurting everyone.

"Things were so crazy, I just didn't know how to bring it up."

She was quiet, and I tried to dissect the silence into surprised, mad, or just tired, but couldn't get a solid impression.

"Is Paul excited?"

"No," I said honestly. We were living in the same house but avoiding one another. It was awful.

"Oh."

"Yeah."

"So, are you still able to come out after Christmas?"

I was the worst mother in the world. "I can't," I said. "I'm so sorry. I didn't get tickets in time, and I have an appointment with a doctor next week. I'm hoping I can come out in January sometime, though. I'm sorry, Ember."

We were both quiet for a few more seconds. I rescued us by asking about Tennyson, which lightened the mood. December said that Mom had left that morning, but Jared's sister was able to come for the holiday and help out. She'd fly in tomorrow afternoon. The doctor had said they might be able to bring Tennyson home on Friday, Christmas Eve—wasn't that wonderful?

After finishing the call, I didn't give myself the chance to chicken out of calling my mother. I could admit I was hoping she was still traveling so I could leave a voice mail, but she'd just walked in and answered.

"I already guessed," she said after I told her the news.

"Guessed?" I said with a jolt. "How could you have guessed?"

"A mother knows these things," she said simply. "Now, have you been to the doctor yet? Are you taking your prenatal vitamins and drinking your raspberry leaf tea? There are considerations for a woman your age, you know."

It was a relief when everyone finally knew, and even though Paul was still distant and avoiding me, I was lifted by the other people, whose support was in place.

I finally went Christmas shopping. I spent more than an hour trying to decide what to buy for Paul. I settled on a new bathrobe, a portable propane heater/stove for his camping and hunting trips, and an antique pewter picture frame. Not that I knew what to put in the frame. I stared at the stock photo of a couple on their wedding day with envy.

I wrapped the gifts for Stormy and Paul and left them on the kitchen table; we hadn't bought a Christmas tree, and it seemed silly to do so now. I mailed December's and my parents' gifts, even though they wouldn't get there in time for the holiday. I was making progress, though, and feeling stronger and more capable.

Paige and I talked only once, though she texted me now and then to check up on me. I was still embarrassed about my breakdown on Monday, and she didn't seem to know what to do with me exactly, but I was glad that things had healed at least a little bit.

Paul continued to be a phantom. He worked at the office most of the time, and in the evenings he watched basketball, went to his brother's house, or read a book. The living room had become his domain. By silent support of his secession, I spent a lot of time in Stormy's room, waiting for him to come to me. Which he never did. Sometimes he cooked, and whenever he did, he made me a plate, for which I thanked him. I took it as a sign that we were still a team, sort of, but we didn't eat together, and I missed him terribly despite him being within a dozen feet most of the time.

On December 23, "Christmas Adam," as we called it, Paul came home to tell me he was going hunting with Charlie over Christmas Day.

I stared at him until he met my eyes. "It's been two weeks," I said. "We can't dance around this forever."

He was putting new batteries in the GPS I'd given him for our anniversary, so he looked at that while he talked—or didn't talk, as it were.

"I'd rather have an answer than keep doing this, Paul. It's killing me to be ignored by someone I care about so much." I hated how vulnerable I felt saying that out loud.

He kept fiddling with the equipment until I put a hand over it. He stared at my hand for a few beats before looking me in the eye. He still didn't say anything, so I did. "If you want me to leave, I'll leave. But I can't live like this. It's killing me."

We stared at one another for a full twenty seconds. "You don't need to leave," he said, and I felt a spark of hope sputter from the ashes in my chest. "I already am."

The ashes sent up a plume of dust. "What?"

"I've talked to Charlie. After the hunting trip, I'm going to stay with him for a while. I need some space."

"Space? That's all you've had for the last two weeks. It's time to face this head-on and make a decision."

He lifted his chin and looked at me with a challenge in his blue eyes, which suddenly seemed so icy, so cold. "You don't want me to make a decision right now, Daisy, I promise you that."

"Oh?" I asked, folding my arms over my chest. "Maybe I do. I can't live this way."

Red splotches formed on his neck, something I'd never seen before, but then I'd never seen Paul get angry, and now anger was peeling off him in waves, crashing into me.

"This is not what I wanted," he said. "I didn't sign up for it." His voice was rising, the timbre deepening at the same time.

"Neither did I," I said. "But we made vows to one another, we promised to weather the storms together. Doesn't that mean anything?"

"We had plans. And this changes everything."

"I know that," I shot back. "But it doesn't have to *destroy* everything. Think of Mason and Stormy and all they've brought into our lives. This"—I put my hands on my belly—"is a child, one *we* created, and while I can sympathize with the shock and even the disappointment of everything it changes, it's here, Paul. It's a part of us."

"I love Mason," Paul said. "But she picks and chooses when to see me, and she comes only if I buy her something or take her somewhere. I'm not in her life—I have no power in her life—but I worry about the choices she makes and I feel ultimately responsible for her. She tied me to a woman I wish I'd never met, and I take very little satisfaction in being a father to her. Parenting was not what I thought it would be, Daisy, and I've always been grateful I only had one. I have been counting the days until Stormy got out of here, and since she's left, it's finally felt like I'm free to live the life I want to live. I thought you felt that way too."

I'd never heard him say anything like this before. It took me a moment to recover and continue the dialogue. "I admit I've enjoyed the freedom too." I was far too raw to lie about it. "But I also miss her, and a hundred times a day, I find myself going over the mistakes I made with her."

"Another kid isn't going to repair that," Paul said.

Another zinger I hadn't seen coming, but I stood my ground. "I know that," I said sharply. "But it's a part of us, and worth us trying to do better than we've done before." I was still shaken by what he'd said about Mason. Was he really so burdened by his daughter? Is that why he didn't fight for her to visit more often?

"I don't want it," he finally said, blunt and razor sharp at the same time. He continued to stare me down. Then he looked down at my stomach. "There are places that don't care how long it's been."

"No!" I said boldly. "I'm having this baby, Paul. That's not up for discussion. The only question is whether you'll raise it with me."

"And I told you that if you're forcing a decision from me today, my answer is no. I don't want to be a father again."

"What about being a *husband*?" I said, holding back the tears as his words twisted inside me like shrapnel. "What about *me*?"

"You're telling me that if I stay, you're forcing a child on me. I'm telling you I don't want it. Why is your choice more important than mine?"

"I'm not going to force this child on you, Paul. It wouldn't be fair to either one of you." My head was tingling. "But it's still my choice to keep this baby. I'd rather do whatever we can to raise it together than do it by myself."

I wanted to say more about his level of commitment, about him walking away and leaving this child fatherless. I wanted to beat him with my disappointment and share the agony I felt at his refusal to amend his future. But I didn't. I was frozen and couldn't utter another word, feeling the emotion I was holding back pressing against the dam. I couldn't hold it back much longer.

He remained silent. After a few seconds, he gathered up his things and disappeared into the bedroom.

As my tears overflowed, I put a shaky hand over my mouth and ran into Stormy's room, slamming the door. I sat on the bed, waiting for my heart to explode, but then realized, when the sobs didn't come, when Paul didn't come, that I had been watching my marriage crumble for weeks. Though his words cut and bruised me horribly, they weren't as big a surprise as I'd have imagined them to be an hour ago. He'd been pushing me away ever since I'd told him. He hadn't talked to me, he hadn't asked how I was feeling or if I was going to the doctor. He'd simply retreated into himself. Maybe he was leaving *right now,* but he'd abandoned me two weeks ago.

I finally cried, but it wasn't the wracking, heart-wrenching sobs I'd expected, but a drizzly mourning of what I thought our marriage was. I had been wrong all along. Paul didn't want me as much as he wanted a specific kind of future. As soon as I threatened that future, I was a liability rather than an asset. I wondered what he'd have done if I'd been in a car accident, or been offered a promotion that required a move away from his comfort zone. Would he have supported me in either of those things, both of which would also have worked against his *plan?* It burned to realize I could be so wrong about the man I'd fallen in love with. Again.

At some point I fell asleep on Stormy's bed. When I woke up, it was dark. The house was still. It was over. It was done. And while it was heartbreaking, at least I knew where I stood. I got up from the bed and considered my future, a huge, blank canvas waiting for my first few brushstrokes to begin a new image, to guide a new scene. I glanced at the clock radio on Stormy's dresser.

It was 1:13 on Christmas Eve.

Merry Christmas.

Chapter 37

THE NEXT MORNING CONSISTED of vacuuming, organizing some cupboards, and some yard work I'd been putting off. It was hard to believe it was Christmas Eve until I turned on the TV for company and was assaulted by bells and ho-ho-hos.

I turned it off and wondered what Stormy was doing for the holiday. Before I'd told her about the baby, we'd talked about her coming over, but I hadn't talked to her since then, and Jared's family would be getting together too. Did I really expect her to choose me, who she was angry with, or to be surrounded by her cousins and grandparents? Should I call her and ask?

Maybe I should call Jared. I entertained that thought for about two seconds. What would he say? Would I have to tell him about Paul? I couldn't ignore the fact that, for the third time in my life, a baby was pushing the man I loved away from me. Why? Why me? What was I doing wrong that I couldn't make this work? I had to shake off those thoughts. I was seeing this through, and understanding wasn't the most important thing right now. I *had* to stop feeling sorry for myself.

When I ran out of distractions and felt anxiety creeping in, I thought of Paige. I hadn't talked to her much since she'd given me Dr. Cortez's number, and I worried I had been in too much of a fog to really thank her properly—I sensed she was being cautious with me as well since I'd been such a mess. I was pretty sure she wasn't working today, so I called her cell phone.

"Hi, Daisy," she said when she answered. I could tell from the whooshing background noise that she was driving, but I didn't hear the boys.

"Hey," I said. I updated her on the appointment I'd made with Dr. Cortez and thanked her again for the referral. My mother pointing out how ungracious I had been in the past spurred me to make sure I was very clear on my gratitude.

"I'm glad everything's working out," Paige said. "You'll like Dr. Cortez. He's a really great doctor."

"Good," I said, trying not to remember that Amy had said the same thing about Dr. Christiansen. "So what are you doing for the holidays, driving back to Utah?"

"No," Paige said, and I noted the flatness in her voice. A controlled kind of flat. "The office opens back up on Tuesday. I'm on my way back from Vegas."

"Vegas?" I was confused.

"I met Doug halfway between his place and mine. He's taking the boys for Christmas."

"Ohh," I said, everything lining up. "Are you okay?"

She was quiet long enough that I knew she was trying to keep herself reined in. "I'm sure I'll be fine," she said.

"Uh-huh," I said. She didn't take the bait, and I expounded. "What time do you think you'll be home?"

"Probably around six—why?"

"Do you have plans?"

"Does drowning in a tub of pralines and cream count?"

"Totally counts," I said with a chuckle. My idea was set.

"Then I have plans."

I wondered how much it took out of her to try to make a joke when her heart was breaking. Actually, I thought I already knew the cost. I'd done it before. Many times. I was doing it now.

"You drive safe, okay?" I said.

"I will," she said with a sigh. "Let me know how your appointment goes next week."

We ended the call, and I looked at the clock. Plenty of time to brighten someone else's day—funny how that brightened mine, too.

At 5:40, I pulled into Paige's apartment complex. She wasn't there yet, so I listened to NPR and waited. It was almost 6:15 before she pulled in. She must have recognized my car because she stepped out while looking at me.

With my belly growing, it was harder to pull myself out of the car than it used to be, but I smiled once I stood. "I brought Chinese," I said, not adding that we'd probably need to reheat it. We met on the sidewalk outside the doors to her complex.

She held up a plastic bag. "I worried I wouldn't have enough ice cream so I stocked up. Sorry I'm late."

I shrugged. "I hear pralines and cream goes really well with Schezwan chicken."

Paige smiled, but I could see she was feeling a little battered. "Thanks for coming."

"I've been a single mom most of my life." Whoa, what a weird thing to say. It was true though, which was even weirder. "But this is the first holiday I've spent without at least one of my kids."

"I'm so sorry," Paige commiserated as she opened the door.

"Stormy didn't even come to get her presents," I admitted as we walked inside. "What happened in Vegas?"

Paige's eyes filled with tears. "It was awful," she said, her voice squeaking. She wrapped her arms across her chest, the bag of ice cream banging against her hip as she entered the building while I held the door. "Nathan was bawling when Doug left with him. I cried for the first fifty miles. Cursed for the next ten. I can't believe a judge felt like it was okay for a three-year-old to be taken away from his mother for so long. This summer Doug plans to take him for *eight* weeks. I'm going to petition the courts to wait until he's older. He can't leave me for two months. He's so little."

"I'm so sorry," I said.

She looked up at me. "Want to know what's really pathetic?" She didn't wait for an answer. "I wore sweats and a baseball cap when I left this morning." She was currently dressed in very flattering straight-leg jeans, a gauzy teal top over a white T-shirt, and cute little silver ballet flats. "I stopped at In-N-Out to change my clothes and do my hair and makeup before we met up," she said, waving to her makeup-free face, which she'd obviously cried off many miles ago. But her hair looked great, smooth and sleek. "Why did I do that, Daisy? What was I trying to prove?"

"That you're okay," I said.

"But I am so not okay," she said, tears overflowing as we stepped out of the elevator. She didn't even try to wipe them away; she just dug her keys out of her purse and unlocked the door to her apartment. We went inside and she hung up her purse before staring at the rug in her entryway. "This is all so wrong. It's *Christmas.*"

She was preaching to the choir, which meant I had nothing to offer other than commiseration. "It really stinks."

"Like a dead skunk—which I passed about thirty miles ago."

I couldn't help but smile. "Paul left. I don't know when or if he's coming home."

"I'm sorry, Daisy," she said, finally wiping at her eyes.

"Yeah," I said, trying to shrug it off. "Kind of a dead-skunk holiday for me, too."

I shook my head—I wasn't trying to turn the attention to my own problems. "The point is that we're both on our own for the holiday. I thought maybe we could watch *It's a Wonderful Life.* It's playing on two different cable stations, I think."

"Ugh," she said, shaking her head. "I'm not up for that."

"What about *Scrooged?*" I said from behind her as we headed toward the kitchen—that ice cream needed to get in the freezer. "It's the best irreverent Christmas movie out there, next to *8 Crazy Nights,* but that's actually about Chanukah."

Paige gave me a small smile over her shoulder as she pulled open the freezer and put the ice cream—bag and all—inside. "I don't think I could handle *The Muppets Christmas Carol* right now."

"How about something like *Jurassic Park?*" I asked, following her into the living room and kicking off my shoes—I swear my feet were already swelling. "You can stream in Netflix, right?"

Her smile got a little wider. "Now *that* sounds perfect."

Chapter 38

ON CHRISTMAS DAY, PAIGE came to my house—not as many toys to make her frown or Christmas decorations to remind her of what she was missing. We had a *Lord of the Rings* movie marathon—extended versions—and used the break between movie one and movie two to make brownies.

Her ex called halfway through the second movie, and I paused the action while she talked to her boys. She was such a tender, nurturing mother, and I tried not to compare my style to hers too much. I'd never been very good at the soft and squishy parts of motherhood. Maybe because I had been so young when I started, or because I had to keep a roof over our heads. But Paige was doing that too. I had always looked forward to a weekend without the girls, and while I'd never been alone for a holiday before, I'd wished I was more than once—it was so much work trying to keep them sufficiently entertained.

"Man, I miss them," Paige said.

I hadn't realized she'd finished the call, or that I was on the brink of tears as regret washed over me.

"Has she called?" Paige asked, seeing right through me.

I shook my head while swallowing the lump in my throat, embarrassed to be so transparent even though I appreciated that we could understand one another. "It's okay, though," I said, letting out a breath and pulling myself back together. "Now let's watch Aragorn kick the snot out of those Uruk-hai."

After the second movie ended, we decided to throw together some pasta, and in the process we started talking about the Christian symbolism in the movies. I was impressed with things she found that I hadn't seen, but I called a few she hadn't considered such as the way Saruman tempted Gandolph to use his powers to support Sauron just as Satan tempted Christ, and how Aragorn makes the sign of the cross over Boromir as he's dying.

"Huh. Didn't catch that one either," Paige said. "You really do know your Christianity."

I shrugged but felt pride instead of frustration with my religious background. On my way home from Paige's last night, I'd passed a Catholic church all lit up for midnight Mass. I hadn't stopped but part of me had wanted to. Maybe next year.

"So do you," I said, taking my plate of fettuccine to the table. "I didn't realize Mormons were Christian until we met."

"Yeah, lots of people don't think we're Christian. I don't really know why—the name of our church is The Church of Jesus Christ of Latter-day Saints."

"I didn't know why either," I said, twirling some fettuccine onto my fork.

"So you were raised religious?" Paige asked, and I could hear the careful nature of her comment. I remembered the defensive position she'd had to take during the first book group and wondered if she got that a lot.

"I was raised Catholic," I said. "Very Catholic."

"You're not practicing anymore?"

"No," I said, trying not to feel uncomfortable, but I did. When was the last time I'd discussed religion with anyone? "I had some negative experiences."

"Yeah," Paige said. "I've had a few moments of that myself." She paused then looked up sharply. "Not that I'm saying you shouldn't have stopped going or anything. I'm not trying to be judgmental."

She spoke fast and scared, and I smiled. "I didn't feel judged," I said. "Church just didn't work for me. It doesn't bug me to say that."

"How about God? Do you believe in Him? I'm just curious."

I thought about what my mom had said, how church was a vehicle to God, and how well that blended with the conversation we'd had at book group when we'd discussed *The Poisonwood Bible*. "I believe in God," I said. "I'm not sure I like Him all the time, though."

I could tell Paige was uncomfortable with that, but she didn't say anything, so I quickly changed the subject back to the movies. "And what about the whole *Return of the King*? It's only the base foundation of all Christianity, awaiting the Second Coming. Am I right?"

It ended up being a very good day. We were both hurting, and yet we had found some sisterhood together. I was grateful. At the end of the night, after we had beat the Tolkien discussions to death, Paige asked me what I was going to do now that Paul had left.

"The house is Paul's," I said. "I'm not on the mortgage, and he makes the payments. I keep hoping he's going to come home and have a different opinion, but I feel silly holding my breath. I guess I need to look for an apartment." I paused, letting the idea settle like a hammer on my toe. I took a deep breath and tried to shrug as I pinched off a corner of a leftover brownie. "This is still so *Twilight Zone*."

Paige gave me a sympathetic smile. "The office isn't open on Monday, so I have the day off. What if we go look at apartments and maternity clothes?"

"Sounds horrible," I said, brushing crumbs from my fingers.

"We could get pedicures, too," she said.

"Okay, you talked me in to it."

I was only half paying attention when Paige and I went out on Monday. We found two apartments that looked good. One wouldn't be ready for a month, but the other one was available now and not far from Paige. I was so not happy about returning to apartment life, but I tried not to make a big deal about it due to the fact that Paige was in an apartment, and I didn't want to sound like a snob.

We also found a few maternity boutiques. I pretty much bought whatever Paige said looked good since it all looked ridiculous to me. I was such a zeppelin. The pedicures were the best part—I chose red for the season I didn't feel much enamored with. At the end of the day, I gave her a big hug, thanking her profusely for making the holiday bearable.

"Right back at ya," Paige said. "You totally saved me."

I went back to work on Tuesday despite the fact that half the office didn't come in. I heard nothing from Paul, and Wednesday became almost the same day as Tuesday, except that I wore a different whale costume to work. On my way home Wednesday night, I stopped at the apartment complex near Paige's place in Tustin. The manager met me at the door of the available apartment, and I walked through it with new eyes, trying to quell my resentment of having to make yet another change in my life.

"Let me think on it a little longer," I said, forcing a smile as we headed out of a place that didn't seem as though it would ever really feel like home. Would the people below me have late-night parties? Would someone down the hall cook with onions too often? I hated living in apartments.

I went home to a dinner of leftover fettuccine in an empty house. I texted Stormy to tell her I loved her. She didn't text back. I cried myself to sleep for the fourth night in a row.

Thursday afternoon I left the office early to go to my appointment with Dr. Cortez. He tried looking for the baby's gender, but the appointment was instead dominated by the discovery that the placenta was covering part of my cervix—placenta previa, he called it.

"It should move up as the baby grows and expands the uterus," Dr. Cortez said, the hint of a lilt to his words. "But avoid lifting or aerobic exercise until your next appointment, okay? And give me a call if you have any cramping or spotting."

"Okay," I agreed. I didn't realize until I was getting dressed that I hadn't even looked at the monitor when he did the ultrasound. Not that I'd ever been able to tell what it was on the screen anyway, but why hadn't I even looked?

I was invited to a New Year's party by a neighbor I talked to only a few times a year. Paige had a date with a guy named Derryl that she didn't talk about much but smiled over every time she said his name. I was glad she was going out, but a little jealous too. Livvy called and invited me to her house for the holiday. I was touched, but had already committed to my neighbor's party, which turned into a total bore. I was in bed by ten, spent New Year's Day catching up on a scrapbook I'd abandoned five years earlier, and breathed a sigh of relief when I went to bed that night.

The holidays were over. I had survived.

At work, I finally let myself think about the fact that I hadn't seen or heard from my husband in a week and a half. Nothing. I suspected that he'd come home for clothes once or twice while I was at work last week, but he'd managed to avoid me entirely. I called the manager of the apartment complex I'd looked at and asked if the unit was still available.

"Yes," he said eagerly. "You could move in tomorrow."

"How about Saturday?" I had the brief reminder that Saturday was book group night and grimaced. I'd thrown my copy of *Silas Marner* at Paige and never gotten it back. But I wanted to go. Maybe it could be my reward after I moved all day. I'm sure the girls in the group wouldn't mind that I hadn't finished the book.

I made an appointment to sign the contract the next morning. Then I dejunked every closet in the house while playing my *Forrest Gump* soundtrack at full blast. I didn't have any boxes to pack things in yet, but left my closet fodder in piles and stacks throughout the house so that only Paul's stuff went back in the newly cleaned closet. I cried the whole time.

The next morning I lay in bed too long. Everything had become so real and so heavy. I couldn't get out of bed. I couldn't go to work. I couldn't *do* this. But I did get out of bed, feeling sore and heavy, and got ready for work. I did what I had always done—pulled myself up by my bootstraps and got on with my life, even though I felt dead inside. I stopped at the apartment complex on my way into the office and signed the contract. I'd pick up keys on Friday. Wow.

At the office, I took the stairs in hopes that I could stave off the insane weight gain that had me in its sights. By the last floor, my belly was hurting, and I was breathing hard. Was I already *that* big that it hurt to do normal things? No more Szechuan chicken and pralines and cream for me. In between work projects, I called the utility companies to get things switched over and hired a moving company to come to the house at eight o'clock Saturday morning. Every time emotion threatened to overcome me, I took a breath and pushed it away. There was too much to do to waste time with so many *feelings*.

At eleven, I took a break to use the bathroom. That's when I realized I was bleeding.

Chapter 39

"GOOD NEWS AND BAD NEWS," Dr. Cortez said as he pulled the rolling stool up to the exam table an hour later. I'd been instructed to lie on my left side while he went over the results of the ultrasound, and I tried to stay calm.

I felt numb and didn't dare ask any questions for fear that I'd be inviting an answer I wasn't prepared to hear.

"The bad news," he said in that lilting voice of his, "is that the placenta has not moved as we had hoped it would. In fact, it's covering more of the cervix than it did at your previous appointment, which is why you had the bleeding. The placenta has pulled away from the uterine wall."

"And you can't fix it," I summed up. The mental canvas I had been painting on was suddenly blank again.

"No, we can't," he said with a shake of his head and a sympathetic expression. "There is no prevention or cure for placenta previa, but there is still some good news."

"Okay," I said.

"The baby is fine," he said, smiling for the first time. "Heartbeat is normal, and development is right on schedule. The other good news is that the tear from the placental displacement was minor. It will heal."

I took my first deep breath in nearly an hour and stared at the ceiling.

"But . . ." His voice trailed off.

My eyes snapped back to his licorice ones. "But?"

"I'm ordering you to stay down."

"Stay down?" I repeated as though confused, but I knew what he meant. I just couldn't comprehend how it was possible.

"Bed rest," he summarized. "*Full* bed rest for at least two weeks, then we'll reevaluate, see if we can lift some of your restrictions. For now, no intercourse, no lifting, no walking except to the bathroom and the kitchen a few times a day. Three-minute showers."

"That means not going to work," I said. How could I not work? I wasn't worried about the intercourse part—that was *not* an issue any longer. But I had just signed a contract to move on Saturday. I couldn't stay in Paul's house forever.

"I will write a note to your employer." He looked up at me. "It'll be okay."

That's when I realized I was crying. I hurried to wipe away the tears and nodded, embarrassed to be so emotional, not that I was all that surprised—I was always emotional these days.

"Do you have people who can help you?" he asked.

I almost shook my head. My husband had left me. My daughter wasn't speaking to me. My extended family lived on the opposite side of the country. I was more alone than I'd ever been in my life.

"Yes," I lied, thinking about online grocery delivery. Movers. A housekeeper.

"And, Mrs. Atkins," he said, still looking at me with that bold stare of his. "I will take good care of you."

I looked away as more tears sprang up, but my glance stopped at the cross at his neck. I stared at it for a moment and then asked, "Do you pray, Dr. Cortez?"

He smiled widely, showing bright white teeth. "Every day," he said. "I pray for my family, for my patients, and for the Lord to help me be the man He sent me here to be. Do you pray, Mrs. Atkins?"

"No. Not anymore." I looked at the cross again.

"With God, all things are possible, Miss Daisy. His peace He will give you, if you will only ask."

"Ask? That's kind of the problem I have."

He smiled warmly at me. "Finding one's faith is a journey that can take a lifetime, and there is no saying where anyone is at any given time in their life. But"—he lifted one finger to make his point—"I believe that a life with a belief in God and in His mercy and justice is better than a life without it. Asking for His peace and comfort does not make us weak."

Dr. Cortez gave me permission to drive myself home, but made me promise to arrange for help as soon as I could. I drove slowly, and when I got home, I went straight to Stormy's room to lie down. It took all of five minutes before the weight of the entire situation pressed in on me. More tears. How would I do this?

How can I make it work? I can't take four months off of life. How will I function? How will I do the basics? Laundry, grocery shopping, earning a paycheck. I raised my hands to cover my eyes as though hiding from someone who might see me losing it, see me breaking under the pressure.

And then I felt something flutter in my belly, a feeling like cresting the first hill on a roller coaster, or stepping into a high-speed elevator. I held my breath and went very still, my hands going from my wet eyes to my rounding stomach. I'd wondered a time or two over the last few days if I'd felt the baby move, but I hadn't been certain. I wasn't sure I was ready to acknowledge it. But . . . there. I felt it again.

And there.

I closed my eyes and felt myself smile as I focused intently on this reminder of why I would take four months off of my life. Tears ran down the sides of my face. I pressed both hands against my belly and took a deep breath.

Ask.

The word was just there. Maybe it was Dr. Cortez's voice, I couldn't be sure.

Ask.

Could I bear the rejection if my request was met with silence?

Things were silent anyway. Dr. Cortez had said that a belief in God's justice and mercy was better than a life without it. Did I dare believe that? Did I want justice to get its due? Only if I didn't trust mercy. Did I trust mercy? Did I believe it? Did I deserve it?

Ask.

I exhaled slowly, closed my eyes, and with my hands on my belly, I began to pray.

"Our Father, who art in heaven, hallowed be thy name . . ."

Chapter 40

"WELL, I SUPPOSE WE'LL HAVE to make the best of it," Sam, my supervisor, said when I called the next morning. I hadn't had any lightning bolts following my prayer last night. I hadn't felt anything, really. But the prayer hadn't hurt. That was a start, right?

Sam continued. "I'll get with Amy and Lenny to see how we'll split things up. Can you work from home?"

I was stuck on the idea of having to work with Amy. That would be awkward to say the least. "I'll have my laptop," I said. "I can do plenty through that, but I won't have access to any office documents or files."

"Understood," he said. "Perhaps we could put Naomi from underwriting in your office, and she can be your hands and eyes here."

"That would work," I said, relieved even though the idea of having someone else in my office made my skin itch. Another call was coming in, and I pulled the phone away from my ear long enough to see that it was Jared. Why was he calling? I didn't take his call and talked to Sam for another ten minutes. Then I called Jared back.

"I just got a text from Stormy," Jared said. "What's going on?"

Ask. Such a small word for such a big thing. Stormy had been the safest person to tell, but I'd known it was just like telling Jared directly.

I explained it all to him, hating the weakness and vulnerability I felt at having to divulge all the tragic turns of events I'd been navigating. I assumed he knew about the pregnancy—no doubt Stormy had already downloaded her feelings on that subject—and although I hesitated to tell him about Paul, there was no point in pretending things were different than what they were.

"Wow," he said. "You sure know how to pick 'em."

It wouldn't have been so funny if he hadn't once been one of those I'd picked. It was nice to laugh with him before he turned serious again. "You going to be okay?"

I thought about that, struck by the sincerity of his comment. "Yeah," I said. "In the long run, I will be. Right now I'm just trying not to panic."

"Aren't you moving to a new place?"

"How did you know that?" I hadn't actually *talked* to Stormy since I made the announcement, and I hadn't brought up the move with her in the few texts we'd sent back and forth.

"December told Storm you were looking at apartments last week. Did you find something already?"

It was so tempting to lie to him and pretend I had everything under control.

Ask.

"I did find a place. In fact, I'm supposed to move in on Saturday," I said. "I signed the contract less than two hours before all this happened. Amazing timing, huh?"

"This Saturday? Are you still following through on it?"

"I already have movers coming, and I thought if I used the office chair, with rollers, I could do most of the packing before then." How idiotic could I be? Did I really think I could finish separating my things from Paul's without having to stand? It made me sad to think about disentangling our lives from one another. It was all so surreal.

"Storm and I could come help. I could knock off work early. January's a lousy month for sales since the holidays tap everyone out."

I wanted so badly to say that I didn't need or want his help. That I was perfectly capable of doing this myself. But I wasn't. And I knew it.

"Really?" I hadn't really asked for his help, but I hadn't refused him either, and that was a step in the right direction.

"Sure. I assume you won't be going anywhere, so we can come anytime, right?"

"I'm a lump," I said. "But I feel bad putting this on you." He was my *ex*-husband. He didn't owe me anything—not even child support now that our child had chosen to live with him.

"Don't feel bad," Jared said. "It's about time Storm got over herself, ya know, and you need us, right?"

Need. That was almost as bad as *ask*. Like it or not, however, I could not do this alone.

"I really do," I finally said.

"Good deal. We'll be there."

They came at six, and Stormy acted as though everything was fine between us. I lacked the energy it would take to discuss things and played along. Stormy came back and forth between my room, which used to be her room, and the rest of the house, asking questions while Jared provided the manual labor. He'd even brought boxes. At seven thirty, Paige showed up, though I didn't know it was her until she tapped on the bedroom door where I was laid out like a very round Queen Bee while people buzzed around me. I hated it so much.

"You going crazy yet?" she asked as she came into the room. She had a reusable bag from Trader Joe's in one hand; whatever was inside it was heavy, which meant it was not potato chips—bummer. I had hesitated to tell her anything at all, but knew she'd be hurt if I didn't include her. She immediately said she'd do what she could to help. The process made me realize how hard it was for me to take anyone's charity, and that made me feel bad. Had I lived my life as such a rock and an island that I couldn't reach out? What kind of relationships did I expect to have if I didn't let anyone be necessary to me?

"I passed crazy a long time ago," I said in answer to her question. "Now I'm on to neurotic. After that comes insanity, and I should reach it by Sunday at the rate I'm going."

Paige laughed and sat on the bed while I pulled myself up to a better sitting position. She looked great today, her eyes were bright, her smile genuine, and her hair caught the light just enough to set off the golden tones. "I brought you some books."

"You did!" I said as though I'd won the Publishers Clearing House sweepstakes. I sat up even more and tried to peek in the bag.

"Some of my favorites, including . . . this one." She pulled a book from the bag and handed it to me. *Silas Marner.* The first half of the book had been read, but the second half of the pages were in mint condition save for a fold on the back few pages. It was my book, the book I'd thrown at Paige when I had chosen her as the root of all my problems.

"I'm so sorry about that, Paige," I said, embarrassed that I had been so unhinged. "I was out of control."

"Crazy pregnant lady," Paige said, smiling and shrugging. "You should have time to finish it before book group."

I looked up at her. "I wish I could come," I said. "Especially after all you and Livvy have done for me. And I want to know how Athena's doing, and Ruby's been so sweet to me. I hate missing it."

"I know. That's why we're going to bring it to you."

"What?"

Paige grinned even wider. "I talked to Ruby, and she was up for a road trip." She must have seen the dismay on my face. "I know you won't be moved in, per se, but it'll be fun, and, seriously, the alternative is being alone while you know we're all talking about you anyway. I'll come over early and straighten up."

"I move that day," I said. "I'll have nothing but boxes."

"Not a problem," she said, standing up. "It's done. And the boys are playing with some kids from church for the next"—she looked at her watch—"hour and eighteen minutes. I'm at your service until then."

I blinked at her. I didn't even have to *ask*. "I don't know how I'll ever pay you back for this."

She picked up a few pieces of garbage and tossed them into the trash can. "I can be bought with fine chocolate and pedicures, not necessarily in that order." She put her purse next to the bed and headed for the bedroom door. "I assume General Stormy is giving orders?" She looked over her shoulder to give me one more parting smile before I heard her join the undecipherable voices in the other room.

I'd read another fifteen pages of the book when my mattress slumped. I looked up to see Stormy sitting there. If anything her eye makeup was thicker than it had been when she was living here. And there was a red lock of hair on the left side. I reached up and fingered it while biting my tongue.

"It's an extension," she said, using both hands to unclip it. "Dad won't let me color it for real."

"Two points to Dad," I said, settling against the pillows and trying to act casual. The last conversation we'd had resulted in her bolting from the house and ignoring me for weeks. She looked at the book resting on my belly.

"What's that about?"

I looked at the cover for a minute. "A man who thought he had everything until he lost it, only to find the greatest treasure in a child."

"Sounds stupid," she said blandly.

I smiled. "It's rather insightful."

She gave me a flickering look and then started playing with the extension in her hand. "So, the baby's okay and everything?"

"Yes," I said. "In another month, you'll be able to feel it move."

She made a face. "Creepy."

I laughed. "So, how are you?"

"Okay," she said, then looked around the room. "I'm going to miss this house."

"The first house we ever lived in," I said. "Maybe the last." Buying a home in Orange County on my salary alone was a pipe dream. "I'll miss it too."

"You don't think Paul will change his mind?"

I considered that for a minute, then shook my head. "I'm not sure I'd trust it if he did." It hurt to say that, though; I missed him so much. At least, I missed the Paul I thought he was. "You'll like my new place. It has a pool and a gym."

"Dad's complex has a pool and a gym."

"Well, mine's closer to the mall."

"Not that much closer."

Something struck me as strange about the comments she'd made— why the comparison? "You'll have your own room, of course," I said. "And it's in Tustin, so I'll be closer than I am now."

She looked up at me, and I read concern in her face. "Who's going to take care of you?"

No one! I wanted to shout. I wanted even more for it to be true.

"Well, I'm hoping that after a couple of weeks, I'll be able to get around better than I do right now. And Paige is only a couple of blocks away. She's offered to help." I didn't say that I was hoping to hire a housekeeper to come in for an hour or two a day. It would be hard on my new budget, but worth it if it meant not having to put everyone else out.

"With play practice and everything, I can't come out very often."

"But that means I'll enjoy your visits more than ever, right?"

"It's too bad you didn't find a place closer to Dad," she said. "Then it would be way easier."

My heart skipped a beat. She wanted me closer? I hadn't even considered her and Jared when I was thinking of places to move. Now that the idea had been broached, I mentally kicked myself for not having thought about it. I must have been quiet for too long because I saw her expression change, and she stood up. "Anyway, is that rooster dish set yours or Paul's?"

"Mine," I said. Paul had given it to me for Christmas last year.

"Okay."

She left me to my thoughts. Was it too late to cancel the apartment? Did I want to cancel? I pulled my computer onto my lap and went online, just to see what was available in Jared's area. The idea had me on fire.

Paige came in to say good-bye around eight thirty. I explained that I was thinking about switching apartments, then braced myself for what Paige would say. She'd helped me get this apartment, and I knew she didn't have a lot of extra time to spare for me right now. However, she heard what I *didn't* say out loud, which was that Stormy wanted me closer.

"It hasn't been three business days since you signed the contract, so you should still be within the grace period. Do you have his number?"

"I'm sure it's on the paperwork in the kitchen."

Paige got the papers for me, but after she handed them over, I paused, my thumb hovering over the phone buttons. Did I want to do this? Spontaneity wasn't my strong suit. "What if I can't find a place?" I asked.

She waved toward my computer. "You just found half a dozen places," she said. "And you should be as close to Stormy as she'll allow. If you can't move in as quickly as you need to and need a place to stay . . . well, we'll figure something out."

"You're amazing," I whispered.

She tossed her hair over one shoulder and blinked rapidly. "I know."

I punched in the number without another hesitation. The call went to voice mail, but I left a detailed message, stating that other considerations had come up and I would need to cancel the contract. I was glad Paige wasn't mad about me having wasted her time. She seemed to understand that I hadn't factored in Stormy wanting me close to her, and that bit of new information trumped all else.

Around nine o'clock, Jared and Stormy came in. They'd gotten almost everything boxed up and said they'd come back on Thursday to do a final pack. I turned my laptop to face her. "You got me thinking," I said.

Stormy was confused for half a second, and then her eyebrows lifted and she took over my computer completely, scooting next to me on the bed to look at the listings I'd found.

"This one's closest to work," I said, pointing to the one I was most interested in. I was talking to Stormy, but looking at Jared. Would I be stepping on his toes by moving so close?

"Nice place," he said with a smile. "Let me know if I can help."

"This one," Stormy said, turning the laptop to face me.

Jared took a few steps closer so he could see the screen as well. "Is that Harbor Glen?"

"What's Harbor Glen?" I asked, looking between them both.

"It's across the street from my complex," Jared said.

Stormy quickly followed up. "If you're gonna move down there, you might as well be close, right? And they have double hot tubs. I know a girl who lives over there. It's nice."

I looked at Jared again, but he didn't seem bothered by the idea of me moving so close.

"Come on, Storm," he said, waving Stormy toward the door. "Your mama needs her beauty rest."

Stormy stood up and put the laptop on the bed, giving me a coy smile.

"Is that what this is?" I said, feeling lighter than I had in a long time. "Well, I'm on my way to being a total knockout, then." I flipped my flat, two-days unwashed hair over my shoulder much like Paige had done earlier, only she'd looked cute, and I looked homeless.

Stormy laughed before disappearing through the doorway. Jared hesitated and looked back at me. "Let me know if you want me to go look at places or anything," he said. "I think it would be great if you were closer. It would be good for Stormy."

Chapter 41

I STAYED UP UNTIL ALMOST ELEVEN, working on things for Naomi to do at the office in the morning and avoiding the urge to sleep when I wasn't tired. The evening had me all riled up. I'd already sent an e-mail inquiry to the Harbor Glen manager, and I planned to call the manager for the other apartment complex first thing in the morning to officially cancel my contract.

It didn't help my insomnia that I missed having Paul beside me, and yet I was annoyed to be wanting him. I pushed those thoughts away and chose to obsess about work instead. I hated not going to work. I held on to the hope that in another week I'd be able to return to light duty. Maybe I could go to work for a few hours a day, so long as I always took the elevator.

I slept in the next morning—what was there to get up for?—but was awakened by the sound of a door opening. I blinked several times to fully wake up and then pulled myself up in bed.

"Hello?" I asked, looking at the clock: 8:31. Stormy was in school—or at least she'd better be. Who else had a key?

Paul suddenly appeared in the doorway, hands in his pockets and tension in his shoulders. He had a duffel bag over his shoulder.

I immediately began smoothing my hair, despite being rendered speechless by his unexpected arrival.

"Hey," he said, looking cautious and . . . dare I say repentant?

"Hey," I said back. He must have forgotten something and needed to pick it up. But why the duffel bag? Seeing him made me want to cry for several different reasons.

He pushed himself away from the doorway in a kind of forced lazy movement and dropped the duffel bag with a soft thump before coming into the room.

I could not ignore how attracted I was to him, how much I still loved him. How much I wanted him to stay.

"Your friend called me," he said. "Last night."

"My friend?"

"I think her name was Paige?"

Paige called him? I wasn't sure what I thought about that. How did she get his number?

He stopped a few feet away from the bed. I smoothed the blanket over my belly, which suddenly reminded me why he'd left in the first place. I wondered what Paige had said to him.

"I'm sorry about everything," he said. "I was out of line."

I was speechless for the second time in less than a minute, but I quickly gathered my thoughts and asked, "What about your future?" I was hesitant to forgive too quickly or too easily, even though his words washed over me like sunshine.

He looked at me with those little-boy eyes that always accompanied an apology. "You're my future, Daisy."

My heart betrayed my intent to keep perspective on this turn of events and began to soar. What woman in my situation wouldn't want to hear those exact words from the man she loved and feared she had lost? I felt myself smile as my eyes blurred with tears. Last night I'd told

Stormy I wouldn't trust Paul even if he did return. I was a complete liar. He was here, and I just wanted him to stay.

"Really?" I whispered, choking on the word. Was this real, or was I still dreaming?

He sat on the bed and reached out to tuck my horrible hair behind my ear. "I missed you."

The tears overflowed, and he used his thumb to brush them away before leaning in for a kiss. I put my hands on either side of his face and lost myself in the kiss for several seconds. It deepened, he moved closer, wrapping his arms around my back, and I melted into him, carried away by the chemistry and desperation to renew this connection.

I'm not abandoned. I'm not alone.

The kiss became more intense. His hands began to move; my body began responding. And then I remembered, and pulled back.

"I can't," I said, breathless and brimming with regret.

"Can't what?"

"Be with you like . . . that."

"Why?"

"Bed rest," I said, hating it more than ever at this moment. "I can't do anything that endangers the pregnancy." But he'd come back . . . "I'm sorry."

How could I say no to him?

He pulled away and smiled, but I knew it was forced, at least a little bit. "I understand," he said with a nod.

He understood!

"I've got some stuff to do at the office, but I'll come back this afternoon if that's okay."

"Yes," I said, wiping at my eyes and bobbing my head. "Of course it's okay."

He gave me one more kiss, then winked at me on his way out of the room, leaving the duffel bag in the doorway of the bedroom. I was jubilant.

As soon as the door closed behind him, I grabbed my cell phone from the bed and texted Paige.

Paul's back!

It was almost ten minutes before she responded.

For good?

I felt bad for bothering her at work but not bad enough not to reply. I paused and looked at the doorway where Paul had disappeared. Was he here for good? I hoped so. Why would he have come back if not to stay?

Daisy: I think so. You called him?

Paige: Yes. I thought he should know. Is that okay?

Daisy: Totally okay. I can't believe he's here!!!

Paige: Congrats. So . . . are you still moving?

Was I? I'd totally forgotten about the phone call I needed to make to follow up on canceling the first apartment.

Daisy: I'll call the manager at 9:00 to make sure he got my message, but I was going to cancel it anyway.

Paige: Maybe hold off on renting the new one until you know what's going on with Paul.

Daisy: Good idea. Thank you for your help.

Paige: Of course.

I lay back on the pillows and considered this shift. I wanted so badly for everything to be okay between Paul and me and for us to move forward the way I had initially hoped we would when he learned about the baby. I put a hand on my belly and took a deep breath, daring to believe that this child was a test of our true devotion to one another and that his return meant we were passing with flying colors.

Paige texted me again.

Paige: What about book group? I'd hate to do it without you,
   but don't want to intrude.

Daisy: We can do it here. That would be perfect!

Paige: Okay. Good luck. Call if you need ANYTHING.

Daisy: I will. Thank you SO much.

I texted Stormy, and she called me at lunch. I didn't try to read her tone too much. I didn't want her to be disappointed that I wasn't moving closer, and I hoped she could appreciate how big this was for me. In the end, she was supportive. What more could I ask from a seventeen-year-old than that?

Paul came home at one o'clock. He'd picked up my favorite chicken salad sandwich from a deli around the corner. That's the kind of guy he was—the kind who remembered how much I liked their chicken salad. He worked in the other room for the rest of the afternoon. I had a million questions I wanted to ask, but I didn't dare. I didn't want to upset the fragility of him being here. I was banking on the fact that we'd have lots of time to discuss details.

I finished *Silas Marner* and put my hand on my belly, thinking about the man Silas had become through the love of a child. I was a different woman because of December. Different still because of Stormy too. What kind of changes would this new baby bring into my life? It was a relief to consider the positive possibilities now that I had overcome the hard thoughts and emotions.

Paul made cheese enchiladas for dinner and brought a plate to me on a tray before bringing in a chair and a TV tray for his own meal. I felt like a smitten fourteen-year-old girl the way I was smiling at him. "Thank you."

"You bet," he said as he began to eat. It was delicious; Paul was a wonderful cook. Partway through the meal, he asked how I was feeling. It was the first time since all this had begun that he'd asked about that. I took it as a good sign—an important milestone.

"I feel okay," I said. "Stressed about missing so much work, of course, and already bored to tears from being in bed all the time, though Paige brought me some books and that's helped. I might bat my eyelashes and see if you could bring the bedroom TV in here."

"I could probably do that," he said, using his fork to stab a piece of cheese-drenched tortilla. "How long do you think it'll be until you get feeling better?"

Feeling better?

"I go back to the doctor in a week, and then he'll do another ultrasound to see where things are at. Hopefully, the placenta has moved, and I'll be able to get up a little bit."

Paul took another bite, looking at his plate. He seemed confused by what I'd said, so I reviewed it, wondering if something was hard to understand. It was likely all confusing—this was upper level woman stuff, not his forte.

"Maybe you should come sleep in our room. I can keep my hands to myself."

I smiled, loving the invitation back to our marital bed. "The question is, can *I*?"

But I did go back to our room, back to our bed, and I reveled in Paul's presence against my back, his soft snores in my ear. He'd returned, and I was so happy about that, but something niggled and stretched somewhere in the corner of my mind, something that didn't fit. I didn't want to shine the beam of my searchlight into that corner. Couldn't I have faith in being happy? Hadn't I prayed for help?

Finally, I closed my eyes and let my breathing match his. It had been a very hard month; I needed to let go of the pessimism that things never worked out and enjoy the fact that Paul was here with me, for me. I needed to be grateful for that and stop waiting for the next shoe to drop.

Chapter 42

BY THE END OF THE WORKDAY on Friday, I felt like Naomi and I had figured out a good rhythm. The IT department gave me instructions that Paul helped me follow that allowed me to access the company database remotely, and that was a huge benefit. Being busy was good medicine. Paul was too.

I highlighted specific parts of *Silas Marner* and read another book Paige had given me—she had excellent taste. Considering the circumstances, I thought things were going smoothly. Paul and I were getting along, I was feeling good, and the baby was moving around a lot.

The only downside was that Paul and I hadn't really talked. Not about what had happened, or what would happen in the future. We talked about work and current events and his hunting trip with Charlie, but nothing about us and the boxes still packed and stacked the way that Jared, Stormy, and Paige had left them. It was almost as though there was an electric fence around the topic of the state of our relationship, and anytime we got close, we could hear the voltage buzzing and we slowly backed away. I didn't like it, but I also didn't do anything to change it. I didn't want to be the one who put my hand on the fence only to find out it had been set to "Kill."

Friday afternoon I picked up another of Paige's books—*The Help*. I'd heard about it but couldn't remember if what I'd heard was good or bad. I remember hearing the movie was good but that it was the kind of film you went to see with your best girlfriends and I didn't really have any of those—not the movie kind. Actually, Paige and Livvy would fit that bill nowadays, which was a fun discovery. Would they come over for a movie night if I rented it? Would Athena or Ruby want to come too? It was a big book, which was why I'd avoided it until now. But I still had more than a week left before I went back to Dr. Cortez; I had time to finish a big book.

The book was set in the south of the 1960s. I had a hard time getting into it, but didn't know if that was because of the book or because I was distracted by Paul being here and that we hadn't talked about what was between us.

Eventually, however, the story grabbed me by both hands as though sitting me down in a chair and saying, "Listen." The women in the book were nothing like me—two of the characters were black maids, the third was a single white girl who'd been raised by a black maid. They all lived in Mississippi. Yet the more I read, the more they felt like me. Or maybe I saw bits of myself in them. Which didn't make sense and yet fit perfectly.

I had to use a bathroom break to stock up on tissues when one of the characters had a miscarriage. It resurrected the pain I'd felt when I'd lost the baby during my divorce from Jared. Even though I had told myself I didn't want the baby and that it was better that way, it was still a loss. Still heartbreaking. To see the pain I'd felt reflected in someone else broke me open, and I sobbed, having to put the book down for a little while at one point in hopes of getting myself back together.

It wasn't a stretch to think about the little life inside of me now, a life I hadn't wanted and had prayed and wished would go away. But it hadn't gone away, and right then I was so grateful that prayer hadn't been answered. It made me wonder if having prayers go unanswered was sometimes the very answer we needed. It took some working through of my own situation before I could return to the story. The book was such a reflection of the good and bad and ignorance of people—on both sides of the Civil Rights issues of the time.

Despite the fact that he'd just returned, Paul had a conference in Sacramento on Friday. He'd warned me he'd be home late. When Paige found out, she offered to bring dinner, and when Stormy found out Paige was bringing food and the boys, she said she wanted to come too. I, of course, cried when the plan came together. Everything was working out, and I was so grateful for the support I didn't even know I had.

Stormy showed up at six, and we had half an hour or so to chat before Paige showed up with dinner from my favorite Mexican grill for us and chicken nuggets and fries for the boys. The boys were far more excited to see Stormy than they were about their food, though, and I loved seeing how much they adored her. I knew she'd been tending for Paige, but I didn't realize how comfortable they all were with one another. She might be a better big sister than I thought she'd be, and yet little tremors of jealousy flitted about within me as well. I wanted Stormy and me to be okay—totally and completely okay—but we weren't. Not yet. I envied the friendship she had with Paige, unencumbered by all the complexities of our current situation.

Paige handed everyone their food—I hoped the expense hadn't been too much for her—and assured the boys that she wasn't leaving; apparently they equated Stormy's presence with their mother's absence.

Stormy grabbed a blanket and spread it on the floor of the bedroom. "Let's make it a picnic!" she said, sitting cross-legged. The boys plopped down beside her and dug in while I arranged my pulled pork salad.

We'd only just started when Nate came to his mom for a bite. He was so cute, and I had that reminder of second chances. Or in my case, third.

"Oh, I could just eat him up. Your boys are such sweet things," I said.

"They are," she agreed, looking at them with a faint smile on her face. "I'm lucky to have such great little men, aren't I?"

What if I had a boy? Would I know how to take care of him? Would he be as cute as Paige's boys?

"So, Paige . . ." Stormy said, popping a fry into her mouth and looking up at us. There was a sparkle in her eye that warned me she was up to something. I braced myself.

"Yeah?" Paige said as she took another bite.

"Tell us about your boyfriend." Stormy grinned.

"Wait, your *what*?" I blurted out as Paige's face turned bright red.

She tried to look casual, but her face had already betrayed her. "I don't have a boyfriend."

"Then what do you call that cute guy you've been hanging out with?" Stormy challenged.

"You've never seen him," Paige said strongly, losing the casual air she was trying to hold on to.

"Then he *does* exist," I threw in, looking between the two of them.

"Oh, yeah, he does." Stormy looked a bit too pleased with herself. "And he *is* a boyfriend, Paige, like it or not. What else would you call him?"

I put down my fork and crossed my arms expectantly. "Yes, what do you call a man—a *cute* man—you're hanging out with regularly? Is it that Derryl guy you went out with a while ago?"

Paige threw Stormy a frustrated look. "I thought you could keep a secret."

"Oh, come on," I said, waving away her attempt at annoyance. "I'm stuck in bed with nothing but the TV and an occasional book to keep me company. I need a good story. Fess up."

She gave in, but busied herself with her meal instead of looking at either one of us.

"His name is Derryl Freestone."

"And?" I demanded when it seemed as though she might stop there.

"And we met in the building's cafeteria during lunch. He works on the third floor."

"Wait—that's a law firm, isn't it?" I said, smiling even wider. "He's a *lawyer*? Is he a partner?"

"Not yet, but he thinks he might make partner in the next year, depending on how one of his cases turns out."

She didn't elaborate, but I could see that all kinds of thoughts were going through her mind. I was happy for her, really happy. Any man who ended up with Paige was very lucky indeed, but I sensed her concern and insecurity. I understood that too. When one happily ever after falls apart, it's hard to believe in it the next time around.

"I, for one, am thrilled to hear it. You need some spice in your life—a man." I nearly added how wonderful Paul was, how he'd convinced me that it could work a second time around, but it still felt rather fragile.

Nathan popped up again and took Stormy's hand. "Come here."

She obliged, lifting Shawn off her lap and following the two boys out of the room and to, I presumed, the kitchen, where, a moment later, sounds of drums rattled—likely plastic and metal containers hit with wooden spoons.

"She's really good with my boys," Paige said. "You've got a great girl there."

I didn't answer at first. Stormy was great, but I wondered if that was more in spite of me than because of my influence. I was very insecure about my parenting.

"You've done a great job raising your daughter," Paige said, as though trying to make the point.

"I've made some mistakes, and we still have our differences, but overall, I got a good one with her, that's for sure." Would Stormy ever move back home? Would we ever live together like mother and daughter again?

"Do you mind if I ask you a question?" Paige asked, saving me from my worries for a moment.

"Not at all," I said, relieved to have our conversation continue.

"How long after your divorce did you marry Paul?"

"Twelve years." That seemed to surprise her, so I continued. "And no, I didn't wait for some noble reason, if that's what you're thinking. I was just caught up in taking care of my two girls as best I could. You know how hard being a single mom is. It simply took that long for Paul to show up and sweep me off my feet." Paul had been such a blessing. I wanted so badly to believe that this crisis was behind us and that we would both grow from it and be better for it.

"He's really that great?" Paige pressed. Her question hit me harder than I wanted it to, but she seemed to read that through my expression and hurried to continue. "I mean, doesn't the honeymoon period wear off? Two people can't remain all twitter-pated and lovey-dovey forever, right? What happened when that wore off? I made a bad choice for a husband the first time, but he sure looked like a knight in shining armor in the beginning. I don't know that I trust my judgment for a second round. For that matter, I don't know that I trust men in general. Derryl's great—he's fun and sweet, and yes, he's good looking. But . . . things change after marriage, you know?"

"Oh, I know," I said with an emphatic nod.

"Right," Paige said, nodding eagerly. "Daily life gets in the way. The best face you've kept on display while dating has to drop at some point, and the real you comes out. And when that happens, what will I discover I'm stuck with? Will I end up with another Carol in my life or something equally as bad?"

"Carol?"

"Doug's new wife." She played with her food and sighed. "Maybe I'm not making any sense."

"No, you're making total sense," I said. "You're afraid because you can't really know a person before marrying them."

Tears rose in her eyes and she nodded. "That's it exactly. I enjoy dating Derryl, but I'm not sure it's for the right reasons. He's got money, for starters."

"And he's cute, from what I hear," I said with a smile.

She nodded, but her mood was still heavy. Did she feel guilty that he had money? Paul had money, and I'd never seen that as a drawback. Then I thought about the rough patch Paul and I were in. I hadn't seen it coming, and I thought I knew him pretty well. There were no guarantees, but how could I tell her that without sounding hopeless?

"Doug called before Christmas," she said, "and Stormy answered. She told him where I was—and who I was with." She leaned toward me conspiratorially, as though whatever she was about to say was something she didn't want anyone overhearing. "And when I heard about it, I was *glad*."

"News flash, Paige—you're human. Your ex is moving on and has a new woman in his life. It's totally normal that you moving on with a new man would feel good."

"But it's more than me feeling good about my life."

"I know. Dating another man is a way to wound your ex—show him that you don't need him. I've been there," I said with a shrug. "I remember. I was bitter for a long, long time. What you're feeling is okay."

"But it's *not* okay," she said, shaking her head. "Nothing's okay. This wasn't how my life was supposed to turn out. My boys need a dad. But is Derryl the person who should fill that role? I really, really like him. Maybe even love him." She squeezed her eyes shut and shook her head again. "I don't know how I feel. Am I in love with *him* or with the *idea* of him and everything he's changed in my life? I love the *idea* of not having to work anymore. Of being home with my boys. Of maybe having another child or two. Of not worrying about money. Of . . ." She sighed, obviously struggling to make sense of all her conflicting thoughts and feelings.

I reached across the bed and took her hands in both of mine. "Hey, you listen to me."

She looked up, and I held her gaze. "Just take it one day at a time, one step at a time. Derryl might be the one. He might not be. Either one is *okay*. And you don't need to know which one he is, not yet. There's plenty of time to wait. Don't rush it. You've only known him a few months."

She nodded, looking relieved. I was glad I'd said the right thing. "You know what else?" I nodded toward the door, where the boys and

Stormy had disappeared. Something crashed in the kitchen, followed by a shriek of laughter. "Your boys are growing up fast. Just since I've known them, they've gotten bigger. Nathan has doubled his vocabulary. Shawn's reading more and even learned to ride a bike. Don't let this time with them slip away. Once it's gone, it's gone, and there's no getting it back. Don't waste their childhoods worrying about the future and the what-ifs. The future will work itself out, one day at a time. But if you live in worry of it, the present will pass you by, and next thing you know, your boys will be snarky teenagers who don't want to talk to their mother."

My own words hit me. *Don't let this time slip away. The future will work itself out.*

Stormy's laughter echoed down the hall, and the smile I'd intended became a little more forced. Maybe if I'd done things differently, Stormy and I would be different, but like I'd told Paige, you don't get those days back. Which meant I needed to double my efforts to make these days really count. I wasn't done mothering my daughters, and I needed to stop seeing a finish line somewhere. As long as I was here, and they were here, there was opportunity. The idea wrapped me up and gave me a lump in my throat.

"I'll try to remember that. Thanks." A new round of tears welled up in her eyes, but she didn't seem as burdened as she wiped at her eyes. "Enough of tears. I'm a neurotic mess."

I laughed as we turned back to our meals again. "Aren't we all?"

Chapter 43

PAUL CAME HOME AROUND eight thirty—Paige and Stormy had already left—and we snuggled in bed with popcorn while watching a movie together. It felt so perfect, so comfortable and normal and right, but we still skirted that electric fence, smiling at one another and being kind, but not going too deep. I didn't know how long I could do this, but I wasn't ready to discuss it either. My conversation with Paige kept coming back to me. *One day at a time. Don't miss the present by worrying about the what-ifs.* I fell asleep beside Paul and woke in time to watch him sleep for a little while before he got up. I enjoyed those moments immensely.

He eventually got going for the day, running errands, taking care of household chores, catching up on work he'd missed because of yesterday's conference. I lay in bed and got lost in *The Help* again. By the time I finished the book that afternoon, I had a whole pile of tissues beside me. I didn't know what to think of it. On the one hand, it was beautiful and educational and so well written. On the other hand, it was raw in places, and it made me so angry. The most uncomfortable part, though, was that, once again, it didn't have a happy ending. Maybe it was happy enough, but it wasn't happy-happy. I had wanted a happy-happy ending. I had wanted big changes and amazing discoveries. Instead, every character went on with their life pretty much as they had been in the beginning, only wiser for what they had experienced together. Good things were on the horizon for some, but bad things were coming for others. It wasn't fair.

And yet one line stood out to me. Toward the end of the book, one of the characters reflected on the fact that while things weren't perfect, she felt that everything had turned out the way it was supposed to.

Why did that make me uncomfortable?

Paul started straightening up for book group while I continued to ruminate on *The Help*. I hated feeling like an invalid, and then I felt like an escaped convict when I got up to take my shower for the day. I hadn't had any additional spotting since Thursday, which, to me, seemed like proof that remaining on bed rest was silly, but I didn't dare risk it, so I took my three-minute shower and then pulled my hair into a sloppy bun to save me from having to do anything with it. I did my makeup in bed and felt better once I could smile at myself in the mirror and admit I looked human for the first time in three days. I was pathetically excited about book group tonight. Paul, though gracious to prepare the house, disappeared into the bedroom as soon as the first attendee, Paige, arrived.

I'd chosen to wear a powder-blue top Paige had helped me pick out a couple of weeks ago. It looked huge until I put it on and frowned at how snug it was. The stretchy maternity capris were just as unflattering, but at least my toes were still cute from my last pedicure. If nothing else, I had glittery toes. I was on the love seat when Paige came in holding a pie tin; she was wearing a green top that made her eyes sparkle. She set her purse by the door and headed into the kitchen.

"What did you bring?"

"Lime cheesecake," she said from the other room.

"Key lime?"

"No, uh, lime Jell-O cheesecake. It's out of this ward cookbook I have."

"Ward?"

"Oh, a *ward* is a Mormon congregation," she said, reappearing. I didn't ask any more questions but wondered if they realized how strange it was to depict a group of religious people as a *ward*. She hugged me before pulling back and looking me over. "You look great."

"I'm telling your minister you're a liar. What's his number?"

"I don't have a minister. Mormons have bishops. And you aren't getting his name *or* his number." Paige laughed and sat down, pulling her trim little legs up underneath her and leaning her elbow on the arm of the couch. She opened her mouth to say something just as the doorbell rang, and she popped up to answer it.

It was Ruby, decked out in a shimmery blue blouse over black pants. She immediately swooped in, and I reached up to get as much of her powder-smelling hug as possible. When she pulled back, she asked all kinds of questions about how I was doing and what I needed. I assured her that I had all my needs met, grateful that she didn't know about Paul's leaving and subsequent return.

Athena came in right behind her, still looking burdened and beautiful. She didn't come over and hug me, but we didn't really have a huggy relationship, so that was okay. Ruby hugged her, however; Ruby had a huggy relationship with everyone. She informed us that both Shannon and Ilana were unable to make it. I was disappointed, but I hadn't connected with them as much as I had with the others so I didn't necessarily miss them. I hoped the change of location from Ruby's house to my house hadn't made it too far out of their way.

Livvy was the last to arrive and apologized profusely for being late. It took me a moment to realize what was different about her.

"Your hair," I heard myself say after I figured it out. "It looks awesome."

My announcement made her the object of everyone's attention, and she reached up and smoothed her hair that had recently been colored a beautiful burnished brown. It was a very nice fit for the red flush that had crept up into her cheeks. It was cut in an A-line bob and was perfect for her.

"You like it?" she asked.

We all assured her that it looked wonderful, and I could tell from her smile that she appreciated the feedback but was hesitant to believe it completely. "I was ready for a change," she said by way of explanation, still standing just inside the doorway.

"Well, it was a good one," Paige said.

As though suddenly realizing she was still the center of attention, Livvy quickly sat on the couch between Paige and Athena, but she was smiling. I wondered what had happened since that day she'd come to my rescue three weeks ago. She looked different, and it wasn't just the hair.

"So," Ruby said from her spot on the kitchen chair Paul had brought in earlier. She looked directly at me. "You need to give us a bit of an update, young lady. An awful lot has happened since we met in December."

That was the understatement of the New Year. I gave them a quick recap, pointing out Paige and Livvy's roles in the story, though I didn't delve into the emotional train wreck I'd been all month. They asked for pictures of Tennyson, and I passed my phone around, over which they all oohed and aahed.

"So, anyway," I said, concluding my saga. "I'll see what the doctor says next week. Until then, I am your token bump on a log, but I sure appreciate you guys coming all the way up here tonight. I'd have hated to miss it."

"Of course, of course," Ruby said, waving it away. "Athena was gracious enough to have picked me up on her way. We had a wonderful visit." She turned her attention to Athena, who suddenly had a look on her face that seemed to hold a certain hesitation. "Athena's had a big month too."

All eyes were on Athena, which was fine by me since that meant no one was looking at me anymore.

Athena smiled, shy and uncomfortable, and the silence stretched for a few seconds too long. I knew Ruby was waiting for Athena to confess all, but obviously Athena wasn't ready for that. I felt bad she'd missed the November book group and had so many things put on her plate since losing her mom that I hadn't gotten to know her as well as I had the other women.

"So," Paige said, breaking the silence. *Silas Marner.* The topic had been officially changed. "As I said last month, I chose this one because it was short—always nice for the holidays—and because it had kind of a Christmas message. I read this the first time in high school, and I liked it then, but I found that reading it now was even more powerful. Now that I have kids of my own . . ." She paused and looked at me as though for some support. I smiled, though I didn't know what I was encouraging her to do, exactly. "Like Silas, I've felt mistreated by some people I trusted."

Ouch. And yet it was fair, even if it embarrassed me. I also knew she wasn't talking about me specifically. She had far more hurts to deal with than what I'd added to her shoulders.

She continued. "Both of those things stood out to me in regard to

Silas's story, and I felt like I was reading it on a different level than I had before. What did you guys think?"

We all looked at each other, waiting for someone to speak. Ruby was the first who did so. She talked about how she'd always loved the classics but hadn't read this one for years and years, but it made her remember what it was about classic literature that she so appreciated. Her thoughts somehow ended up on her college years—I didn't know she had her master's degree in English literature—and what she felt set *Silas Marner* apart from the other books of its day. It was a fascinating lecture. When she finished, she turned to me and raised her eyebrows.

"Oh, I really liked it," I said, smoothing my hand over the front cover.

"Well, not at first," Paige said, trying to hide a smile.

My gaze flicked toward Paige, and my mouth curved up. "But once I really gave it a chance, I was struck by the fact that some of the most horrible things that happened to Silas were actually building blocks that prepared him to be the man he was by the end of the book. That was refreshing to me."

"I noticed that too," Athena said. "Up until he found Eppie, it was like he wasn't really there. I mean, it was as though he didn't even remember his life or his relationships before he came to Raveloe—like they were a dream. It was like he was asleep, so absorbed by his gold, caring and seeing nothing else. And then Eppie came into his life and became everything to him—she brought all of his life lessons to a head and solidified his life. Does that make sense?"

"That's a great way to put it," Ruby said. "Solidified, became whole."

The comments brought a lump to my throat; all I could do was nod. Was that not an analogy for life, trying to find wholeness? With people we loved, with accomplishments and personal growth?

"The people we love have so much power," Athena said, but a sadness had crept into her voice. "I told you about my mom's life. She was an amazing person. She loved the people in her life. She gave them everything she had. I miss that . . . I mean, her." She looked up and smiled at all of us in a nervous way. "I mean, I miss her."

But we'd all noted the slip. Athena was young, but not that young, and I wondered if she were worried about not having that kind of love in her life again.

"How's your dad?" Livvy asked.

Athena took a breath and shook her head slightly. "I finally did it. He went into the care center right after Christmas," she said quietly, looking at her hands in her lap.

"You did the right thing," I said, wanting to reassure her.

"Thank you," she said.

Livvy patted her knee. "I'm sure he's being very well taken care of."

"He is," Athena said, blinking rapidly, as though the crack in her voice hadn't already betrayed how difficult this was for her to talk about. Livvy put her arm around her, and Athena finally dropped the veil she'd been working so hard to hold up. "He's all alone in there. I feel like I should have done more, especially with my mother gone."

"Dear Athena," Ruby interrupted, leaning forward. "Your mother would have done the same thing."

"You don't know my mother," Athena said.

"How is he when you visit?" Paige asked.

"He's in his own world," Athena said, sounding tired. "I don't remember the last time he called me by name."

"It's a terrible disease," Paige said in a sympathetic voice. "But you did the right thing."

Athena looked around at us as though realizing that we weren't just here, we were *here*. We cared. I knew she didn't have the kind of relationship with her mother like I did with mine; she missed her so much. I tried to remember what I knew about her family. I knew she had a sister, but if Athena was shouldering the burden of deciding on the care for their father, it was no wonder that she felt so alone.

"We can trade off and visit your father with you," Ruby offered. "Maybe having some company will help you put things in perspective."

We all nodded in agreement, and I hoped I'd be off restrictions so that I could do my part.

"Thanks, everyone," Athena whispered.

Livvy handed her a Kleenex she'd seemingly produced by magic.

"And while I'm spilling my heart, Grey and I broke up," she said, dabbing at her eyes. She held up her hand before any of us could start in on the questions. "Don't worry, I'm fine. It turns out he wasn't so perfect after all."

"Are they ever?" I said automatically as everyone else shared their sympathy, then I glanced at the doorway to make sure Paul hadn't overheard me. I wanted to know if the door between Athena and Grey was completely closed or still partway open, but Ruby cut in, for which Athena looked relieved.

"Livvy," Ruby said. "We haven't heard your thoughts on the book."

"Oh, um, I liked it," Livvy said. She smiled but it was plastic. "You guys have pretty much summed up my thoughts. It was a touching story."

"It was, wasn't it?" Ruby mused. "I'm very glad you chose it, Paige."

"Me, too," I said, casting a look at Livvy. There was a crease in her forehead, and she looked a little distracted. I had a feeling she hadn't even read the book.

"Good," Paige said. "I'm glad everyone enjoyed it. Daisy, it's your month to choose one."

"Oh, really?" I said. The baby chose that moment to do a flip, and I put my hand on my belly to re-center myself. I still wasn't used to the sensations of pregnancy. "Um, well, Paige brought me some books. One of them, *The Help*, was really good. I know there was a movie, but I never saw it." I looked around and saw that Paul had set my copy of the book on top of the TV when he'd cleaned up. I pointed at it.

Paige picked it up and handed it to me. "I really liked this book and the movie," she said. "I only know about the Civil Rights movement from the History Channel and movies, but I felt like this really got to the heart of the situation. I had no idea what it was really like, for both sides."

"I like her writing a lot," I said, hoping I sounded reliable. "And it's about some very different women, which seems like a perfect fit for us." I made a little circular wave to encompass all of us.

We set the date for next month's meeting, and I felt flutters of anxiety in my stomach at the thought of what would happen in those four weeks between now and then. So much had happened in the *last* four weeks that it was almost scary to look that far ahead.

Paige served up the Jell-O cheesecake. It was pretty good, though Paige apologized for it profusely, stating she hadn't gotten to the store so she'd had to come up with something she already had the ingredients for. We chatted some more, then one by one, the ladies said their good-byes while I sat with my feet up like some kind of diva. It was so hard not to show them to the door like a proper hostess.

"I left a piece for Paul," Paige said when she came into the living room after retrieving her pie tin. She licked some cream from her finger. "It's on the counter."

"Thank you," I said. "I can't thank you enough for all you've done for me the last few weeks. I'd have been lost without it."

"You are very welcome," Paige said, tilting her head and smiling at me. She looked around the living room as though searching for something, then her gaze settled back on me. "So, did you unpack?"

"Not yet," I said. "I think Paul moved all the boxes into Stormy's room."

Paige furrowed her brow. "But he didn't unpack them?"

She made a good point. He'd been back for three days. Why hadn't he undone the moving efforts? I didn't know what to say to Paige though, and for an instant I resented that she'd even raised the question. I shrugged to emphasize that it wasn't a big deal to me. "It's been crazy." But it *hadn't* been crazy, not really. It had been calm and placid and careful.

Too calm? Too placid? Too careful?

Oh, stop it! I told myself and smiled even wider at Paige, who was watching me as though she could read the thoughts in my head.

"So, what was up with Livvy?" Paige asked, picking up her purse. "Was it just me or did she seem a little out of it?"

"Yeah, she did, didn't she?" I said. "Her hair looked great, though."

"Yeah, it did, but she seemed deep in thought and . . . troubled, I guess. I hope she's okay."

"I'll call her on Monday and check in on her. I haven't talked to her this whole week, but she was calling me every few days before then to check up on me."

"She's a sweetheart, isn't she?"

"She really is," I said, "but she's got issues."

"Oh?" Paige asked, adjusting the strap of her purse on her shoulder.

I didn't feel like it was my place to share my thoughts about her husband, especially since Livvy hadn't verified anything, so I shrugged again. "Don't we all?"

"Don't we, indeed," Paige agreed. She gave me a parting hug and then waved before closing the door behind her.

The house, so recently filled with women whom I had come to care about, seemed quiet and empty without them. I'd almost forgotten about Paul until I heard the bedroom door open. I twisted in the chair and smiled at him when he came into view. I wanted that smile to quiet the niggling little worry in the corner of my mind, but it wasn't working. Even though she hadn't meant to, Paige had got me thinking in a direction I'd been trying to avoid.

"How'd it go?" he asked.

"Great. They are really wonderful women," I said. "Paige left you some pie."

"Cool. Can I get you anything?"

"No," I said. He turned away but stopped when I called his name. "Paul?"

"Huh?" he asked, turning back to me.

"Thank you for coming back."

He smiled and nodded before heading into the kitchen, and I felt my smile drop. I had hoped for more reassurance than that.

Chapter 44

I WAS DETERMINED TO STAY out of bed for the rest of the night. I was so sick of the walls of my bedroom that being in the living room seemed like a vacation. I did move to the couch so I could stretch out on my left side, since I'd been sitting up all evening, and I even watched a basketball game with Paul and told myself it was interesting. After the game we watched the news.

The silence was getting to me, especially in the wake of the great discussion I'd had with the book group ladies. Paul and I really hadn't talked much since he'd returned, and I missed our conversations. We'd gotten used to being together again, and he must know I wasn't angry at him anymore.

Was I ever angry, or just sad?

"So the book we read for book group last month was really great," I said.

"Oh, yeah?" he asked, turning away from the toothpaste commercial. "What was it?"

"*Silas Marner.* It's a classic by George Eliot, who was actually a woman. She took on a man's pen name, because back then women weren't thought to be capable of writing. They weren't thought to be capable of much, actually."

"Ah," he said with a grin. "Sounds hoity-toity."

I smiled. "Kinda, huh? It was good though. It's about a man who finds his real treasure."

"His real treasure?" Paul asked, engaged.

I gave him a brief recap but noticed that his attention waned. "So by the end of the story . . ." I stopped.

Paul had already turned back to the TV.

"What?" I asked.

"I'm here, aren't I?" he said sharply.

"What's that supposed to mean?"

"It means I came back."

I'd figured out that much, so why did he have to point it out? "I know," I said, confused and not sure I was ready to pursue the conversation. "Anyway, it was a really great story. It gave me hope."

"Hope for what?" he asked, still looking at the TV.

Did I dare dig into this? Was I ready? I took a breath and decided that I was. "Hope for us, for our family."

He looked at me quickly, but he didn't say anything. Instead he stood and headed into the kitchen with his empty pie plate in one hand and the empty bottle of beer in the other. He came back with another bottle and leaned in the doorway.

I didn't like that I was looking up at him due to my reclined position. It was so tempting to smile, to compliment him on something, and let this opportunity pass, but I didn't. I couldn't.

"What's going on in your head, Paul?" I asked. "I'm trying to read you, but I'm not making heads or tails of it."

"I don't know what you mean." He tipped the beer and took a long swig. "I'm an open book."

I could feel all the niggling worries I'd had begin to funnel down, lining themselves up like dominos. "You never apologized for leaving."

My statement was inviting an apology, but he didn't take the bait. He took another drink, and I went on. "And you haven't said a word about the moving boxes. Should we unpack, or are we doing a trial run here?"

He looked toward the TV; I watched him carefully. He hung back, keeping the distance, not wanting to get too close.

"Why did you come back, Paul?" I tried to prepare myself for an answer I might not be ready for.

"Because Paige said you were having problems. I was worried about you."

"Were you worried about the baby?"

Another swig of beer. No words.

"Paul," I said, trying to stay calm even though I could feel a black hole opening up in my chest. "Were you worried about the baby?"

He took a deep breath. "I want you to be okay," he said, almost as though he were surrendering. "I want our life back."

"Our life without a baby in it," I summarized. The implosion began, and the hazy shapes that had shifted back and forth in my mind began to take on a sharper focus. A painful one. "You came back because if I lost the baby, like last time, we could still have the life we'd planned out before this happened."

"I'm going to bed," he said, pushing away from the door frame and turning toward the bedroom. A minute later the bedroom door closed, and I stared at the wall while mentally scattering the dried petals of hope I'd cultivated and grown since he'd walked back through that door.

I thought back to *The Help,* to the line that had stood out to me so strongly. Maybe everything was working out the way it should.

Not with a happy ending, but the way it was supposed to happen.

The thought cut deeply, and yet the pain I expected to feel at the discovery didn't hurt the way I imagined it would. Is a happy ending worth it if it's not right? Is a happy ending always the *best* ending?

It wasn't that Paul wasn't the man I'd married, I suddenly realized, but he wasn't the man I could raise a child with. He had come back for *me,* which in its way was sweet and affirming of how much he loved me, but it wasn't enough. Not anymore. I was now a package deal, and by rejecting this baby, he'd rejected us both.

Chapter 45

"Partial bed rest is still a restriction," Dr. Cortez said to me the following Wednesday after finishing the ultrasound and verifying that the baby was okay. "The placenta is rising, and that's good, but you still have a partial eclipse, and that carries a big risk. You need to spend eighty percent of your day sitting or lying down. No lifting. No going into the office. No intercourse. No stress."

I grunted. No stress? What a joke.

"I have good people around me," I said with a sincere smile. "And I don't want to take any risks." Livvy had driven me to the doctor's office when she realized I was planning to go alone, and she was in the waiting room.

"Any cramping, bleeding, or pain, you call my office, okay?"

I nodded. "Okay."

"Do you want to know if it's a boy or a girl?"

My breath caught in my throat. I nodded, and he smiled widely while shutting the chart. "A boy."

A boy, I repeated in my head. "I've never done boys."

"Life is full of new horizons," he said, standing up and putting out a hand to help pull me up. "Congratulations."

I walked to the waiting room, and Livvy looked up at me expectantly.

"My sentence has been commuted," I said, treasuring the knowledge that I was having a son for a moment before I said it out loud. I should tell December first, I decided. She'd been last for everything else. "Sort of."

"Sort of is good," Livvy said, standing up. I'd updated her about the situation with Paul on the drive over and about the new apartment I'd found across the street from Stormy and Jared. So far, I'd done everything online, but Jared was going to bring me the contract to sign tomorrow. Paul was still staying in the house, but I'd returned to Stormy's room until I could get moved into my new place, which, I hoped, would be next week.

Paul and I were cordial, but distant. I cried myself to sleep at night, and he seemed to be feeling sorry for himself. The gap between us widened a little more each day, like watching someone slowly die of an illness without a cure. He was there, but he was gone. It broke my heart, and yet I took solace from . . . something. Maybe from Ruby continuing on despite the loss of her husband. Maybe from Athena making difficult decisions about her father's care. Maybe from Livvy keeping a smile while I knew she was waging a battle all her own. And maybe from Paige, who didn't have the life she'd worked for but was raising her boys and trying to figure out a new future.

"My kids can help with the move," Livvy said as she buckled her seat belt, reminding me to blink back the tears that had started to rise.

"I feel horrible having so many people help me," I said, truly meaning it. "I have a moving company I can call."

"We'll come over anyway, just in case. It's good for us to help each other," Livvy said. "And it's good for you to be helped too—it's what connects people. Service and compassion."

Livvy's words reflected my own discovery of the price of my

independence, and at that moment, I dropped the wall of not asking for help. What was I so afraid of? The fact was that the last few months had been a crash course on humility. For all my perfect planning and hard work, there were still mountains left for me to climb, but I had faith—that word resonated in my head—that the vistas I would bask in would be worth the journey. It was a journey I had never taken alone, but for some reason I'd wanted to believe it had been a solitary trip. I reached over and gave Livvy's arm a squeeze. "Thank you."

She smiled in a way that affirmed she felt good helping me. Allowing her to do so was a positive thing in her life. Go figure. "You're welcome."

We drove in silence for a minute, and I thought about the last few months and the changes that had taken place in my life. There was no denying that the women I'd met through book group had made a difference in my life; something I certainly hadn't expected when I'd decided to go that Saturday night last October. I thought about the books we'd read and how each one of them had impacted me. *The Poisonwood Bible* had been full of such incredible insights. *My Name Is Asher Lev* had led me to reflect on my relationship with both my childhood religion and my current belief system. It also helped me see my parents a little differently. I could now see that they truly believed what they lived. It worked for them, and, lucky for me, I didn't have to be cut off because I didn't choose it for myself. *Silas Marner* had been overwhelming on so many levels. Of all the books we'd read, that one had made the biggest impact on me, as it seemed to parallel my current challenges and led me to some rich discoveries. And *The Help* showcased the way every woman had something hard in her life, but a different kind of hard.

I glanced at Livvy and the thoughtful expression on her face. I sensed a kind of anxiousness coming from her, that things were changing in her life. I didn't know what they were, exactly, but I had no doubt they were good changes. I wanted to be there for those changes; I wanted to do my part to help her just as she'd done her part in helping me. I wondered what she would think of *The Help*. Would it impact her the way it had me?

"I've already read *The Help* if you want to borrow Paige's copy," I offered.

"Next month's book?" Livvy asked.

I nodded. "Have you read it?"

"No," she said. "In fact I didn't finish *Silas Marner* before the meeting. I meant to, but I . . . lost it. But then after you guys were all so touched by the story, I found a copy at the library. It really had some good messages."

"It did," I agreed. "Did it ruin the story for us to have discussed it before you finished?"

"Not at all," Livvy said. "Just the opposite—I knew what to look for. I've always believed it's the choices we make in our lives that define who we really are at our core, and I felt like the book emphasized that. I can see that I've made a lot of good choices in my life, but I've made some mistakes—actually, I've made the same few mistakes over and over again, and I'm going to do better now."

I knew there was more to her story, but I sensed she didn't want to tell it right now. I was okay with that.

There are public demons and there are private ones, and sometimes, like in my situation, they get turned around on us; Livvy was entitled to her privacy. And, honestly, the details didn't really matter. I'd seen her change over the months, and that was enough for me. I realized there was something I needed to say to Livvy, and I took a deep breath.

"I think you're a wonderful person, Livvy," I said. "And I misjudged you."

She looked over at me, a little startled by what I'd said. I hurried to clarify. "The first week we met, I saw you as . . . less than you are. I didn't see past my own fears and stereotyping to get a sense of who you really are. I'm ashamed of myself for having done that because I can't imagine how I would have dealt with all of this if you weren't so . . . *you*."

"So *me*?" Livvy said with a nervous laugh. "That's not always a good thing."

"Well, it's been good for me," I said, leaning back against the seat, glad that I'd been able to say what I needed to tell her. "I want to be the kind of mom who loves her family, Livvy, who wants to take care of them, and who takes pride in what she's done. I haven't really been that kind of mom. My goals and priorities have been mixed up, but I have another chance." I looked at my belly and thought of Stormy and December and little Tennyson.

What would I name this one? Christian, maybe, after my dad, and as a reminder that I didn't need to turn my back on everything to be myself. The thought made me smile.

"Second chances are priceless," Livvy said in a soft voice.

"Yes, they are," I agreed.

I'll get it right this time, I said to myself and to whoever else might be listening.

You're not alone, a voice said, and I felt a lump in my throat and tears in my eyes. I glanced at Livvy and thought about the other book group ladies, about my daughters, my mother, and even Jared, of all people. For all my insistence on doing everything myself and proving that I was capable, I really *couldn't* do it by myself, at least not well, and I didn't have to. That was a big discovery.

"I'm feeling like ice cream," Livvy said as she slowed down at a light. She looked over at me and lifted her eyebrows. "What does the pregnant lady think? Drive-through on the way home?"

I laughed. "The pregnant lady thinks that's a great idea." I put my hands on my belly. "We both do."

Rolo Cookies

½ cup butter
½ cup shortening
1 cup white sugar
1 cup brown sugar
2 teaspoons vanilla
2 eggs
2½ cups flour
¾ cup cocoa
½ teaspoon salt
1 teaspoon baking soda
approximately 48 Rolo candies, unwrapped*

Preheat oven to 375 degrees. In a large mixing bowl, cream butter, shortening, and sugars until smooth. Add vanilla and eggs. Mix until smooth. Add flour, cocoa, salt, and baking soda. Mix until combined.

Using approximately a tablespoon of dough, wrap the dough around a Rolo, covering the candy completely. Repeat until all Rolos are used. Place Rolo-wrapped dough balls on baking sheet, 2 inches apart.

Bake for 6 to 8 minutes, or until tops of cookies are just beginning to set. Do not overbake; the caramel will harden when cookie cools if you do. Let cookies cool on pan for at least 3 minutes before removing them to a cooling rack. Wait until cookies are completely cooled before eating; otherwise, the caramel might burn you. Store cookies in an airtight container with a piece of bread to keep cookies soft.

Makes 48 cookies.

*Also works with bite-sized Snickers bars instead of Rolo candies.

Paige

Coming September 2012

the Newport Ladies Book Club

Paige

a novel

ANNETTE LYON

Chapter 1

I SAT ON A PADDED BENCH on one side of the chapel with my boys. The building felt like home in some ways. There was the typical VISITORS WELCOME sign outside. Inside, the walls had paintings I'd seen in other chapels. I could guess with relative accuracy where the Primary room was, where to find the Relief Society room, the tithing slips, and even the restrooms.

But this wasn't home. The congregation—my new ward—was filled with strange faces.

During the opening hymn, I watched the woman conducting. I scanned the bishopric up front, the priests—and what looked like one of their leaders—at the sacrament table. A few rows ahead of me, I spotted a couple who looked close to my age. His arm rested on her shoulders; her head rested on it. Suddenly, she lifted her head, and he leaned over as if to hear what she had to say, but she didn't speak. Instead, she kissed his cheek and smiled, adjusted their little girl's position on her lap, then rested her head on his arm again.

My singing voice caught in my throat, and I looked away. Not another sound came out as I stared at the floor and struggled to rein in my emotions. Six months ago, Doug and I had looked just like that.

I hadn't known about Carol yet, although, in hindsight, the signs had been there. I'd simply excused them all away. When Carol's husband had been convicted of embezzlement, she'd been left alone and desperate for work. We'd hired her part time to help in the office at Doug's dental practice.

I'd taught her how to bill insurance companies and how to order supplies through our vendors. And Doug. He'd shown a level of compassion I was proud of—at the time.

Later I noticed the cell phone bills with calls and texts to a number I didn't recognize. A trip to a dental convention that cost twice as much as usual, with the explanation that Ben, the colleague Doug usually traveled and shared costs with, had brought his wife, so Doug roomed alone.

He hadn't been alone.

I touched a finger to one eye and then the other, bringing away moisture that I wiped on my black skirt. I lifted my chin and breathed in and out. Did anyone in this crowd have similar secrets? Were any other women under the same illusion I had been, carrying on as if their lives were the Mormon ideal, not knowing that a storm was about to break and tear everything apart?

And how would they accept me into the fold?

One reason I'd fled to California was to escape the people Doug and I knew in Utah, all the people who didn't know the details of Doug's affair and our divorce. Many of them had known me since grade school and the two of us since college. Some took sides. Others stared in silence. Some judged.

As if I didn't already judge myself. The divorce might have been final, but I could still hardly believe it. What did I do wrong? What could I have done to prevent my husband from straying? Wasn't I a good enough wife?

Doug had hired a shark of an attorney, leaving me without a whole lot besides Doug's crusty old car from high school, custody—besides some holidays and weeks during the summer—and a little child support, which wouldn't kick in for a couple of months.

Where was Doug right this minute? Was he at church today, pretending to be Mr. Righteous? He might be sitting in a new chapel too—in Colorado, where he'd moved with Carol. His arm might be over *her* shoulders. She might be reaching up to kiss his cheek. Smelling his cologne—the scent I'd known and recognized as *mine* for years. The thoughts sent a physical pain into my chest and made my eyes burn. I swallowed hard in a vain attempt to get rid of both. Sometimes, especially at church, I avoided thinking her name, mostly because *Carol* had become a swear word to me. And I did use the name that way, more often than I cared to admit.

I'd originally felt sorry for this woman. I'd *helped* her. I'd held her as she'd cried about her husband's betrayal. The irony made my stomach turn.

The meeting ended, and I gathered the crayons and coloring pages the boys had been playing with. As I took three-year-old Nate's chubby little hand, I prayed he'd go to a strange Nursery without a fight. Shawn, who was approaching his seventh birthday, followed behind. Several people smiled as we passed. I tried smiling back, but it was hard. Ever since the divorce, I'd pulled into myself. Going into public—even doing my hair and makeup—was hard. Now I was surrounded by strangers, people called "brother" and "sister." People I was expected to socialize with. I felt anything but social right then, and the idea of ever viewing these strangers as anything like family seemed about as likely as a fairy godmother showing up to fix my problems.

Soon I'd have to introduce myself. I wasn't sure I could do that, even though I'd practiced a basic statement in front of the mirror.

Nothing sounded right. How could I introduce myself when I didn't even know who I was anymore? I was a new ex-wife. I was a failure— an angry one.

Every time I thought of the affair, I blamed it on either me or on Carol. Somehow, never on Doug. Blaming him made sense to my brain, but I couldn't do it in my heart, even though deep down I knew hearts never made any sense.

As we headed for the crowded hallway, I chattered to the boys to keep my mind off of Doug and . . . *her*. And the fact that they were married now. Just days after we'd completed the final paperwork.

"They'll sing the same songs as in our old ward," I assured the boys for probably the fifteenth time that day. "Nate, the Nursery will have some brand-new toys you've never seen before. I wonder if they have a train or some action figures."

"Like Superman?" he asked.

"Maybe," I said.

"Or Batman?"

"Sure," I said, hoping against hope that the Nursery *did* have some action figures. I'd settle for a Teenage Mutant Ninja Turtle—anything that could pass for an action figure—because then Nathan would be happy.

We arrived at the Nursery classroom—they had just one, which I wasn't used to; my Utah ward had three Nurseries.

"Are you new?" a tiny slip of a woman asked with a sing-songy voice—for Nathan's benefit, I assumed.

"We just moved in this week," I said. I'd smile if it killed me. "This is Nathan. He's three."

The woman squatted to his level, making him cling tighter to my leg. "Well, hello, Nathan. You're such a big boy."

I caught Shawn rolling his eyes next to me and was grateful for a reason to hide a laugh. Even though he'd just started first grade, he was well aware of any time adults talked down to him as if he were a "little kid." Even though he was. I could imagine what he'd say the minute we stepped away from the classroom: *Nate's not a baby, Mom.*

I squeezed his hand conspiratorially and introduced myself to the Nursery leader. "I'm Paige Anderson."

"Shelly Bateman." She looked so young that without the ring on her finger, I would have assumed she couldn't drive yet. A girl about a year old toddled over, holding her arms up and grunting. Shelly picked her up. "And this is my Ashley. She's not old enough for Nursery, but since it's our calling, she gets to be here with us."

Us? I peered into the classroom and noted a twenty-something man sitting on a miniature chair dwarfed by his legs—his knees were nearly in his ears—playing cars with three little boys on a low, eight-foot-long table. He was making screeching and roaring noises that rivaled the toddlers'.

"That's my husband, Jeremy," Shelly said. "We just had our second anniversary last week! Two whole years now—can you believe it? We're officially no longer newlyweds." She waited silently in expectation. I wasn't sure whether to congratulate her on the milestone or share how long my husband and I had been married . . . which I couldn't.

I opted for distraction. "Wow. Two years," I said. "That's great. Goes fast, doesn't it?" I switched gears to Nate. "Isn't her little girl Ashley cute? She's got brown hair, just like you. So if you need anything, just talk to Ashley's mom or dad. He's over there. Look—lots of other boys to play with. And I bet there's an action figure in the toy bin by the window."

I was rambling like an idiot. Somehow, Shawn became my leveling influence. He took his little brother's hand and tugged him toward the other side of the room. "Let's go look for an action figure."

Nate clung to Shawn's hand but looked back at me. I waved and smiled stiffly. When he detected no sign of me ditching him, he followed his brother to the toy bin and rummaged through the piles.

"So . . ." Shelly said, turning back to me. She hitched Ashley higher on her hip and smiled in the way only an inexperienced two-year newlywed can. "What brings you to Newport? Your husband's work?"

Ouch. I had to swallow before answering, if nothing else to keep from crying but also to give me a second to form a coherent sentence. *You've practiced this already. Just say what you rehearsed.* But that's not what came out.

"No, no husband anymore. It's just me and the boys." My rambling tongue abandoned me. That was all I could say—and it wasn't at all what I'd meant to say. I couldn't leave it at that, so I managed, "We moved to the Newport area after the divorce because I've got some family here."

I didn't mention that the "family" nearby was actually Doug's parents. June and Rex Anderson still saw me as their daughter and had been nothing but supportive throughout the mess of the last several months. They'd promised to help with the boys. Doug and I had lived in the area for dental school, so it didn't seem entirely foreign. My parents had recently left on a mission, and my four siblings were scattered across the country. June and Rex were the most stable family I had. A month ago, when I put money down on a lease, moving here—and away from all the familiar, judging faces—had sounded like a good idea.

"Oh, I'm . . . I'm so sorry," Shelly said. "I didn't mean to pry . . ." She glanced at her husband, but I couldn't read her face. At first I wondered if she was contemplating whether *they* could ever split up. But when she turned back to me, her face was a mask of sympathy. Surely she and her beloved Jeremy would make it.

I was that naïve once.

In truth, I'd go back to that innocent belief if it meant having my family back together. I didn't want sympathy. I wanted my family back. What could I have done to save it?

"Spider-Man!" Nathan cried with gusto. "Look, Mama!" He ran back, flying the toy toward me.

"That's great, buddy!" I said, happy for a distraction.

Nathan made Spider-Man scale my arm like a skyscraper and then shot a web to the wall and swung over to it. I squatted down and touched his arm to get his attention. "Hey, do you think you'll be all right while I take Shawn to Primary?"

Spider-Man was busy shooting webs all across the room, so Nathan didn't even hear me. I straightened and laughed. "I'll take that as a yes. Come here, Shawn. Let's get you to class."

In the hall, Shawn ran to the Primary door and peered inside, where they'd already begun and some kid was giving a talk. The boy's mother whispered into his ear, and he bellowed the words into the microphone, nearly swallowing it whole. The boy was a brunette version of Aaron Moody from my last ward. For the second time in just a few minutes, I found my mouth curving into a smile—still an unfamiliar, albeit not unpleasant, sensation. The Church really was the same everywhere you went.

A stout woman with an auburn bob approached us in the hallway. Her face lit up when she saw us. "I heard we had a new family in the ward," she said. "I'm Sister Parker, the Primary president. Let's see if we can find where you belong." She held a binder to her chest and leaned toward Shawn. "What's your name?"

He held my hand a bit tighter and glanced up at me as if to ask whether he had permission to talk to a stranger. I nodded for him to go ahead.

"I'm Shawn."

"And how old are you, Shawn?"

"Six."

"He'll be seven next month," I added, knowing that would affect which class he was put into.

Sister Parker consulted a page in her binder. "That puts him in Sister O'Reilly's CTR 7 class. You'll love Sister O'Reilly. She's an artist and draws the neatest things on the board during her lessons." She addressed the last part to Shawn as she pulled out a paper from her binder and handed it to me. "I'll take him to sit with his class. After church, you can pick him up at his classroom. It's right down this hall and into the foyer—the room on the left." She juggled some papers in her binder and slipped out a bright pink sheet. "Would you fill this out? I like having an info sheet on all the families in the ward. Helps me get to know the children better."

"Sure," I said, taking the paper as I surrendered my son. Shawn went with her happily, and I waved as he trotted into the room beside Sister Parker. I took out a pen from my bag and started filling out the getting-to-know-you form. It would make me even later to the adult Sunday School class, which was just fine with me—I might avoid getting introduced. I pulled out a copy of *The Friend* for something to put the page against. I leaned against the wall and clicked the ballpoint pen top. I read the first line.

Parents:

I wanted to scratch out the last letter to make the word singular. My pen dug into the page.

Parent, singular. He's got one.

The Primary president didn't really want to know about both of Shawn's parents; the form blindly assumed children would have two parents in the ward. *Doug doesn't belong on this paper.* Sure, he was technically the boys' father. But here, in our new life, my boys didn't have *parents.* Just a mom. Me.

The first line wasn't filled out yet, and already I could feel a meltdown threatening to erupt. I closed my eyes, admitting to myself that as much as I hated Carol, Doug was just as much at fault for what happened between them. It would be nice to blame the seductress who took my husband. As if he'd been powerless against her wiles. As if she hadn't seduced him without his total willingness to go along.

She made me feel special, Doug had said by way of explanation. *She accepted me for who I am.*

He'd put the failure of our marriage in my lap. If I'd been a better, more attentive, supportive, loving wife, maybe, just maybe, Doug wouldn't have strayed. Forget covenants; it was all my fault.

I didn't want to live with those thoughts. I couldn't. Although guilt and shame plagued me day and night on a conscious level, I found that blaming *her* for shattering my happily ever after was easier than the other option—believing I'd failed as a wife. That if I'd been enough for Doug, he wouldn't have been pushed into another woman's arms.

Steadying my hand, I filled in the first line of the getting-to-know-you form.

Parents: Paige Anderson

I applauded myself for not crossing out the extra *S*, but my vision blurred, making it hard to read the next line.

I hate you, Doug. Hate, hate, hate you. You're such a . . . Carol.

Shadetree Photography

About the Author

Josi S. Kilpack grew up hating to read until she was thirteen and her mother handed her a copy of *The Witch of Blackbird Pond.* From that day forward, she read everything she could get her hands on and accredits her writing "education" to the many novels she has "studied" since then. She began her first novel in 1998 and hasn't stopped since. Her seventh novel, *Sheep's Clothing* won the 2007 Whitney Award for Mystery/Suspense, and *Lemon Tart,* her ninth novel, was a 2009 Whitney Award finalist.

Josi currently lives in Willard, Utah, with her wonderful husband, four amazing children, one fat dog, and varying number of very happy chickens.

For more information about Josi, you can visit her website at www .josiskilpack.com, read her blog at www.josikilpack.blogspot.com, or contact her via e-mail at Kilpack@gmail.com.